THE GREEN BICYCLE

Haifaa Al Mansour

PUFFIN

PUFFIN BOOKS

UK | USA | Canada | Ireland | Australia
India | New Zealand | South Africa

Puffin Books is part of the Penguin Random House group of companies
whose addresses can be found at global.penguinrandomhouse.com.

puffinbooks.com

First published in the USA by Dial Books for Young Readers,
an imprint of Penguin Random House, LLC,
and in Great Britain by Puffin Books 2015

007

Design by Jennifer Kelly
Text set in Tactile ITC Std

Printed in Great Britain by Clays Ltd, Elcograf S.p.A.

A CIP catalogue record for this book is available from the British Library

ISBN: 978-0-141-35668-6

FOR MY PARENTS, FOR MY HUSBAND,
AND FOR ADAM AND HAYLIE

CHAPTER ONE

Wadjda wasn't thinking about her ticket to heaven. You could see it on her face.

She wasn't even singing about it, really. Just moving her mouth to the lyrics, her body swaying in rhythm with the melodic chanting of the other girls in her class. Though she mouthed the words, her bright brown eyes wandered the school auditorium restlessly, as if she were trying to catch sight of something more interesting.

Though Wadjda wore the same dull, beat-up grey uniform as the rest of her class, she stood out somehow amid the sea of girls, with their straight, perfectly styled hair, neatly pressed clothes and confident posture. The long hair surrounding her face curled softly, making her look untidy – mischievous, even. If anyone noticed her there, slouched in the middle of the back row, she'd have been easy to identify as a misfit.

"It's time for battle; it's the only choice," the girl next to her, Salma, sang. Her voice rose with enthusiasm. "The war is boiling."

It seemed like they were always singing about their duty

to be virtuous young girls and to fight faraway infidels, or anyone who wasn't a Muslim. As a believer, it was the biggest, best thing you could do. It was better than going on al-Hajj, the holy pilgrimage; better than *zakat*, giving money to the poor; even better than freeing a slave. It was the surest way to get to heaven's highest state.

But that didn't make singing about it any more interesting. Sighing, Wadjda let her eyes keep drifting. One by one, she read the posters scattered across the walls of the empty auditorium. During *Dhuhr* prayer, the space would be transformed into an all-girls' mosque. So each poster was inscribed with lines from the Quran, or from the Prophet's well-known sayings about women. The closest one read, *My fellow Muslim sister: Be careful from the human wolves – men. Protect your honour from those who will kill you.*

Wadjda smiled, trying to imagine her friend Abdullah as a wolf. *Well*, she thought, *he's got black hair – kind of like a wolf's. But there's nothing ferocious about him. He's more of a hamster!*

Laughter welled up inside Wadjda, but she hid her giggles beneath the swelling of the song. She'd missed quite a few lines, and Salma was glaring at her. Glancing guiltily around, Wadjda tried to join back in.

They were singing along to a male voice on a cassette tape, which the teacher had turned on for the girls to follow as they practised. But, try as she might, nothing more than a whisper emerged from Wadjda's mouth. Even if she'd been louder, she told herself, her voice wouldn't have carried past the first row, where three girls stood, singing their hearts out, chests lifted and chins high. They had the best voices by far, and always got placed up front.

Unlike the girls in Wadjda's row, who'd been stuck in the back for a reason. Yasmeen hit an especially shrill note and Wadjda winced, fighting the urge to put her fingers in her ears. It was definitely better to be quiet-bad than loud-bad.

By this point in the practice session, everyone was tired and restless. They were probably all thinking about lunchtime, and how best to position themselves in the cafeteria queue for a falafel sandwich. There was a limited number, and they always sold out. The struggle to snag one before the bell rang was maybe the closest thing to real battle that Wadjda's classmates would ever experience.

"Girls! Stand in your spots!" Ms Noof shouted. Huffing impatiently, she surveyed the three rows of eleven-year-olds on the homemade-looking wooden stage. The teacher's bulky figure was all but lost in her oversized skirt and long, plain blouse. It was the kind of outfit Wadjda saw advertised along Thirtieth Street in Al-Olaya, the commercial heart of Riyadh. She liked to watch the Yemeni salesmen there haggle with their costumers, who were mostly no-nonsense teachers like Ms Noof.

Although all Saudi women wore essentially the same black uniform in public, with a veil wrapped round their heads and either a masklike *niqab* or a sheer black fabric called a *shayla* over their faces, underneath they liked their patterns as crazy and bright as possible. From all the weddings and social gatherings where Wadjda saw her teachers – sometimes, Riyadh felt like a small town, rather than a sprawling city – she knew Ms Noof loved animal prints. Wadjda liked to pretend that, if the school allowed it, her teacher would be wearing a leopard-spotted blouse with matching heels.

At her call, the girls snapped into place. Their feet, all in plain black leather shoes, lined up in perfect rows across the stage. The large banner looming above them made Wadjda feel very small indeed. WELCOME TO THE 4TH GIRLS' SCHOOL IN RIYADH EAST, it read. That wasn't true, strictly speaking. Theirs wasn't the fourth school in the eastern part of the city. But, while all the boys' schools were named after famous Muslim warriors and scholars, the girls' schools were labelled with random numbers.

Wadjda twisted her lips and sighed. *Just another one of the lessons girls in Riyadh learn every day*, she thought. From the moment she'd started school, she'd been told that modesty and quietness, a life in which no one knew anything about her or talked about her, *ever*, were the highest virtues she could hope to attain.

"Again, from the beginning." Ms Noof leaned down to push play on the tape recorder, lurching over the small machine like an elephant trying to scratch its toes. Hoisting herself up, she let her gaze fall on the group, scowling at each girl in turn.

From the tape deck came a screech of static. Then the song blared out of the speakers. Though she was trying hard to pay respectful attention, Wadjda couldn't help raising her eyebrows. *They have sound effects now?* She hid her smirk behind her hand. *I didn't think this could get any more dramatic!*

Yet, even the movie soundtrack noise of distant medieval battle – the thump of galloping hooves, the whinnying of horses – couldn't keep Wadjda focused. She was tired of following along with the rest of the class. Her eyes wandered again to the dusty red carpets laid out in front of the stage, travelled across the rows of empty wooden chairs scattered around the room.

They must have taken them from the science lab, she thought. The faded green paint made her remember hours of experiments, back when her class had its turn with the lab. She wondered if she could find the chair into which she'd carved her initials, and if the wood still smelled faintly of chemicals.

Two of the older girls entered the auditorium then, pulling Wadjda away from her daydreams. Fatin and Fatima were cool without trying to be. Whenever she saw them, a gigantic grin filled Wadjda's whole face. Fatin was sassy, always ready with a funny comeback or snarky remark. While Fatima seemed calm and quiet on the surface, underneath she was a true criminal mastermind. Her elaborate pranks were school legend, even if she never talked about them – or talked at all, really.

Once, Wadjda remembered, Fatima had taken a shoe from every one of the teachers while they were praying. She'd hidden them all over the playground, burying a sneaker in the sand and tucking some heels into the nooks and crannies of the dusty lot where the girls spent their free periods. When the teachers finally figured out what had happened, they had to go scrambling and dashing around the playground, digging in the sand like pirates on a treasure hunt. Though Fatima never admitted it, all the girls knew such a brilliant scheme was something only she could pull off.

Aside from the fun and laughter Fatima and Fatin provided, Wadjda liked the two older girls because they didn't comment on her messy hair, make fun of her unusual

6

clothes, or mock the badges she collected and pinned to her schoolbag. Fatin had even bought one of the colourful bracelets Wadjda made and sold for spare money. It was a special bracelet, with a Justin Bieber charm on it.

Fatin and Fatima should have been in class, but today – like every day – something more fun had apparently distracted them. Fatima hushed Fatin, giggling and poking her in the shoulder, as they slipped by the choir. Though Fatin carried a map and Fatima a globe, it seemed obvious that these were props, a way of pretending they had a reason to roam the school. In all likelihood, they were up to something.

Wadjda tried to get their attention, rippling her fingers in a little wave as she lip-synched the song. Fatin and Fatima gave her an ever-so-slight nod in return. A smile of satisfaction lit Wadjda's face. She turned, hoping the other girls in her row had noticed.

They had. But someone else had noticed, too.

Ms Noof.

And now Wadjda's teacher was scowling right at her.

With her hands on her hips and her brow crinkled in angry lines, Ms Noof looked like a storm about to break – right on top of Wadjda's head. Wadjda's heart skipped a beat. She couldn't get in trouble now: she hadn't learned the lyrics of the song by heart. What if Ms Noof called her out in front of her classmates? She didn't want to think about what would happen. Wadjda darted her eyes to the floor, tucking her hands into her uniform pockets and rocking back on her heels. To fake an innocent look, she made her eyes very wide as she sang.

It didn't work. Ms Noof hit stop on the tape recorder. The song ground to a halt, cutting off a triumphant rattle of drums. The girls' voices trailed away into silence, and they looked up, seeking guidance.

"Wadjda! Step to the front, please." Ms Noof set her hand against her hip and gestured with one finger. Wadjda bit her lip and reluctantly dragged herself forward. As she passed through the front row, her high-top Chuck Taylors came into view. Wadjda's Chucks were no longer too new and black, nor were they too worn and holey. They had just the right beat-up grey colour she'd hoped for during her countless hours running in the streets with Abdullah. The shade was highlighted by faded purple laces.

Among the other girls' black leather shoes, though, her high-tops didn't look so perfect. Wadjda closed her eyes and rubbed her sweaty palms against her sides. She wished she could hop offstage and sprint away to anywhere but where she was right now.

Noura, smiling the sweet and perfect smile of a sweet and perfect girl, bumped Wadjda's shoulder, hard, as she took her place in the back row. Wincing, Wadjda gave Noura a lethal glare. Then, slowly, she turned to face Ms Noof. Wadjda's eyes felt like lead weights, drawn to the floor by a powerful magnet. By the time she found the courage to raise them and meet her teacher's gaze, Ms Noof had come close, towering over her. Wadjda knew there was no bigger sin than her lack of enthusiasm for the song. She would not be easily forgiven.

"Why don't you show us all your beautiful singing voice? Start with the first verse." Wadjda could see the smirk in her eyes.

The rest of the girls giggled. A finger poked Wadjda hard in the back. Wadjda looked over her shoulder, trying to find the culprit, anger and embarrassment swirling through her. The feeling mixed itself up with the crystal-clear certainty that she was, yet again, a complete loser. Her face flushed, burning so hot and red she was sure her classmates could see. Stupid blush. Stupid song.

Again, Wadjda fixed her eyes on the floor. Again, she scuffed her feet back and forth. Determined, she opened her mouth, ready to sing – but no, down went her eyes, and her mouth clamped shut. The whole class was laughing at her. How could she sing?

"Well?" Now Ms Noof was smirking openly. "If you don't want everyone to hear that *beautiful* voice of yours . . ." She trailed off and gestured with her head towards the door.

Wadjda left without speaking. In her absence, the group looked more unified, a perfectly matched set of neat, well-dressed girls. Ms Noof smiled like a satisfied general inspecting her troops and finding them ready for action.

"All right, girls. Let's go over it again from the beginning!"

I can't believe I got kicked out of class. Again.

Wadjda's foot connected with a rock, sending it arcing through the air. It didn't hit anything, though. It just plunked back down in the dirt, sending up a cloud of dust.

Nine a.m. The day had only begun, but already the merciless sun burned down, sending its punishing rays right through Wadjda, who stood alone in the centre of the courtyard. Shielding her eyes, she searched the horizon for relief. Not a cloud in the sky. Even her school's menacingly high fence didn't cast much shade, though it stretched up far above Wadjda's head. The sun had already positioned itself directly over the playground, and there was no relief from its scorching brightness.

As if things weren't bad enough, waves of heat poured from the back of the split-window AC, too – straight on to Wadjda. Sweat sprang out all over her body. Sighing, shaking her loose clothes to move air across her skin, Wadjda paced the dusty ground, searching for shade. She'd been banished to this spot before. She'd also visited the principal's office enough times this year to know she had to tread lightly and mostly stay put. The last thing she wanted was for her mother to have to come to school for another meeting. She would do anything – literally, anything – to keep that from happening.

Through the white noise from the AC, she heard the voices of the girls echoing in the auditorium.

"It's time for battle; it's the only choice. The war is boiling, calling. The horses are prepared; the battle will start. War heals wounds better than suppressing anger!"

Wadjda sighed. Giving up her search for shade, she slumped back against the hot wall and let the song wash over her.

"If our religion is humiliated, heaven calls and our fate is written. *Allahu Akbar* is our song; it is our light and the fire we fight with!"

CHAPTER TWO

The warm smell of cardamom and saffron teased Wadjda awake. Traditional blond Saudi coffee was boiling in the kitchen, and she could hear the soft sounds of her mother moving from room to room, preparing for the day ahead.

Wadjda loved the familiarity of their house. It was old and cosy, the place where she'd been born. She couldn't imagine living anywhere else. Of course, it wasn't perfect. The walls were so thin that the slightest noise echoed through the whole space. The electricity went out now and then, sometimes because her mother didn't pay the bill, but mostly because a fuse blew or a switch broke. Over time, Wadjda had learned to fix these things. Between the constant repairs and the monthly mortgage, her mother was always complaining about the house being a money pit. But while their home had its issues it was Wadjda's safe spot, the only place where she and her mother could be themselves, relaxed and happy and tucked away from the world outside.

It was barely five in the morning. Despite the early hour, Wadjda was already in her grey school uniform, tugging a brush through her hair. She liked to get up early, before her mother set out on the long journey to the remote school where she taught. She liked being there for her mother, liked to take care of her and make sure things were all right. Getting up at the same time was a silent act of support.

With the flick of a switch, Wadjda turned on the radio. *Her radio.* She smiled and brushed her fingers across its metal sides. This was the thing in her small room that she loved most. Music moved her, lifted her. As she straightened the sheets on her bed and threw her slippers underneath, she rocked her hips and shook her shoulders in time with the beat. It was going to be a fun day, and Wadjda was ready for it to begin.

It was going to be hot, too. Already, the sun was burning through the small window above her desk. Wadjda had covered the window with wallpaper, but even that thick sheet failed to block the intense desert heat. Climbing on to her desk chair, Wadjda added a few pictures to the collage she'd started on top of the wallpaper, using images cut from magazines. Her father brought them back from the oil company on the east coast where he worked.

Scrambling down, Wadjda flipped through one of those magazines now, looking for pictures of girls her age. They smiled out at her from the glossy pages: two girls on skateboards hovering at the top of a jump; a girl strumming a guitar; a group of kids sitting on the beach, boys and girls together, arms slung round one another's shoulders. The heat burned against Wadjda's fingers as she climbed up again, pressing these new pictures on to the wallpaper. Her collage was her checklist, a reminder of all the things she would do as soon as she got the chance.

On the radio, the DJ introduced the next song. Wadjda dashed to her tape deck and hit record as the new single from Grouplove began. She wasn't sure what the DJ had been saying about the song, or what the band was singing about – her English couldn't quite keep up with the fast pace of the lyrics. But she loved the feeling the song gave her. Flinging out her arms, Wadjda spun in a circle, closed her eyes and let the beat move her. She knew the song was good. The DJs had played it more than a dozen times in the last few days. Only a hit would get so much attention.

Wadjda prided herself on her taste in music. Nine times out of ten, the songs she picked to record went on to become hits. And, as much as she loved music, she loved sharing it even more. The mix tapes she made sold for real money at school – five Riyals each. And this latest mix was so good that her classmates would probably buy it even if she charged a lot more!

The thought of selling the tape made Wadjda pause in her dance. *Better be safe.* Quickly, she clambered up on to the bed and ran her fingers along the length of cord she'd strung in through the window, making sure it connected properly to the back of the radio. The cord led to the roof, and from there to the makeshift antenna Wadjda had rigged up to capture songs from stations all over the world.

She'd found the antenna discarded next to a garbage bin on one of her rambling walks home from school. *Who still uses these?* Wadjda had thought, squatting in the dirt. *I bet it's someone old, because there's a satellite dish on every roof in Riyadh!*

Not till later, when she was sitting in their satellite-dish-less house, straining to make out the song buzzing through her radio's fuzzy speakers, did Wadjda realize the antenna was perfect – for her. But what if she'd missed her chance? In Riyadh, if you didn't take something when you saw it, it was usually gone by the time you went back.

Still, she had to try. The next day, she erupted out of school the minute she was dismissed and raced through the streets, her heart thudding against her chest. Magically, the antenna was still there. Waiting for her like a gift.

Dragging it all the way to the roof took hours of panting, sweaty work. But it was worth it. The antenna was Wadjda's tunnel to a faraway world. The music it carried into her room created a private space, a place far from the shrieky Turkish soap operas her mother adored, from the gloomy news reported daily on TV. Wadjda's radio played music made especially for her.

Turning over the English name of the song she was recording in her mind, Wadjda carefully wrote down her own version of its title, translating it phonetically into Arabic. The full track list was labelled WADJDA'S AWESOME MIX TAPE, VOL. 7. Next to the growing stack of cassettes, she counted out handmade bracelets. Jewellery brought in decent money from kids who didn't like music. And, just in case, Wadjda specialized in everybody's favourite treats – candy and crisps – which always sold out. The school strictly forbade leaving the grounds during the day, so it was impossible to sneak away and get snacks during lunch. Wadjda had the market cornered.

Her mother hated the idea of Wadjda selling things to her classmates. "Like a common beggar," she'd say, shaking her head. But she didn't seem to mind the extra money when they needed things around the house. Over time, they'd come to an understanding: it was all right as long as they didn't talk about it – and as long as Wadjda didn't get caught.

Today, if she sold all the bracelets and tapes, and maybe a few bags of candy and crisps, she could easily clear fifty Riyals. More than enough for a large pizza and two Cokes on Thursday night, when she and her mother always ordered dinner in. Wadjda smiled, pleased, and searched the floor for her high-tops. The song was nearing its end. Bobbing her head in time, she looked through the half-open door of her room and saw her mother, drying her hair in the living room.

Wadjda thought her mother was the most beautiful woman on earth. Her silky hair fell to her slim waist like a black river. It was so thick that it was hard for Wadjda's mother to control it all under her *abayah* and burka. She had to buy a special cap to keep it from falling out of her veil in public. Thick lashes framed her wide, dark eyes. When she outlined them with black lines of kohl, she looked almost cartoonishly glamorous, like a star from a Bollywood film. *She should be in a movie*, Wadjda thought.

Of course, her mother would never allow herself such a dream. It wasn't proper. Still, there was something impossibly elegant in her movements, even as she struggled to do simple tasks, like attach a broken brush accessory to the top of her hair dryer. A smile stole across Wadjda's face as she listened to her mother curse under her breath. Finally, her mother tossed aside the broken part and dried the rest of her hair without it.

But Wadjda was wasting time. The clock read 5:30 a.m. Time to go. She jumped up and left her room – but seconds later she was back by the radio, shifting from foot to foot, drumming her fingers against the dial as she waited for the song to end. At last, she hit stop on the recorder and dashed out, hoping her mother wouldn't curse her for making them late, yet again.

Today, though, her mother was also rushing, twisting her hair quickly round her fingers and adding little coloured clips to hold it in place. Wadjda waited near the door, underneath a gold-framed picture of her father. The picture had been taken on her parents' wedding day. Her father practically glimmered, his crisp white *thobe* and checked *ghutra* complemented by the beautiful brown *bisht*, or traditional cloak, draped over his shoulders.

Had the *bisht* been more expensive than her mother's simple wedding dress? Wadjda had seen her mother's gown in the wardrobe, had even run her fingers gently across the white silk, but she didn't know if there were any pictures of her mother wearing it. She couldn't remember ever seeing one around the house.

Following her daughter's eyes, her mother glanced at the picture, too. At the sight of her husband, she suddenly looked so tired. Wadjda frowned, feeling the familiar twist in her stomach. Something troubling was happening between her parents, but she didn't like to think about it. Thinking about it made it real.

Now her mother looked away, sighing. She'd almost

finished her hair. Each strand was locked into place, creating a strange mixture of curls and bows. *Only my mother could pull off a look like that*, Wadjda thought. On her, it was beautiful.

"Turn off the stove before the coffee boils over," she called. Wadjda ran to the kitchen and twisted the knob, letting the gas sputter out. The sandwich her mother had made her waited on the counter – Wadjda's favourite, a delicious mix of melted cheeses rolled tight in white Arabic bread. Her mother had made her *kerk chai*, too: tea and warm milk. Smiling, Wadjda breathed in the rich smells of cardamom and saffron.

Her mother ran into the kitchen and tended to her coffee, adding a few scoops of cardamom and a pinch of saffron. Smiling down at Wadjda, she said gently, "Lots of caffeine in there. Hopefully it'll keep you going – at least through morning period."

Wadjda nodded. Recently, she'd heard one of her teachers say that caffeine was bad for kids. In Riyadh, though, people didn't give habits up easily – not even bad ones. For as long as she could remember, Wadjda had been drinking tea and coffee. She liked the little kick she got from *kerk chai*. These days, she needed it to get through her endless boring classes. And her cousins and friends drank it, too, so surely it couldn't be that bad.

Outside, a car horn honked. With a jolt, Wadjda and her mother whirled towards the door. Wadjda's mother moved too fast, though, and splashed boiling coffee across her hand, scalding her pale skin. Sighing in frustration and pain, she wrapped the wound with a wet towel.

"I guess he's already here," Wadjda said, rolling her eyes.

Her mother spoke without looking up from her burnt hand.

"Well, he can just wait. I'm doing everything I can to be ready on time."

But there was worry hidden in her tone. And, when she moved, she *moved*. Her mother poured the coffee into a thermos, grabbed her notebooks, donned her *abayah* and burka, and made for the door, all in a rush. Wadjda hurried along behind, carrying the rest of her mother's supplies in a jumbled heap in her arms.

At the door, Wadjda's mother paused to tug the keys from their hook, knocking a string of blue prayer beads to the floor as she did so. These were Wadjda's father's. He always had the beads dangling from his hands, and he'd roll them over his index finger with his thumb when he talked. Sometimes he even swung them round an extended finger as he paced the house, letting the long blue string slap rhythmically against the fabric of his white *thobe*.

Wadjda's mother picked them up and put them back

in place. For a moment, she covered them with her palm, letting her hand rest tenderly against the beads, the way she touched Wadjda's cheek before bed. Then she turned to Wadjda and pulled her veil over her face, businesslike once more.

"Don't forget your key, and don't lock the upper lock. Your father may be coming home after his night shift." Her tone was the one she reserved for the times that Wadjda came home late or didn't finish her homework – so not really that often, Wadjda thought. Not a *regular* occurrence. Well, not a tone she'd heard for a few days, at least.

As they exited through the front gate, Wadjda frowned, twisting her lips and setting her jaw like a superhero face-to-face with her arch nemesis. Before them stood Iqbal, her mother's Pakistani driver-for-hire. He was in front of his old van, plastering a broken headlight on with duct tape. When he saw Wadjda, he matched her glare with a deadly evil eye. But then he saw her mother, and he began to act showily exasperated.

"It very long way, Madame!" He yelled at her in bossy, broken Arabic. "Other teachers we are taking, very long way. You late every day! No taking you late!"

Rolling her eyes at the familiar show, Wadjda put her hands on her hips and squared her shoulders. Iqbal towered over her, but she did not yield.

"She no late! You just came! I see you – five minutes not even!" She used the same broken Arabic for emphasis.

"I no talk to you, little girl. I talk to your mother. She is late!"

Without letting Wadjda or her mother reply, Iqbal got into the car and slammed the door. A picture of a smiling child in *shalwar kameez*, the traditional tunic and trousers worn in Pakistan, fell to the floor. Iqbal picked it up and cleaned it tenderly before putting it back on the dashboard. Time seemed to pause; he stared into the eyes of the little girl in the picture, looking as if his mind and heart were very far away.

Then he looked up and found himself back in Saudi Arabia, staring right into Wadjda's face, which was pressed up against the glass. Leaning back, Wadjda stuck her tongue out, just to make sure Iqbal knew who he was dealing with. He honked again, waving his hands at her with ever more exaggerated impatience.

"Don't worry about him," her mother said from beneath her face covering. "OK, *yalla*, bye!" She took her things from Wadjda, ruffling her daughter's hair as she stepped into the car. Wadjda heard her parting words faintly: "There's no problem, Iqbal. You take lots of money, so let's have some quiet for the long drive."

The minivan bumped away in a cloud of dust and clanking of engine parts. As Wadjda was about to go back into the house, she saw the minivan swerve wildly to avoid an oncoming car. In its recovery, it almost crashed into the garden wall of a nearby house. Wadjda flung her arms wide in dismay. What was Iqbal doing? Nervous, she watched the battered car disappear round the corner, the familiar fear that Iqbal would drive her mother straight off a cliff somewhere tickling its way into her mind.

In the living room, Wadjda rushed to grab her backpack. But, catching a glimpse of herself in the mirror, she stopped and looked hard at her reflection. Slowly, she lifted her hair, wrapping it round her hand and piling it loosely on her head. Could she ever look as effortlessly elegant as her mother? If Wadjda pinned her curls and tilted her chin slightly to the left, catching just the right light, could she be as beautiful?

Sunbeams flickered across her face and reflected off the glass. Sighing, Wadjda put on her *abayah*, turning away from the girl in the mirror.

Outside, bright sunlight beat down on the rows of concrete houses lining the streets. A tall wall fronted each home, and a thick layer of dust coated everything: the trees, the rubbish heaped in the gutters, even the cracked grey pavements. In Wadjda's neighbourhood, it was difficult to tell one thing from another. Beneath its blanket of dust, the street seemed boring and lifeless, a giant beige blur stretching endlessly into the distance. Aluminium foil or tightly drawn curtains covered the windows, offering the people inside protection from the sun – and from the curious eyes of the outside world.

Here and there, groups of girls walked to school, their bodies completely covered with black *abayahs* and veils. Only different backpacks or eyeglasses distinguished one from another. Taxis and minivans passed by with a roar, leaving dust clouds hanging in the air behind them. Women were not allowed to drive in Saudi, so each car was packed with female passengers, all pressed tightly together, all dressed in black. Clusters of foreign-looking men, mostly Indian and Pakistani, moved towards their places of work. They had on worn, faded clothes, most of which looked as if they'd been beaten with a dusty broom in place of cleaning. The women instinctively kept their distance from the men, moving to the other side of the street or waiting for them to pass so they could avoid any accidental contact.

She couldn't wait any longer. With a sigh, Wadjda turned towards school – and flinched, her body jerking back as – *crash!* – a rock skipped past her, knocking against a discarded soda can and sending it clanking away across the pavement.

Startled, Wadjda looked up to see her father, smiling and tossing another rock up into the air. Her heart swelled. From the accuracy of the throw, she'd known it was him even before she turned round. Her father was always showing her how to skip stones, and there were endless targets on Riyadh's garbage-ridden streets. Discarded cans and fast-food wrappers seemed to fill the pavements as soon as the street sweepers passed through, the new rubbish easily taking the place of whatever garbage had been removed.

Wadjda's father ran his hand through his short black hair and drew his fingers across his neat moustache. Wadjda could almost feel its soft tickle against her cheek. She liked how his uniform from the oil rig had faded, turning a cool, sun-bleached grey. When he'd left home, it had been bright blue and ugly. It looked much tougher after a little wear and tear. *Like my sneakers*, she thought.

"Watch this!" her father called, and flung a rock towards a jumbo-sized fast-food cup, which someone had left on the wall behind Wadjda. Even as she ducked, Wadjda saw the cup fly from its place, lid and straw exploding in opposite directions. Impressed, she grabbed a stone from the dusty road, hefting it in her palm, feeling its weight.

"Oh yeah? Check this out!" She searched for her target, chest puffed out bravely, and zeroed in on a dusty milk carton lying a few metres away. Though she gave it her best shot, the rock fell short. In silence, Wadjda and her father watched it tumble to a stop near her father's foot.

"Close, my girl! Keep practising. You're getting there."

Wadjda couldn't wait any longer. She ran over and hugged him. "Where have you been, *Abooie*?" she blurted, wrapping her arms round his chest and squeezing tight.

Her father didn't answer. He just held her out in front of him, smiling. "Look at this," he said at last, pulling a shiny black rock from his pocket. "It's volcanic, from the Empty Quarter. It'll fly straight and fast – think how that will help your aim! Now, you have school, yes? Better get going."

Wadjda took the rock from his hand, beaming. He patted her on the head. They stood side by side for a moment as Wadjda rolled the glossy stone in her hand. She didn't want to leave, not yet. She wondered about her father's lonely life on the rigs, out in the middle of nowhere. In her mind's eye she saw him pacing the Empty Quarter, imagined a glint of light on a stone catching his eye. She thought about him picking up the shiny black rock, holding it in his hand and thinking of her. His daughter.

With a surge of glee, she tossed her new prize up high once, then again. On the third throw, she snatched it from the air and started off towards school, running fast, her shoes slapping exuberantly against the pavement.

CHAPTER THREE

I look cool, Abdullah thought. *Cool and grown-up.*

He was working on one of the large campaign billboards his uncle Abdulhakeem bin Hamad bin Musaid Al Toofi had asked him to set up around town. The task wasn't hugely important, but any assignment from his uncle made Abdullah swell with pride. It was a big deal to be trusted and given the honour of helping out on his uncle's election campaign. It was the beginning of his training, the first step in a long journey that would take him all the way to the top of his tribe's distinguished elite.

Abdullah's family was an important one, and he knew he would grow up to be a leader in their remote community. In a village as small as theirs, bloodlines and connections were the surest way to reach the top. His uncle was loved by all, and for much more than his family name or tribal affiliation. His enthusiasm for life, and his deep knowledge of the traditional ways of the desert, had earned him respect. He was the ultimate Saudi tribal man – more at home at his legendary camping parties in

"We left the door unlocked. *Ummi*'s been waiting for you all week!" she called over her shoulder.

Her father's eyes flickered at the mention of her mother. Once more, he passed his hand over his hair. Then he patted the dust off his overalls and moved towards the front gate of the house.

the desert, hunting wild rabbits through the dunes and smoking *shisha*, than he was in an office or the city.

But, for all his skills, there was nothing of which his uncle was prouder than his big, bushy moustache. It best represented his strength and power, and on the billboard it easily spanned three feet. Abdullah stepped back, grinning. He'd seen first-hand how much work went into maintaining such facial hair. Uncle splashed on all sorts of products to keep his moustache thick and lush, and he carefully dyed it black before the white roots could grow out and expose his true age to the world.

Sweat trickled down Abdullah's forehead. He swiped at it with the back of his hand, wondering idly why his contented uncle had decided to run for political office. Maybe he was trying to act more dignified. But deep down, though, Abdullah knew he would always be an unruly, free-spirited man. The people of his tribe – and his nephew! – wouldn't want him any other way.

Stories of his uncle were legendary in their village. When Abdullah's oldest sister had got engaged, his uncle had ordered twenty trays of *Muffatah*, enough to feed the whole neighbourhood. Every tray held a grilled lamb, laid out from head to hoof atop an enormous bed of tender basmati rice, dripping with roasted onions, raisins and pine nuts. That epic meal was still talked about by everyone

in their suburb. Abdullah remembered taking a large plate for Wadjda and her mother, too. He'd chosen a good piece of meat for her, carefully selecting the most tender piece of thigh.

At the thought of Wadjda, Abdullah swiped again at the sweat on his brow and straightened his white, tightly woven hat – his *taqia*. To make it look just right, he ironed it himself before Morning Prayer. He'd done a good job today. The *taqia* sat firmly on his head. Feeling more confident, Abdullah dropped the screwdriver into the pocket of his pristine white *thobe* and theatrically pulled out a larger one, giving it a playful spin with his fingers. That'd show Wadjda, he thought – though, to be honest, he couldn't remember a time when he'd actually impressed her. Not when he taught her to knock down a can with a rock from all the way across an empty field. Not even when he showed her how to whistle. He knew she appreciated these things. The flash of her mischievous smile, and the sweet grudging dip of her head, told him so. But she was too proud to say the words aloud.

She'd smile now if she could see the billboard. Why, it was as tall as him! Its two sides came together in a point, like a giant letter *A*, held together by folding hinges in the middle. The board had been placed strategically at one of the busiest intersections in town, across from the largest

supermarket. The roads here met at the midpoint between the boys' and girls' schools, which were on opposite sides of the neighbourhood.

Abdullah had actually finished putting the board up ten minutes ago, but he kept fiddling, tightening already-tightened screws, pretending there was more work to be done. Occasionally, he glanced at a group of drivers who stood nearby, drinking tea, wondering if the poster had caught their attention. No one seemed to notice.

The poster had already begun to accumulate dust, the tiny grains blown in by the low wind that blanketed Riyadh in a constant layer of sand. It blanketed Abdullah's bicycle, too, which leaned against one side of the billboard. His books were clamped to a rack on the back, and Abdullah shuddered, thinking of the hours of boring lessons ahead.

Still no sign of Wadjda. Nearby was the convenience store where she bought junk food and candy to resell to her classmates at double the price. Abdullah checked his watch, tracking passers-by as they moved along the street, their forms appearing and disappearing in the hazy air. Where was she?

At last a familiar shape in the store caught his eye. A jolt of happiness shot through Abdullah. Though he wanted to wave, he didn't. He had to look cool.

Inside, Wadjda stood in the candy aisle, considering the different varieties of chocolate. She looked up and smiled when she saw him. Instantly, Abdullah disappeared back behind the billboard. He patted at his pockets, looking for another tool, knowing he needed to busy himself with a task before Wadjda came out of the shop. He tried to steady his features, but despite his best efforts his face kept breaking out in a smile.

He surveyed the portrait of his uncle once more. Uncle was a big man, a bit overweight, but that was as it should be for such an important person. In the picture, he sat upon a chair that looked like a throne. Beneath him was inscribed, "Vote for me for Municipal Council. Your glorious representation."

Out of the corner of his eye, Abdullah saw Wadjda approach, munching on a breakfast sandwich. He brushed his hair into place, pulled back his shoulders and stood taller. Wadjda didn't seem to notice. She read over the poster and laughed.

"What's this, an ad for moustache products?"

Abdullah almost laughed, too. But he hid his smile from Wadjda, and, when he turned to face her, his look was cool and annoyed.

"Very funny, you. That's a moustache so strong a falcon could perch on it!"

"A falcon? An aeroplane could land on that thing!" Wadjda chuckled.

Abdullah smiled and opened his mouth to reply. Then, over her shoulder, he saw a group of boys approaching. If they saw him talking to Wadjda in public, he'd spend the rest of the day – maybe the rest of the week – paying for it. They'd tease him mercilessly for wasting his time with a girl. He looked around, searching for a way out. Then, in a move so fast it was almost instinctive, he snatched the sandwich from Wadjda's hands.

"Thanks for buying me breakfast!" he called, sprinting off in the opposite direction from the group of boys.

"You jerk! If you want to race, you don't have to steal my sandwich!" Wadjda screamed, and took off after him.

They flew through the neighbourhood, jumping to avoid large cracks in the tarmac, dodging round random palm trees growing up through the pavement, leaping over the dusty garbage and debris lining the kerbs. Cars honked in the morning madness of rush hour. Foreign workers on bicycles glided out of their way, dipping in and out of the stalled traffic like silvery fish making their way upstream.

Wadjda was gaining quickly on Abdullah. From experience, she knew she was faster. It was only a matter of time before she caught him.

But, as she rounded a corner, a gust of wind caught her

veil and it slipped back on her head, exposing a few inches of hair. For two or three precious seconds, Wadjda felt the cool breeze moving across her face and drying her sticky forehead. Then, without a thought or a missed step, she reached up and pulled the veil back into place, tightening it round her neck, making sure all her hair was out of sight.

Brow furrowed, she picked up speed and started to really close in on Abdullah. She leaped over a mangy cat like a hurdler. Her churning feet kicked up a huge cloud of dust and sand as at last she overtook him, snatching the sandwich from his hand, shouting out a final cry of victory. Slowing her run to a trot, she looked back, pumping her arms in show-offy celebration.

This went on for another minute. Then, exhausted, Wadjda and Abdullah stopped running and stood opposite each other, panting. Sweat beads sprung up again on their brows. The already-oppressive desert heat engulfed them. They exchanged a glance. Safely away from the other boys, Abdullah smiled at Wadjda.

But, before she could smile back, he took off, sprinting towards the convenience store where he had left his bicycle.

CHAPTER FOUR

Strutting down the street, finishing her sandwich, Wadjda took a shortcut that passed within a block of the boys' school. The other girls in her class steered clear of this area. They wanted to avoid being accused of bad, or worse, immoral intentions.

Wadjda couldn't have cared less. The best parts of her day in Riyadh were spent roaming the streets, exploring new shops and neighbourhoods, poking her head into forgotten corners. Last week, she'd explored the new roadside shopping mall Abdullah's politician uncle was building. When it was finished, he would lease the many units to vendors. But, for the time being, most of it was empty. Wadjda had tiptoed through the vast space, imagining what it would look like when it was done.

The world's so big, Wadjda thought. Like that cavernous mall, with its sky-high ceilings. And she wanted to see all of it.

She darted through the garden gate of the closest home, passing swiftly across the expanse of land surrounding the house and slipping out again through the exit in the back wall. Her favourite part of this particular shortcut was how quiet it was. The path was her own world – a secret Riyadh no one except Abdullah knew existed. And this morning it felt especially serene. Only the occasional rumble of an engine broke the silence. In the distance, Wadjda could just make out the shapes of passing cars and minibuses. Each one was filled with indistinguishable black figures – female students and teachers.

As Wadjda walked, she tallied one more time the sales she hoped to make. If she could unload at least half the bracelets she'd produced last night, she'd almost certainly pass the twenty-Riyals mark. And that didn't even count the tapes –

Whoosh!

Wadjda gasped, her hands darting to her head. Abdullah had spotted her near the boys' school and reappeared! He snatched the top of her veil and unfurled it from her head as he zipped past on his bicycle. The thin cloth stretched, billowing between them, forming a black line from him to her.

But the veil was tucked too tightly round Wadjda's throat. Abdullah's momentum pulled her forward, and she fell to the ground. Stunned, she shook out her stinging palms, mortified. Her hair was exposed. Again! Instinctively, she raised her hands to cover herself.

A few metres ahead, Abdullah slid his bicycle to a halt. He turned and blinked in disbelief, surveying the strange collection of bows and coloured clips knotted randomly across the top of Wadjda's head. He'd known her forever, so he wasn't shocked to see her hair. She'd only started wearing the veil last year, and it was always falling off when they played. In fact, Abdullah sometimes had a hard time recognizing Wadjda when she was veiled. She seemed more like herself without it.

Now, though, he couldn't help laughing. "What's all this?" he asked, pointing at her hair. He tried to gesture to all the bows and clips, but there were too many, and it looked like he was trying to wave away a swarm of bees.

Wadjda stood and turned to face him, uncovered head held high. Lifting her chin, she tossed her head back the way her father did.

"It's totally in fashion. Not that you'd know anything about that!"

Her words fell on deaf ears. Abdullah continued to guffaw, practically falling over the handlebars of his bike. In spite of herself, Wadjda reached to the top of her head and tried to pin some of the loose clips back into place. Surely she didn't look that silly!

While she was distracted, Abdullah kicked his bike back into motion. Catching the flash of sun on metal,

Wadjda spun and saw him pedalling off. Her veil dangled from his hand. He held it out mockingly, letting the end trail in the dirt.

"I'll get you, you jerk!" Wadjda shouted. In a burst of pure rage, she took off after him. Abdullah looked back, saw her sprinting furiously and started to slow down. He did it partly out of pity – and partly out of fear. You did not want to mess with Wadjda when she was angry. And he'd already messed with her a lot that morning.

Just as Wadjda reached out and ripped the veil from his hands, she tripped and fell to the ground – harder this time. *Ow!* Pain shot from her knees, from her elbows. To make matters worse, she'd splashed down in the only mud puddle in all of dry, dusty Riyadh.

The puddle was notorious to Abdullah and Wadjda. Every day, a handsome young man stood at this spot, washing his car. He washed it right when the girls' high school bus passed by the end of his street. He was there every morning, and again in the afternoons. The second wash was for safe measure, Abdullah always joked.

Wadjda figured that the guy must really like his car clean. Either that, or it had something to do with the big smiles and long gazes she'd watched him exchange with the older girls. It seemed to Wadjda that they were able to communicate quite a bit while showing nothing but their eyes.

Although the handsome young man didn't know she existed, Wadjda liked him – usually. When he washed his car, he blasted music from the speakers, and the bouncy songs gave her walk an upbeat soundtrack. Today, though, wiping mud off her face and clothes, she cursed him under her breath. Her once-neat black veil lay submerged in the swampy mud.

Ahead, Abdullah screeched to a halt and stood, one foot on a pedal, one on the ground, eyes wide. Smeared in mud, hair a mess around her face, Wadjda looked terrifying. She sat up and shot him a fiery glare.

"You moron! You're so stupid! How can I go to school like this?"

He'd gone too far. Abdullah's shoulders slumped. He was about to get off his bicycle to help when some boys emerged from a nearby store. They were the same guys he'd seen at the intersection. Like him, they were dawdling on their way to school.

As the boys unchained their bikes, Abdullah caught the nearest one's eye. He knew he looked embarrassed, so he struggled to disguise his guilt with a mocking smile. "Did you really think you could catch me?" he shouted.

He didn't look at Wadjda, and he used a barking, unsympathetic tone she wasn't used to. Caught off guard, Wadjda looked at him in utter confusion. Then, composing herself, she snapped back, "I did catch you! Even on your stupid bicycle, I'm faster."

The boys were clowning around on their bikes in front of the shop now, spinning in circles, trying to catch one another with great bursts of speed. Part of Abdullah wanted to join the game. Another part wanted to help Wadjda. He looked back and forth, torn.

"Yeah, right. Seems to me like you're late and covered in mud. Hey, maybe if you had a 'stupid' bicycle, you could go home and change! Oh wait: you don't. So I guess you can't."

With that, he stood up on the pedals and kicked his bike forward, pumping his legs hard. In seconds, he'd covered the distance to the group of boys.

The dust from his departure blew slowly towards Wadjda. She stayed where she was, sitting on the ground, keeping her face steady and still. If her lips trembled, or if the tears fell from her eyes, Abdullah would see how hurt she was.

The boys pedalled off, Abdullah riding in circles round the tallest one, showing his skills. He didn't even glance back over his shoulder.

Wadjda let her head drop down against her chest. Time for school. She was going to be late *and* dirty. She took a shaky breath, counted to ten and hefted herself off the ground, dragging her veil up after her. It felt like an iron chain, impossibly long, almost too heavy to lift. When she tried to squeeze out the water, she only got more mud on her hands and arms. The veil was too grimy and wet to even imagine wearing.

With a sigh, Wadjda started to run. In the distance, she could still make out the boys, weaving their bicycles back and forth across the street, happy and free. They moved so fast on their bikes. They flew through Riyadh like birds.

"I'll get one," Wadjda said out loud. It sounded like she was challenging herself.

CHAPTER FIVE

Wadjda crouched in a sliver of shadow cast by a building round the corner from her school, frantically considering her options. How could she sneak in without being noticed? There had to be a way!

She couldn't see beyond the school's front gate, but she knew from experience that Ms Hussa would be directly inside. Somehow the principal was always there, waiting to catch Wadjda when she messed up. If the devil had a name, Wadjda thought, it would be Hussa.

Images of the principal slinking through school like a Siamese cat darted through her mind. Wadjda shuddered. Each day, Ms Hussa stood at the entrance and inspected the girls, raised up on her sleek stiletto heels, gazing down from on high. Wadjda's mother had told her Ms Hussa's shoes were designer and very expensive. It made sense. The principal's style was as legendary as her terrifying reputation. Each day, Ms Hussa pulled her hair back tightly to accentuate her perfect make-up. The style set off her sharp, unmerciful eyes. She seemed to have new clothes every week, and the girls were always gushing about her many different outfits.

Not Wadjda, though. She didn't like expensive stuff, and everything Ms Hussa wore practically had dollar signs scribbled all over it. To Wadjda, Ms Hussa looked like a dummy in a shop, not a real person with her own style. Of course, no one cared what Wadjda thought, especially not about fashion. She was the starkest contrast you could imagine to the glamorous Ms Hussa.

But it wasn't just the fancy shoes and clothes that put the principal above it all. It was the way she talked – like she was smarter and more interesting than Wadjda. It was the way she walked – like she always had somewhere better to be. It was the way she looked for an excuse – any excuse – to put someone down.

Ms Hussa won't need an excuse today, Wadjda thought, examining her filthy clothes. If she had a good enough story, she could get away with a warning about the muddy uniform – *maybe*. Coming to school without a veil was something else. Wadjda had been warned about the casual way she covered her hair three times already. But she'd never forgotten her veil altogether.

And it wasn't just the punishment Wadjda feared. It was Ms Hussa's mean comments, which would burn through

Wadjda like tiny sparks on her skin. The whole school would look on as she squirmed beneath the principal's disdain. Ms Hussa was the head enforcer when it came to labelling misfits, to relegating anyone who made the slightest misstep to a lifetime of insults and social-pariah status.

"Why does she have to be so *awful* about everything?" Wadjda whispered to the empty street.

The wind whistled by, as if suggesting answers. Maybe, it said, it was Ms Hussa's deep-rooted sense of superiority. She was the daughter of one of the town's most influential leaders. They had more money than Wadjda could imagine. Throughout her childhood, Ms Hussa's father had probably told her that the family was better than anyone else's. That she was better, too.

Or maybe Ms Hussa had been hurt once, and now she was alone and angry. Though she was very beautiful, Ms Hussa didn't have a husband. And everyone knew why. Even Wadjda had heard the rumours. Supposedly, when she was young, Ms Hussa had been in love with a boy. But the boy was from a different tribe – and, even worse, he was poor. Still, they liked each other, so they sneaked around. Apparently, they'd been caught together at her house. To avoid punishment, Ms Hussa had claimed her love was a thief and said that he'd broken in.

No one knew if the rumour was a hundred per cent

true, but everyone whispered about it anyway. So maybe that was the answer to Ms Hussa's meanness. Still, Wadjda didn't understand how the ultimate bad girl had grown up to be the biggest defender of the same moral code that made her look so bad.

"You'd think she'd give people chances instead," Wadjda murmured. This time, she spoke loudly enough for the last few girls going through the school gate to hear. One turned her head, and Wadjda shrank back against the opposite wall.

Enough. She needed to get inside. Sighing, she mapped out her options. There weren't many. Could she scale the school's walls? No. She didn't even have to look up to know that was a stupid idea. The gigantic, brown concrete barrier was almost two storeys tall. Unless she magically transformed into Spider-Man, Wadjda wouldn't be able to hoist herself that far. And that wasn't going to happen, at least not in the next few minutes.

Maybe she could bribe one of the other girls for their veil? *No.* The thought of parting with the money it would take stopped her cold. Besides, everyone else at school was scared of Ms Hussa, too. Even for money, they were unlikely to risk her wrath.

The final bell was ringing. She'd have to run the gauntlet and hope for the best. Dashing forward, Wadjda mixed in with the group of girls rushing to get through the gate before it closed. With any luck, she could duck below some of the taller ones and slip past Ms Hussa's incredibly sharp eyes.

As Wadjda passed through the shadow of the front gate, she saw Fatin and Fatima up ahead. As expected, she saw Ms Hussa, too. The principal was in her usual spot, wearing a beautifully embroidered black top over a perfectly fitted long, black pencil skirt. Her arms were crossed over her chest, and she leaned easily against the fence that ran along the interior of the school. This large wooden partition was meant to ensure privacy for the girls during the brief minutes when the school gates were open. A huge image of a fully veiled woman had been splashed across its surface in vivid paint. Underneath, a caption in bold letters read, *This is the perfect* hijab *for all schoolgirls*.

Behind the partition, which formed the final barrier between the all-female school and the outside world, Wadjda could see the girls starting to take off their *abayahs* and veils. Some of her classmates took it to the next level: they wore the *shayla*, a sheer silk garment that covered the entire face. But at school they removed that, too. Because the school was only accessible to women, the girls were free to shed the extra layers of clothing that kept them safely out of sight from the men and boys outside.

As she looked at the laughing, chattering group, Wadjda

felt her heart clench. The overcrowded schoolyards of Riyadh were probably the only big social gatherings of which she and her classmates would ever be a part. Nothing else was allowed. And, awful as it could be, school was the only place where girls her age were in direct contact with life on their own terms. Here alone they could get away from their homes and families and be themselves.

Wadjda inched forward. The girls ahead of her cheerfully exchanged morning greetings, shared the latest gossip and combed their hair into place as they removed their head coverings. *I wish I were like them*, Wadjda thought. Her classmates always seemed to be having so much fun. Was it possible that they didn't worry about their mothers and fathers fighting? That they didn't hear their mothers fretting about bills at the end of the month? Did they not dream of surfing waves or joining a band and playing music like the kind she danced to on the radio? Wadjda blinked, watching the shapes of the girls go blurry and indistinct in the sun and dust. Was it possible, really possible, that they were happy to live the lives everyone told them were acceptable?

In most ways, it seemed like the answer was yes. Sure, when no one was looking, some of the girls might apply lip balm or spritz on perfume. They might sneak a look at themselves using little mirrors mounted on pencil sharpeners. This had been popular since the removal of all the bathroom mirrors, which Ms Hussa called "a profane distraction". Wadjda had rolled her eyes pretty hard at that one. Luckily, no one noticed.

Aside from these tiny rebellions, though, most of the girls Wadjda's age were content to fall in line, follow the rules and avoid the harsh social judgement that came with being labelled "immoral". Wadjda knew that she risked this judgement each time she darted into a back alley seeking treasures or dashed off after Abdullah on an adventure. Sooner or later, she was going to get caught.

And Ms Hussa might be the one to catch her. Wadjda's heart beat faster as she moved into the principal's line of sight. She saw Ms Hussa squinting, trying to see past the two girls in front of her.

HA! A loud bark of a laugh caught the principal's attention. She swivelled towards Fatin and Fatima, who were folding their *abayahs* and getting ready to go to class.

"Quiet, girls! You're just behind the front gate. You mustn't laugh so loudly. Do you want men to hear you? A woman's voice is her nakedness."

A suppressed giggle from Fatin. Silent as ever, Fatima lifted her hand to hide her defiant smile. Twisting her shoulder, she gave Fatin a gentle bump, urging her to respond.

"Sorry, Ms Hussa," Fatin blurted.

Wadjda blinked. If she didn't know better, she'd say Fatin was being sarcastic. But surely even Fatin and Fatima wouldn't dare sass Ms Hussa!

"It won't happen again," Fatin added – with an equal amount of sarcasm.

As Ms Hussa's quiet fury zeroed in, Wadjda made her move. Pivoting on the ball of her foot, she darted to the left, heading straight for the other side of the partition, where the girls were removing their veils. She could see her escape right in front of her . . .

"Wadjda!" Ms Hussa's voice sounded like a thunderclap. Wadjda stopped dead in her tracks. Her whole body slumped. Caught, she turned to face Ms Hussa.

"Where is your head cover? Are you coming to school unveiled?" The words dripped with horror. If Ms Hussa had asked, "Wadjda, did you just kill someone?" she couldn't have sounded more appalled.

But there was more to come. All of the other girls had stopped what they were doing to watch the spectacle. Suppressing a smile, Ms Hussa paced towards Wadjda like a lion circling a wounded gazelle. With elaborate fake concern, she examined the mess of bows and clips scattered across Wadjda's head.

"And who put those awful clips in your hair? You look like a groomed donkey!"

Most of the girls were giggling now. They stared at Wadjda and whispered to one another behind their hands. Wadjda seethed with frustration, twisting the soaking, useless veil in her hands.

Only Fatin and Fatima shot her a look of sympathy.

CHAPTER SIX

The clock ticked loudly. Wadjda watched the second hand circle round. It seemed to be moving in slow motion.

This was her first religion course of the day. Four others would follow before the final bell rang. Some were super boring, like inheritance law as taught by the Quran and the Imams. Only a few classes covered non-religious subjects. Thinking about the long hours ahead, after the humiliation she'd already endured, made Wadjda want to put her head down on her desk and fall asleep.

Most of her classmates, about twenty other girls, seemed to feel the same way. A few sat up eagerly, staring at the board, but most slumped on to their hands and elbows, tired and drowsy with the midday heat. The depressing room didn't help. The desks had once been covered with pretty stick-on ConTact paper, which had helped obscure the scribbles and graffiti marring their tops. Over time, though, the wallpaper had torn away, leaving an even uglier surface on which the girls had to work. No one had bothered to replace it.

The old air conditioner above their heads took the

burning hot air from outside and spat it out, dishwater warm, on to their heads. The fan on the ceiling was the only thing that made the temperature remotely bearable. During the previous class, the girls had covered the single window with cardboard to prevent the sun from beating its way in. It hadn't helped. Every single girl's thick grey uniform was soaked with sweat. Wadjda felt the damp patches under her arms and in a thick line down her back.

It was time to start. One by one, the girls pulled copies of the Quran from inside their desks and set them on top. Each girl's desk contained her copy of the Holy Book and her *abayah*. That was it. *What more would a young girl need?* Wadjda thought ruefully. As far as her teachers were concerned, all other materials were dangerous.

On the blackboard, Ms Noof, who taught the Quran in addition to conducting choir, wrote, *Registration for the Religious Club: Quran Recitation Competition*. The chalk squeaked through the lines and loops of the words. She moved like a lizard basking on a rock in the afternoon heat, all lazy confidence.

"The competition will be held in just over five weeks," she said, looking at each student in turn. "This is a very important event. It is a chance for you to show your faith and great devotion to God. Through her hard work and piety, one student will win."

Yeah, yeah, yeah, Wadjda thought, slumping further down in her seat. The school held one of these events once or twice a year. They always ended up being battles between the most popular girls, who were better at public speaking, and the best students, who were better at memorization. Wadjda was neither. She would usually just sit at the back and count the minutes till those mandatory assemblies were over – the way she was doing now.

"This is a great opportunity," Ms Noof said. She nodded at Noura, who had won the last speaking competition. Noura gave her a sparkling smile back. "It is an opportunity for you to shine in the light of Allah's greatness, to celebrate the guidance He gives us in the Quran."

She turned back to the board and started to set out the verses they would be studying that day. Wadjda's eyes went back to the clock. *Ticktock. Ticktock.*

Finally released at the end of another excruciating school day, Wadjda stood in the middle of the crowd of girls gathered behind the partition. Once again, it was time to venture into the outside world. Sighing, Wadjda pulled her grimy, stained *abayah* over the top of her grey uniform. Beside her, each girl in her class did the same.

As their hands rose and fell, the schoolyard transformed into a sea of black, the dark colour rippling across the crowd like a wave – or a shadow. The grey of the girls' uniforms was swept away beneath the flowing black fabric of their *abayahs*. Veiled, each one became a miniature version of the covered woman on the giant poster looming above them.

The girls covered themselves automatically as they talked and laughed. But the energy and enthusiasm of that morning waned beneath the blaze of the afternoon sun. Its hot rays burned down more and more brutally as the clock ticked past 1:30 p.m. Already the temperature had reached well over 40 degrees Celsius. Yells and laughter faded to whispers and sighs as the girls readied themselves to leave. In small groups, they'd hop on to their assigned buses or into the cars of their assigned driver. Safely delivered home, they would beeline to the nearest possible air conditioner.

But first they had to get there. And Ms Hussa was back in her spot, making sure each girl left the school completely covered. It was required, and she always did what was required. One by one, her sharp eyes ran over the older girls, making sure their faces were concealed, their hands tucked inside the sleeves of their *abayahs*. She checked to be sure they wore socks to cover any flashes of skin at their ankles and feet. Most importantly, she made sure that each student's exit card was up to date and accurate.

The exit cards. Wadjda sighed, rocking back on her heels as she watched the crowd move past her. Every girl at school was required to present one. It listed the family member or driver who would collect her, and the approved mode of transportation she would use to get home.

Ahead, the girls who took the bus raised their cards high as they hurried past. Endless pairs of black leather shoes stampeded out of the front gate, sending up a dense cloud of dust. The gritty haze hung in the air for a moment. Then, slowly, it began to settle back on to the crowd. Each day, these girls competed for places at the front of the bus queue. Football players in the final match of the World Cup couldn't have tried harder to get to the goal.

The students waiting to be picked up by a private car hung back by the partition. They had to present a card that matched that of the male driver on the other side of the gate. This card would then be placed prominently on the dashboard for the entire time the girl was in the car. Since women were not allowed to drive, the whole process was rigidly controlled. No girl must ever go off on her own.

The last group was Wadjda's – the girls who walked home. They already had a note in their files, signed by both parents, stating that they were allowed to travel solo. Of course, if they were seen with a boy, they might still be stopped on the streets. Unless they had a note explaining what they were doing, they'd get in big trouble. Luckily, Wadjda lived close enough that it wasn't an issue. And she was young, too. Most days, no one paid that much attention to her. And even if she'd wanted a ride there was no one available to pick her up.

Ahead, Fatin and Fatima waited for their drivers, fanning themselves with their cards. They smiled at Wadjda, but she was too tired to smile back. Her fury at Abdullah for snatching her veil – and her rage over getting busted and humiliated by Ms Hussa – had given way to fatigue. Her whole body ached, from the bones in her toes to the roots of her hair. With the sun soaking into her jet-black *abayah*, she just wanted to go home.

To her surprise, Fatin and Fatima strolled over. Fatin's brow was wrinkled with mock suspicion. "Looks like someone's trying to get in trouble again," she said in a sing-song voice. Then, in a normal voice, "You must *love* chatting with Ms Hussa. Where's your card?"

Wadjda folded her arms proudly. "I walk home."

They laughed, not unkindly, at her innocent pride. And they smiled at her veil, which was so dirty it looked like it had been dragged for miles behind a car. Fatin and Fatima didn't know Wadjda well enough to ask what had happened, but Wadjda thought they seemed intrigued. *Probably picturing all my crazy adventures*, she thought. *Maybe they're even jealous!* Glowing with pride, Wadjda tightened the filthy cloth round her head and walked out of the gate.

Being allowed to walk home did make Wadjda proud. When she was dashing through the streets of Riyadh, she felt like she'd become real again. Though she had a mile or so of walking, Wadjda felt like she was already halfway home.

Today wasn't a good day, though. Today was *hot*. Wadjda put her head down and trudged forward, trying to move slowly. As she plodded along, the spinning feet of a group of boys pedalling bicycles caught her eye. Their pale *thobes* reflected the harsh sun, temporarily blinding Wadjda.

A lecture she'd heard in science class tickled her memory. Again and again, her teacher had told them that dark colours absorb heat, while lighter colours reflect it back. She ended the lesson by stating that this phenomenon was one of the miracles of the universe. It proved there was one almighty God, Allah, and that he had created everything for a purpose.

Beneath her hot black veil, Wadjda twisted her lips. She wondered if people knew this scientific secret when the tribal code assigned black to women and white to men. Maybe the real miracle of the universe was that she was able to walk home in Riyadh's sweltering afternoon sun without passing out!

The boys were gone now. Their bicycles moved like a flash round the corner. Wadjda squinted into the dusty afternoon and continued slowly on her way. As she walked, she pitched the stone Father had given her at various targets – a can, a stick, a funny-coloured brick on the side of a building – thinking all the while about the different miracles of the universe. It had taken so much to get her to this exact spot, at this exact moment. So what was *her* purpose, now that she was here?

Crick! Her rock hit at an angle, ricocheted off the pavement and tumbled into an empty plot of land. *Oh no.* Wadjda sighed and looked to the heavens for guidance. She felt nothing but the intense heat of the afternoon sun burning her cheeks. If the stone had been a gift from anyone but her father, she'd have abandoned it and kept walking. Instead, she trudged into the barren plot to hunt it down.

Does the universe make sense to anyone? she wondered, sifting through rubbish and weeds. Her parents didn't seem sure of what they were doing, and they were ancient! What if she just kept getting older and older, and she never figured out what she was meant to be doing here?

A few minutes passed. Wadjda grew nervous. Was the rock lost? Her father didn't give her many gifts, and this one had felt really special. Like proof that he thought about his rock-throwing daughter during the long weeks he spent away. She kept picturing him out in the middle of nowhere. He'd had to think of her at least twice, she told herself. Once to pick up the stone and once to bring it back.

Ahead was a spiky green plant, its stubby leaves burned brown by the sun, its twigs coated with yellow dust. Wadjda moved it aside and found her rock nestled against a discarded cigarette pack. A smile lit her sweaty face, making her feel light and cool despite the unending heat. She rose, scanning the ground for her next target. Up went her eyes, up up up, her arm lifting, too, as her gaze ran across the horizon.

And at that exact moment, over the top of the fence on the far end of the field, Wadjda beheld a vision. A beautiful shiny green bicycle, suspended in thin air, reflecting back flashes of light where the sun beamed down upon it.

Wadjda stood, mouth agape. Wonder and disbelief swirled through her, sending tingles of excitement down to her fingers and toes. This wasn't real. It couldn't be! She blinked. She shook her head. She tugged back her veil, clearing her face almost completely, and opened her eyes as wide as they could go.

Still the bicycle floated in place on the other side of the fence, not moving, not rising or falling, just hovering. It seemed to be poised at the point where wooden boards met sky, waiting, ready for a ride.

For what felt like forever, Wadjda continued to stare. Without looking down, she dropped her arm and slid her black stone into her pocket. And still her eyes followed the bicycle. It was like a vision, a dream. The most beautiful dream she'd ever had.

Suddenly, the bicycle began to glide across the top of the fence, its pedals whirling in slow circles, as if pushed by invisible feet. It came to the end and emerged fully into view, and that was when Wadjda saw that her beautiful green bicycle was resting on top of a delivery truck.

Her heart locked on to that bike. Without even realizing her feet were moving, she began to run after it, heart thumping in her chest. The bicycle disappeared down the next block, caught up in the flow of cars cramming the busy street. The truck manoeuvred behind a shiny red Ferrari and a rusted pickup, both of which jockeyed for position in front of an old 1980s-style limousine. All the cars were pushing their way towards the stoplight at the next intersection.

There, the chaos of the traffic spilled out beyond the three marked lanes of the street to create five distinct rows of cars. With horns honking and engines grumbling, drivers crowded their way on to the shoulders on both sides of the road. The only traffic rule in Riyadh was muscle. Driving here was an endless game of chicken. The key was to keep moving forward. You never gave in or let yourself be intimidated by other, more fearless drivers.

As Wadjda watched, the truck turned and disappeared

down the next street. Again, her feet moved her into action, without a moment's hesitation. She sprinted forward, breathless. When she caught up, the truck was parked in front of a run-down toyshop. It was a random store in the middle of a quiet roadside mall on the outskirts of the neighbourhood. Wadjda had never bought anything there, or even really noticed it.

Today, though, men unloaded many large boxes, carried inside bicycle after bicycle, each wrapped in protective plastic. Wadjda fought her way through the crowd of workers, craning her neck. *Where's the green one?* she thought, her heart in her throat. Search as she might, the beautiful bicycle was nowhere to be seen. It had disappeared.

An older man, dressed traditionally in a long white *thobe* and red-checked *ghutra*, made his way through the sea of items. Immediately, he caught Wadjda's attention. *There's something about him*, Wadjda thought. Maybe it was the fact that he was wearing a weird warm vest in the middle of summer?

But what she really noticed was how he looked relaxed, like he was taking things easy. A big smile filled his face and brightened his eyes. Now and then he joked with the workers as they unloaded the goods.

At last, the truck pulled away, and the interesting man disappeared back inside. Sneaking forward, Wadjda pressed her nose to the hot glass. Through the thin layer of dust, she saw him lean over and pick up something heavy. When he emerged through the door again, Wadjda's heart lifted with joy. He was carrying the bicycle! He put it on display right in front. Its green crossbar shone in the hot sun, sparkling like a precious emerald. The gentle afternoon breeze lifted the bright ribbons on its handles. It was in a league all its own, standing out from the other toys and bikes like a shining beacon.

The man, who Wadjda decided must be the toyshop owner, looked admiringly at the bike. He brushed a hand across the smooth black leather of the seat, clearing it of dust. Smiling, he took a sign from his clipboard, wrote, *Only 800 Riyals!* and placed it on the handlebars. Then he went back inside the store and put an old record on an even older record player.

In all this time, he hardly seemed to notice the strange girl hovering outside his door, staring in awe at the bike.

The record crackled to life. Wadjda recognized the smooth, honeyed voice of Talal Maddah, one of the earliest Saudi singers, and her mother's favourite. His sweet song floated out of the shop, filling the street. Wadjda cocked her head to the side, intrigued. The fact that the shop owner was listening to this music made him even more interesting to Wadjda. Talal Maddah had famously – or infamously – died of a heart attack while performing on one of the few live TV shows allowed in Saudi Arabia. He died singing, in front of millions of his fans.

The next day, all the Imams in the country damned him. They said he would go straight to hell, where his soul would be forever tortured.

"Why were they so angry?" Wadjda had asked her mother one day when they were listening to his music.

"Talal Maddah sang songs about love between people." Her mother twisted her lips sadly. "You know such music is *haram*." This meant it was forbidden. "And percussion is OK, but other musical instruments? That's the worst!"

It was true. The Imams thought Talal Maddah's songs were bad and immoral. To the religious authorities, performing any type of music or art in public was a great sin, and in the end one of the Kingdom's greatest artists died poor and cursed. But in this moment, as Wadjda stared at the bicycle, the painful longing of Talal Maddah's songs touched her heart. At last, she understood what he was singing about!

Slowly, so slowly, Wadjda ran her fingers across the bicycle's shiny chrome handles. Its wide seat gave it old-school charm. It was beautiful. It was sturdy. It looked incredibly *cool*.

It's also a girl's bike, Wadjda realized. The dropped

middle bar between the handlebars and the seat – to accommodate skirts like the girls in her magazines wore – made that clear. Wadjda wrinkled her nose, confused. Why would the owner order a girl's bike? What kind of girl would ride a bicycle around the streets of Riyadh?

At the moment the question crossed Wadjda's mind, she saw it all, crystal clear. This was her bicycle. She was the girl who would ride it.

The sun's heat had got slightly more bearable as the great glowing orb dropped lower on the horizon. It was getting late. Wadjda had to hurry home if she wanted any time to herself. But it was so hard to leave. Her eyes shifted back to the sign, fixing themselves on the impossible price.

Again, the man emerged from the store. His eyes widened with surprise – he hadn't expected Wadjda to still be standing there. For a moment, he just looked at her. She looked back, confused and intrigued. He was so much less formal than the other shopkeepers, in his choice of dress and his taste in music. Still, he didn't look thrilled to see her. He nodded his head towards the sign, a quick motion, up and down.

"It costs eight hundred Riyals. Too expensive for you, I'd say."

As he spoke, a hint of a smile danced on his lips, warming his face. Then it was gone. He looked stern again, and weary, like he was tired of kids wandering around his shop all day and never buying anything.

I'll show you, old man! Her wandering had a purpose. Expensive or not, the green bicycle would be hers. Wadjda tilted her chin up and set her jaw – no smiles for her, just determination. She looked at the bicycle. She looked at the shop owner. And she gave a nod of her own, a quick motion, up and down. Her eyes told him, *I'll buy it from you. Before you know it, I'll buy it!*

The owner's expression didn't change. Slowly, Wadjda turned and walked away. Behind her, Talal Maddah's serenade drifted down the lonely street. It filled Wadjda with thoughts of love and existence, of light in darkness – a million poetic things she hadn't understood until this moment, when she saw her green bicycle.

CHAPTER SEVEN

The way home took Wadjda past the massive houses in the fancy part of town. Each one was the size of a palace, a humongous structure with many floors. Fleets of shiny new cars were parked outside. Usually, Wadjda liked to imagine the many servants and workers running around in the mansions, taking care of the family.

But tonight she was distracted. Her mind raced, and she walked with newfound purpose. All she could see was her green bicycle, hovering in the air before her, shining like a vision in the darkening sky.

Moving fast, she cut through the rubbish-strewn land between the villas. The plots had been left empty because of inheritance disputes. Sons argued bitterly about to whom their fathers had left the land. Brothers clashed, fighting for years over the best locations. All this battling made even the nicest neighbourhoods in Riyadh look like they'd been built next door to garbage dumps.

The rest of the street was covered in construction sites. Every day, it seemed, a new building went up. The city was expanding across the desert, filling in acre after acre that had once been rolling sand dunes. Wadjda sped past one of the larger construction projects at the end of the block, which she thought was probably being built by a big shot like Abdullah's uncle.

As she ran, she counted and re-counted the small wad of money she'd made at school that day. No matter how she did the sums, it was still only twenty-five Riyals. Wadjda checked the final amount one last time, in case she'd missed any smaller notes. She hadn't. Frustrated, she stuffed the cash back into her pocket. Then she took the black stone and hurled it across the field with all her strength.

She missed her target – a Coke bottle, way out of range. Wadjda gave a small, angry cry. She needed that bicycle! If she had a bike, she could keep up with Abdullah and the other boys. Finally, *they* would be jealous of *her*. They'd see the sun flash off her beautiful green bike as she pedalled by, getting further and further ahead and disappearing into the sunset, victorious.

Maybe she could make more bracelets to sell at school. It was a lot of work, but jewellery always brought in decent cash. She could make more mix tapes, too.

Ahead of her, a group of men dressed in everything from *shalwar kameezes* to jeans and flannel shirts were at work on a half-finished luxury villa. Like ants, they crawled about, driving nails into the boards of what would some day be the top floor. As Wadjda stepped on to the field, they stopped what they were doing and turned towards her.

Awkwardly, Wadjda began to scuttle across the large open space, her arms wrapped round her body, her eyes on the ground. Lost in thoughts of her bicycle, she hadn't seen the men working above. Now she felt exposed to their watchful eyes – exposed, and completely alone. Cold sweat began to trickle down her back, and Wadjda felt her hands tremble with fear.

"Hey, nice throw! Why don't you come up and play with us? Let me touch those little apples!" one of the men called. The fellow next to him gave a menacing snicker.

Wadjda's heart sank, and she froze, trying to pretend she didn't hear. She imagined the auditorium poster, the one that called men human wolves. Maybe it was right. In that moment, she felt like a rabbit, hopping across an empty field. A pack of hungry beasts stalked behind her, snarling and hungry.

High above her head, the men laughed vulgarly. They were in a group now, lined up at the edge of the unfinished roof, staring down.

Wadjda's face burned with mixed emotions: shame, fear, embarrassment. She felt like she was doing something wrong. But why? On her long walks home, these sprawling plots and narrow streets were her whole world. She knew the alleys and roads like she knew the lines on the palm of her hand. Yet, as the men's laughter fell on her head, it was like she'd stumbled off the path she knew. Like she was trespassing in a foreign land.

As she hurried to the spot where she'd last seen her rock, Abdullah appeared out of nowhere and picked it up. His eyes were fixed on the scaffolding above them, and he glared fiercely at the workers. The giant shell of the building loomed ominously. The silhouettes of the men – far bigger than Abdullah or Wadjda – dwarfed their tiny figures.

Maybe it was the tough-guy look on Abdullah's face, but when she saw him Wadjda's whole body relaxed. She wanted to hug him and cry. Maybe they could throw rocks at the workers together. Not to hit them but to scare them a bit, to keep them from shouting out such awful things.

Thank goodness you're here, she almost blurted, but then she remembered how angry she was. Abdullah had ruined her veil and let Ms Hussa humiliate her! She dashed over and snatched her stone from his hand. Then she picked up another, rougher rock and threw it back towards him as she stormed off in the other direction.

"Take that!" she shouted, aiming the stone well above his head. "And stop following me. I don't want to play with you any more. At school, for not having a veil? The teachers made me stand out in the sun all day!"

Even on the last words, Wadjda was careful not to let her voice crack. Her friend dodged the poorly thrown rock and looked at her, ashamed. Wadjda kept her face cold. She put her stone in her pocket and turned towards home.

"Wait!" Abdullah shouted. He ran back to his bicycle and pulled a package off the rack on the back. Sheepishly, he held it out. His hand was shaking, just a little. "Here," he said. "I got you this."

Wadjda glared at him, suspicious. Eventually, though, she took the package. Ripping back the paper, she gasped as the wind caught and unfurled a new black veil. It was beautiful. A yellow flower made of beads decorated the corner.

For a moment, Abdullah and Wadjda watched the cloth dance in the breeze. Then Wadjda remembered how mad she was at him and stuffed it into her bag.

"This doesn't make us even, you know." A smile tugged at her lips. "You know when we'll be even? When I race you on my new bicycle! Before you know it, I'll be beating you all over town."

"What?" Abdullah scoffed, momentarily losing his apologetic tone. "Are you kidding, Wadjda? Girls can't have bikes!"

"Then I guess it'll be that much more embarrassing

when I win!" Wadjda said, narrowing her eyes in challenge. Again, she began to walk away. Abdullah jumped on his bike, ready to pedal off in the opposite direction, but at that moment a small pickup passed by. Its wheels rumbled across the empty plot, sending up a huge cloud of dust that completely engulfed him.

Looking back, seeing her friend coated in dirt and sand, Wadjda let out a long peal of laughter. Swiping at the dust on his face, Abdullah stuck out his tongue. He cursed and spat as he tasted the dirt. Wadjda laughed even harder.

At last, Abdullah smiled. They were friends again. The thought made Wadjda's heart lift. But it also made her more determined to get her green bike, race him and win!

An annoyed-looking site manager popped out of the pickup truck and stormed towards the workers. He didn't notice Wadjda or Abdullah. Atop the looming building frame, the workers visibly tensed. In a big group, they scurried down to meet the contractor at the entrance to the site.

"All day, and you only built one pillar? Five men working for me! I pay five men, and I get one lousy pillar? You're robbing me blind." The contractor's voice was harsh and mean. He slapped the closest man on the back of his neck, dragging him forward like a little boy caught cheating at school.

"Go to car. Go," he said, switching to condescending, broken Arabic. "We finish work on other building."

As she watched the cowed workers pile into the back of the pickup, Wadjda's heart sank. She felt bad for them, despite their taunts and stares. She wanted to tell them they should be nicer, that they were all stuck in this place together. That they shouldn't take their frustrations out on little girls, that there were real miracles in the universe and a purpose for everyone. That maybe she'd seen hers today, in the form of a green bicycle.

But she didn't. She just watched the truck pull away in a cloud of dust.

CHAPTER EIGHT

The air conditioner in the window over Wadjda's desk bellowed, spitting out icy-cold air. But only the top of her head felt any sort of relief. The oppressive heat of the afternoon had warmed the whole house to baking, and the AC only helped if you were right underneath it.

Frowning, Wadjda climbed up on her desk chair and pinned the ends of a dark blanket over the window. This would offer additional protection from the sun – and maybe help the AC battle back the heat from a few more metres of space.

I hate to cover my collage, she thought. Sometimes when she got home she'd stare at the cut-out pictures while she made bracelets. Sadly, on super-hot days she needed the blanket. Carefully, Wadjda lifted one of its corners and peered at a favourite picture.

Four girls, completely covered in *abayahs*, glided along on ice skates at a public ice rink. The photo might have been taken at their local mall, which had a large skating arena. The beautiful oval of sparkling ice looked like a jewel in the middle of the massive building, which was a super-modern maze of endless corridors. Wadjda had begged her mother to let her go skating there, but her mother always refused. The mall was the centre of social life in Saudi Arabia – and not just for kids. Grown-ups loved it, too. But Wadjda didn't have a driver, and girls her age weren't allowed to go to the mall alone. Plus, everyone knew couples just went there to flirt, so a chaperone was absolutely required.

Frowning, Wadjda threw herself back on to her bed with a huff. If only her mother weren't so scared of taking chances! Her fear kept them from doing even the littlest things out of the ordinary.

And the world's already so small, Wadjda thought. *So limited.*

But then her mother had reason to be afraid. Wadjda had torn the picture out of a newspaper. The accompanying article reported that the religious police had banned girls from ice-skating at the mall. "If anyone is seen renting skates or letting girls from age seven or older on to the rink, they will be punished," the caption read. The rink would be closed, and the migrant worker who had broken the rule would lose his work permit and be sent home.

Girls could easily bribe those same workers to let them in when no one was looking, though. On the playground, Fatin and Fatima had bragged about doing it. A little money went a long way with the guest workers, they said.

Inspired by their bravery, Wadjda kept ice-skating on her Things-to-Do list. Forget the stupid ban!

But enough daydreaming. She needed to shift her attention to something cooler: money. Carefully, Wadjda laid the bills and coins from her stack out on the bed. This was her entire stash, money she'd hustled and earned by selling candy, tapes, bracelets – anything and everything she could make, scrounge or imagine. Tearing a piece of paper from her school notebook, she wrote down *800 Riyals* in big letters. Her new goal!

Using thick, dark pen strokes, she drew a chart underneath to track her road to victory. Then, taking a deep breath, Wadjda started shuffling the notes, counting under her breath. "Ten Riyals, fifteen Riyals, seventeen, eighteen, nineteen, twenty, twenty-one, twenty-two, twenty-three, twenty-four . . . twenty-five Riyals."

No! Not nearly enough. If she was going to raise the eight hundred she needed for the bicycle, she'd have to seriously step up her game. Still, twenty-five Riyals wasn't nothing. Wadjda wrote the number on the chart, leaned back against her pillow and closed her eyes, contemplating her next move.

The house was quiet. The only sound was the hum from the AC. Its steady whir lifted the blanket's edges, set them gently swaying. Weariness tugged at Wadjda's mind. She felt herself drifting into sleep, her breath slowing, mind wandering. She wanted to slip away into a nice long nap so badly. But she couldn't give in to exhaustion. These quiet afternoons were the only time she had alone in the house. If she wanted that bicycle, she needed to work.

Start with bracelets. Wadjda sat up, shook off her sleepiness and started mapping out requests. Several girls had asked for bracelets from their favourite Saudi Premiere League football teams. Al Hilal, the team from Riyadh, was very popular. Their colours were blue and white. Al-Nassr, which played at the nearby King Fahd International Stadium and wore blue with yellow, was a safe bet, too. She'd make extras of each for some quick sales, Wadjda decided.

Carefully unspooling the coloured threads, she stretched out her legs and hunched over her knees to reach her big toes. Using them as the base for her *loom*, she wove the thread back and forth, watching the braided bracelets come into being. Her quick fingers moved faster and faster, tangling the coloured threads in complex patterns.

Lost in the task, Wadjda took a long time to realize that her stomach had started to rumble. Luckily, her mother had cooked *kapsa* the night before. At the thought, her stomach rumbled even more. To make *kapsa*, roasted onions, raisins and almonds were ladled on to tender rice bursting with cardamom, cinnamon, cloves and black lemon. This was then capped off with sizzling grilled chicken rubbed with blackened tomato paste. Towards the end of the month, when her salary was almost gone, Wadjda's mother had to skip the more expensive ingredients, like almonds. It was still early, though, and the *kapsa* was full of flavour.

I should make myself a plate, Wadjda thought.

The sound of the front door opening snapped her out of her fantasy. Yanking the thread from her toes, she leaped from her bed, darting to the spot just inside the kitchen where she did her homework. Before her mother made it through the door, she slid into her seat, laid out her books and lifted her pencil. She held it over the paper and sat up straight, like the very best student in class.

The front door slammed. Wadjda could hear her mother's heavy breathing before she entered the kitchen. As she removed her veil, she fanned herself dramatically with her hands, trying to cool down. Her face was puffy and red, and her hair looked like Wadjda's – all messy ribbons and tousled curls.

"Almost three hours in the car without AC! It was awful. I'm not sure how much longer I can handle it. Oh, *habibti*, I wish I could quit this stupid teaching job." Her mother sank into a chair, took off her heavy shoes and black socks, and rubbed her feet, all with the same dramatic flair. "I swear, this commute's going to kill me. I'd rather sell fruit down at the hospital than make that hideous trip every single day!"

Nodding in support, Wadjda jumped up to turn on the kitchen AC unit. She felt terrible for her mother. Each day, she came home upset about Iqbal, about his car, about the whole terrible journey to work. Iqbal charged her a lot of money, too! *He could at least fix the air conditioner in his piece-of-junk vehicle*, Wadjda thought.

"If only Iqbal blew cold air, instead of hot, *Ummi*," she said, smiling mischievously over her shoulder.

Her mother smiled back at her. Then, with a heaving sigh, she went to the stove to begin dinner. Wadjda loitered around the sink as her mother washed vegetables and got the plate of leftover *kapsa* from the fridge. Together, they started to prepare dinner.

What could she do to *really* cheer her mother up? Wadjda wondered as they worked. And when was the best time for announcing her plan to buy the green bicycle? What was the best way to bring it up? Her mother was unpredictable. Sometimes an idea would catch her imagination and she'd eagerly play along, coming up with elaborate schemes and strategies. Other times, she'd frown and shake her head, and Wadjda wouldn't be allowed to bring up her idea again.

The bicycle was too important to mess up. Wadjda wanted to introduce it naturally into the conversation, like it was no big deal. Of course it *was*, but she'd keep her cool while they discussed it. The cooler the better with her mother.

As she planned and plotted, Wadjda kept imagining the look on Abdullah's face when he saw her riding her brand-new bicycle . . .

Despite her best efforts, a mischievous grin stole across her face. Her eyes sparkled as she leaned against the counter. Her mother looked up from the food she was heating at the stove. When she saw Wadjda's expression, her eyes narrowed.

"I don't like this look on your face. What are you up to?"

For a fraction of a second, Wadjda debated whether or not she should tell her. If her mother didn't approve, it would be next to impossible to get the bicycle.

But she couldn't help it. She threw caution to the wind and blurted out, "I'm going to buy a bicycle to race Abdullah Al Hanofi! Maybe in two weeks, if I keep my business up!"

Her mother dropped the dishes in the sink with a clatter. As Wadjda's words sunk in, she twisted her lips and frowned. It was exactly like the face she made when she got mad at Wadjda's father for spending days away visiting his mother.

"A bicycle?" she repeated.

"Yeah! My business is doing so well, *Ummi*! I sold Tic Tacs for four Riyals today."

"Oh, Wadjda, I've told you a hundred times! You're not supposed to sell things at school. They'll have you standing out in the sun all day for the rest of your life."

Her mother's harsh words startled Wadjda back to reality. She blinked, watching the beautiful images of herself riding the bicycle go up in smoke.

But her mother wasn't done. "I don't want any more calls from your teachers complaining about you!" she said, throwing up her hands in exasperation.

Wadjda could get sad – or she could get mad. She chose the second option. Rolling her eyes, she stomped off to her room. Behind her, her mother was still going, her voice getting louder and louder.

"And you can absolutely forget about getting a bicycle! This plan of yours is ridiculous. A bicycle! Have you ever seen a girl riding a bicycle?"

I'll never tell her anything again! Wadjda thought, slamming her bedroom door, hard. *She never understands. She doesn't even try to understand!*

Though she slumped down on to the floor, her face was set, her eyes full of purpose. Decisively, she picked up her half-finished bracelets, wrapped the strings round her big toes and got back to work.

CHAPTER NINE

adjda entered her classroom early the next day like a woman on a mission. Her task? Scope out potential customers.

The girl who was busily cleaning the blackboard was out. Wadjda breezed past her without stopping. She knew from experience that she'd be a tough sell. Two other girls sat in the back row, bent over, eyes on each other's homework.

"Change the sentence a little," one whispered. "She'll know you copied it!"

Looking around nervously, the girl saw Wadjda and whispered loud enough for everyone within earshot to hear, "Uh-oh! Here comes the salesgirl!"

Whatever. Wadjda waved her off with a sassy flick of the head. Stuffing her *abayah* inside her desk and throwing her veil over the chair, she ran out to the school's playground area. One of the younger girls leaped up and came to meet her, making small gestures in an attempt to get Wadjda's attention.

"Hey, Wadjda!" she whispered. "Did you finish the bracelets?"

"Not all of them," Wadjda whispered back. "I've only got ten today. If you want one, you have to pay two Riyals extra."

The little girl frowned, trying to decide whether it was worth it. Seeing her waver, Wadjda decided to push. If she wanted the bike, she had to seal *all* the deals.

"It's a lot of work," she said softly. "I practically broke my back making them. And I stayed up so late last night – I'm not sure I'll be able to keep going like that!"

The thought of the bracelet supply drying up seemed to help the younger girl decide. She nodded. Wadjda's eyes fixed on her hands as she pulled the money from her uniform pocket. With each Riyal, she felt like she could see her bicycle more clearly.

They made the exchange, and a few more girls gathered round. A small, victorious smile spread across Wadjda's face as she handed out bracelets and collected money. A light breeze blew, stirring her curls. It wasn't hot yet. The sun was still pretty instead of scorching. *It's going to be a good day*, Wadjda thought.

Coming to school early was one of her secret joys. The mornings were a pretty safe time to make her sales, which was good. The consequences of being caught with a mix tape full of love songs would be dire. The thought of that conversation with Ms Hussa . . . *Yikes!* A chill ran down Wadjda's spine, and she shook her head to banish the image.

Then, in the half hour after she sold her stuff but before classes began, she could relax and embrace her well-earned free time. Running around, playing on the playground, kicking up sand – through it all, Wadjda couldn't stop smiling. Her jeans peeked out from under her uniform as she sprinted. Her trusty sneakers made her faster than everyone else. It wasn't as free as a bicycle ride through the streets, but it was close.

In the far corner of the yard, a group of girls played hopscotch. This quiet spot, just past the area where the girls came in and took off their *abayahs*, was Wadjda's favourite. She ran over, sat and leaned in to get a better view. As she watched, though, she grew increasingly impatient. The girl on the hopscotch grid, Salma, was moving like she was on tranquilizers or something. And the bell would ring at any minute!

Finally, Salma finished her pass and stepped ceremonially off the grid. Grinning, Wadjda leaped into place. She took her lucky stone from her pocket, tossed it in front of her and started to hop. Completing a smooth turn, she bent to scoop up her rock.

To her left, one of the other girls, Noura, raised her head. Her face twisted up with fear, like she'd just seen a horrible monster.

"We need to go inside!" she cried. "Men are watching us!"

All the girls froze. Then they looked up, frightened, and scanned the horizon above the school's imposing walls. Noura pointed with one hand, shielding her eyes from the sun with the other. Her finger was shaking. Wadjda raised her hand, too. She could barely make out a group of construction workers atop a building far in the distance.

"They're a million miles away, silly," she said, laughing. "No way they can see us from there. What, do they have Superman powers?"

"If you can see them, they can see you," Noura retorted. Wadjda snorted and turned her attention back to hopscotch. Noura flushed red.

"Fine," she hissed. "All the *good* girls are going inside. The bad ones who want to expose themselves to men can stay and play out here by themselves."

She waved dramatically for the girls standing nearby to join her. One by one, they rose and followed Noura back into the school. Salma went last. Though she looked sad to leave the game, Wadjda knew she would never dare to break a rule.

As she swung the heavy doors closed, Noura looked back at Wadjda with a victorious smirk. Wadjda met her sneer with a look of anger – and stuck out her tongue, too, for good measure.

"Go, you *sheikha*," she called, using a title reserved for

the most pious of religious women. "Who cares? You're terrible at hopscotch anyway!"

But Noura and the other girls were already inside. Shrugging, Wadjda tossed her stone, balancing on one foot, ready to hop. Before she started, she looked up – and saw Fatin and Fatima. They held a magazine between them, their heads bent over the pages. They were walking towards the back of the school, out of sight of the teachers.

Those girls! Wadjda shook her head, amazed. They walked around like they owned the place. If she didn't like them so much, it would make her angry – or jealous.

"Hey, you guys shouldn't be outside. Men can see you!" Wadjda yelled. Pointing, she indicated the workers, tiny moving specks far in the distance.

Fatin covered her face in pretend fear and looked over at Fatima. Fatima widened her eyes as if with terror. "Men?! Watching? What a scandal! Oh no, maybe they'll tell everyone they saw Wadjda al Safan playing provocatively in the schoolyard!"

All three girls burst out laughing, and then quieted, worried their teachers might hear.

"So, what's the latest mix?" Fatin asked. Beside her, Fatima grinned and nodded. Wadjda scrambled through her bag and pulled out a tape.

"It's got everything," she said. "There are songs on here

from every corner of the universe!" She held the tape up, swaying it back and forth before their eyes like a car salesman swinging the keys to a new Ferrari. "Hear the hits of tomorrow, today! All this can be yours for just ten tiny Riyals!"

Fatin let out a burst of laughter. Taking the tape, she looked over the tracklist on the back, nodding approvingly. "You little devil. I don't know where you get this music, but I'll definitely buy one later. And, hey, what about bracelets?" She flipped to a page in the magazine and held up a picture of a football player. He was tall and lanky, with hair that flopped over his face, and tanned, muscled legs. "Look at this gorgeous creature. I want a bracelet of his team – Al Hilal."

Wadjda took the magazine and inspected the picture, eyes bright. "No problem," she said, not looking up. "I'll make you a special one for tomorrow." Now she met Fatin's eyes, smiling broadly. "But it'll be ten Riyals, too!"

Fatin patted her on the head and took back the magazine. Beside her, Fatima was grinning. "Tomorrow, then, little hustler."

Wadjda pulled her head away playfully. "Don't mess up my hair!" she said, trying to imitate a teacher's cranky voice. "And, hey, you're not supposed to bring magazines to school! Ms Hussa'll kill you."

Fatin was turning to go, but she paused and gave Wadjda a sinister look, waving her fingers like an ogre. "Look who's talking!" she said. "Your bag is a twenty-four-hour convenience store."

All three girls burst out laughing, and then Wadjda resumed hopping, a big smile on her face. Across the courtyard, Fatin and Fatima plopped down by the corner of the building, safely out of view of the main door. They pulled nail polish from their pockets and started painting their toenails blue, the magazine open on the ground beside them.

For a moment, there was peaceful silence, punctuated only by the scuffing of Wadjda's feet on the ground. She was halfway through a circuit on the hopscotch grid, her left foot still lifted, when Ms Hussa slammed open the front door of the school. The bang of the door against the wall was tremendous. Wadjda gasped, and her hand shot to her mouth.

"Look out!" she hissed to Fatin and Fatima, gesturing wildly with her free hand. "Go!"

"Wadjda!" the principal yelled at the same time. The mean look on her face showed that she wasn't messing around.

Moving like a well-oiled machine, the two older girls jumped up, gathered their things and rushed through the back door before the word left Ms Hussa's mouth. Fatin dropped the bottle of blue nail polish under the bench as she slipped by.

Ms Hussa didn't notice. She was hovering behind the safety of the door, peering up at the distant workers on their faraway rooftop. Her ducked head and timid posture reminded Wadjda of the instinctive way most women she knew gazed out at the world. Sometimes, Wadjda found herself hiding behind the safety of a door, too.

It's weird that it feels so dangerous just to look out and see who's around, Wadjda thought. *It should be easier to take on the world than that.*

Ms Hussa pulled her veil tightly over her head, as if protecting herself from a storm, and wrapped her veil round her face as she marched out into the playground.

"What are you doing there?" she snapped at Wadjda. "Can't you see the men watching? Go to class right now, or you'll be punished like the little troublemaker you are!"

Wadjda leaped into action, snatching her bag and running towards the same back entrance Fatin and Fatima had used. As she passed the bench, she saw the bottle of blue nail polish glinting in the sun. Without breaking stride, she bent and scooped it up, cupping it in her palm like a treasure.

CHAPTER TEN

The end of a long, hot day. *Finally*. Wadjda couldn't wait to head home. She dragged her veil up over her face, shouldered her backpack and was headed to the gate when an older girl, Abeer, pulled her aside.

Abeer was nice enough. A little stuck-up, sure, but now and then she'd buy things from Wadjda. And she never teased her or called her names, so to Wadjda she was better than most. She was pretty, too, with piercing dark eyes. Although her hair was always pulled back in a long braid, she let her fringe fall free to frame her face. She was one of the girls who risked Ms Hussa's wrath by hiding a small mirror in the schoolyard and checking the traces of make-up she was able to sneak on during break.

Today, Abeer was already in her *abayah*. Delicate lines of *kohl* circled her eyes, making them look even prettier and more mysterious. Though she seemed ready to go home, she wasn't heading towards the bus queue outside. And Wadjda couldn't remember ever seeing Abeer walk to school.

She must be waiting for someone to pick her up, Wadjda decided. Her brother, her father, maybe a private driver?

Abeer looked from left to right, then checked over her shoulder. Tucking her fingers inside the edge of her veil, she pulled it tightly round her face. Her eyes darted left and right again. In her quietest voice, she whispered to Wadjda, "Can you take this paper out to my brother?"

With a furtive movement of her hand, she removed a folded note from her pocket and slid it between Wadjda's fingers. Wadjda looked at her – then it – suspiciously.

"What is this?" she asked, fumbling to unfold the paper.

"Shh!" Abeer whispered, holding a finger to her lips. "It's a . . . a permission slip to pick me up from school. I forgot to give it to him this morning."

Though she was trying to look casual, Abeer's eyes kept darting around the courtyard. Why was she so worried? Wadjda knew her predicament all too well. In Saudi, if you weren't lucky enough to be born a boy, you needed a paper permission slip from your guardian to do just about anything. From what Wadjda had seen of life so far, girls were doomed to spend most of their time finding ways round the system.

She sighed, folding Abeer's note into her hand. Every girl Wadjda knew had experienced some silly problem with a random paper or approval form going missing. There was no choice: you had to go round it and fix things your own way. And it didn't get any easier as you got older. Once,

Wadjda and her mother had tried to take the train from Riyadh to Dammam to attend a cousin's wedding. They were sent home because they didn't have a permission slip from her father allowing them to make the journey.

Livid, Wadjda's mother called her friend Leila for help. Leila lent her the permission slip she used, along with her family ID card. Since the family cards didn't have pictures, women just used whichever one they could get their hands on. Still, it wasn't easy. Her mother had told her over and over that her name wasn't Wadjda. It was *Aisha*. And her mother wasn't her mother. She was her big sister.

Back then, the whole thing felt like an undercover spy adventure. Wadjda was so excited that she giggled when they bought tickets using their fake names. The sound slipped out before she could help it! Mother's sharp look through the slit in her burka, however, made her stop immediately.

Now Abeer raised her eyebrows at Wadjda and tilted her chin towards the note. *Well?*

Wadjda looked back at the gate. A line of girls in black passed beneath the principal's gaze, ants snaking their way to the hill. Ms Hussa was in her usual spot, examining each as she passed. Her face reminded Wadjda of the train officer, who had mechanically stamped their papers and shoved them back into her mother's hand. Next, he called indifferently, and "Aisha" and her "older sister" had boarded the train to Dammam.

Back on the playground, Ms Hussa tossed her hair and straightened her expensive skirt. Occasionally, she stopped one of the girls, made her pause and turn. She was checking to see that only their dusty black shoes showed underneath their *abayahs*. As Wadjda watched, the principal held up a girl whose backpack had a picture of the *Twilight* movie stars on it. It was cool. Wadjda wouldn't have minded having one herself.

Ms Hussa did not agree.

"On the Day of Judgement, God will ask you to breathe life into these pictures. Can you?" Ms Hussa's tone was impossibly superior. She held up the backpack, shaking it in front of her student's face. "Pictures of human beings and living things are forbidden, let alone these . . . vampires." She shoved the bag back into the girl's arms. "Be careful. The West is always trying to infect Muslim youth with its poisons. You shouldn't be watching such movies."

The ten thousand times she'd been stopped for a similar lecture filled Wadjda's mind. Images flashed through her memory, like scenes from a TV show on mute. Each time, she knew, she risked going too far. There was a line in the sand, and if you crossed it you couldn't go back. She'd known this since she was very young.

As if in slow motion, she looked down at the note in her hand. Only now did she realize the crime she was being asked to commit.

Abeer saw that Wadjda was catching on. Still whispering, but more forcefully now, she leaned in to look directly into Wadjda's eyes.

"Listen. I'll give you ten Riyals if you help me out."

Wadjda looked back at Ms Hussa, then up at Abeer. Again, a vision of the green bicycle passed through her mind. She could practically feel the pedals turning beneath her feet, could almost see Abdullah's awe as she shot past him towards the finish line of a race. She had to earn eight hundred Riyals. She *had* to.

Determined, Wadjda lifted her chin and held up two fingers. "Twenty," she said.

Abeer's nostrils flared. For a moment, Wadjda thought she'd say no. But then she sighed and started going through her purse, counting out notes. She ran her fingers along the wrinkled bills to straighten them. One by one, she pressed twenty Riyals into Wadjda's waiting hands. Then, having made her payment, Abeer spoke with the authority of a manager tasking an official employee. "He's outside on the corner, in a pickup truck."

Wadjda nodded, stuffing the wad of notes into her pocket. Her body began to tense up – it changed her posture, made her look stiff and weird. She had to get it together! This would only work if she seemed normal. Taking a deep breath, she shook out her shoulders and arms, and started walking towards the gate. Halfway there, she tried to casually sling her backpack over her shoulder, but it didn't work. She looked like an alien who'd just discovered backpacks, trying to figure out how to put one on.

Behind her, watching Wadjda walk awkwardly away, Abeer frowned. This was a disaster! But there was nothing more she could do. She ducked round the corner, throwing her black *shayla* over her face and leaning her head against the hot stone.

Groups of girls in black flooded past Wadjda and out of the front gate. Ms Hussa was still in her place. In fact, Wadjda saw, she was actually still scolding the poor backpack girl, who was anxiously watching her bus fill up. Though she was clearly trying to pay attention, her eyes kept darting up to peer over Ms Hussa's shoulder.

As she got closer, Wadjda heard more of Ms Hussa's seemingly endless lecture.

". . . you will change your bag! Images are forbidden. In fact . . ."

This seemed as good a time as any for Wadjda to sneak past. But, even as she decided to make her move, Ms Hussa straightened and folded her arms, indicating that she was finished. The relieved student pulled her veil over her head and dived into the sea of black *abayahs* crowding the door of the school bus.

Sighing, Ms Hussa turned – and saw Wadjda walking towards her.

"Wadjda!" Ms Hussa used the tone reserved for special cases. Quickly, Wadjda stuffed Abeer's note into her bag and trotted over. Ms Hussa paused, squinting down at her, and then looked over to the corner where she'd been loitering. Abeer had plastered herself against the wall. She looked like she was trying to sink back into the stones.

The principal stared at Wadjda, studying her for what seemed like hours. Sweat beaded on Wadjda's forehead. Her heart pounded in her ears like a drum. Surely Ms Hussa would hear.

The seconds ticked by. Still nothing. Wadjda looked up slowly –

And saw Ms Hussa holding out a pamphlet. Their eyes met, and the principal flapped it in front of Wadjda, gesturing impatiently for her to take it.

"Come with an *abayah raas* like this tomorrow, or I'll reserve your usual place in the sun," she said. "Here. Show your mother."

Wadjda took the pamphlet. On the front was a picture of a completely black figure. The figure had no features –

no eyes, hands or feet. Its *abayah raas* covered its body from head to toe. Veiled in this way, the person looked like a ghost, like someone had taken a Sharpie and scribbled over the picture until nothing remained but blackness. Wadjda knew it was a woman; it had to be. But, looking at the picture, you couldn't tell.

Her heart sank all the way to her feet, and she felt her hands go cold. The *abayah raas* was the grown-up version of the covering she already wore. It looked way more inhibiting – not to mention intimidating – than the veil. And Wadjda already had trouble keeping *that* on her head! Still, she did her best to smile. She even held up the pamphlet and gave an enthusiastic nod, as if to acknowledge its importance. Ms Hussa stared back at her, face stony.

There was nothing more to say. It was the *abayah raas*, or the beating sun. As she turned away and finally let out her breath, Wadjda felt the heat start to drain from her ears. Slowly, her muscles began to relax. Her feet couldn't get her out of there fast enough. She had things to do.

CHAPTER ELEVEN

Outside the school entrance, a bus stuffed to overflowing with girls moaned past. As it rumbled by, Wadjda peered through the dirty windows, but saw nothing but black, faceless shadows.

In its wake, a choking cloud of dust swirled in front of her. Coughing and fanning with all her might, Wadjda squinted up and down the street, looking for Abeer's "brother".

There. A handsome young man standing beside a pickup caught her eye. He was waiting in a quiet corner behind the school, *thobe* carefully ironed and pressed. His black hair curled slightly around his ears. Wadjda looked him over sceptically. He seemed like a regular high-school kid – like Abeer. His car was decorated with bumper stickers quoting folk poetry about love. Stupid sappy stuff like, *I haven't slept since I glimpsed your eyes through your burka* or *Love is killing me. Every minute I long to see you.*

Slowly, Wadjda approached him. "Are you Abeer's brother?" she asked, wanting to be sure she was talking to the right guy.

The young man gave a small choked laugh. When he opened his mouth, his silver braces shone in the sun.

"Yeah, sure, I'm her brother. Have you got the paper?"

Cautiously, Wadjda reached into her backpack. She retrieved the note and held it up, making sure to keep it a tantalizing distance away.

"Yeah, sure," she repeated, copying his tone. "She said you'd give me twenty Riyals to deliver it."

In an instant, the young man's oh-so-cool posture changed. "Really?" he asked, arching his eyebrows. Wadjda thought she could see him trying to hide a smile. She waved the paper haughtily.

"Yes, really!"

Now the young man couldn't keep from laughing. Though he immediately reassumed his relaxed posture, his eyes were sparkling. "OK, OK. Here's twenty Riyals," he said, pulling a brand-new bill from his wallet. For a moment, he held it out in front of her, teasing Wadjda as she'd teased him with Abeer's message.

Wadjda barely noticed. Her eyes were fixed on the bill. She couldn't believe he was going to give her the money! Giving him Abeer's note without a second thought, she snatched the twenty Riyals and held it to her heart.

"Wow, even your money reeks of cologne! I'll have to wash it."

Again, a laugh broke through the young man's cool exterior. He got into his car and waved goodbye. As Wadjda watched, he drove round to the front gate of the school. She turned towards home, smiling in spite of herself.

Behind her, she heard the guard call over the school's PA system, "Abeer Al Rassi, please come to the gate. Your ride is here."

Her work was done. *Almost*. Though it wasn't exactly on her way, Wadjda decided to pass by the toyshop – just to be safe. As she skipped through traffic and leaped over cracks in the tarmac, she could already imagine the green bicycle, glimmering in the afternoon sun.

When she arrived at the shop and saw the real bike, it was even better than her imagination had promised. She stood, frozen, in awe of its greatness. Today it looked even bigger and more powerful. She'd get better and better at riding it, learn to go faster and faster –

If only she could reserve it somehow! The thought of someone else buying her bicycle was heartbreaking. As the baffled-looking owner peered out at her, Wadjda licked her finger and rubbed an *X* into the dust coating the bike, officially claiming it as hers.

*Harrumph*ing, the shopkeeper opened the door and stomped out, ready to chase her away. Wadjda met his frown with a smile. Her whole face beamed with joy. She nodded happily towards the *X*, imprinted in glistening spit on the bike's side.

"Don't sell this one. I reserved it!"

The toyshop owner couldn't help but shake his head. "Ha! That's ridiculous." Balling up his sleeve, he used the folded cloth to rub the spot clean.

Wadjda scrunched up her nose in annoyance and shot back, "I *will* buy it. With my own money, too!"

The shopkeeper looked down at her, a slight glimmer in his eyes. But then the call for *Dhuhr* prayer rang out, interrupting the moment. As if woken from a dream, he turned away and began closing up shop. Brusquely, he pulled a long black blanket over the goods lined up in front of the store, obscuring them from view.

Wadjda watched the billowing black cloth settle over her bicycle. She could still see its brilliant green colour in her mind's eye.

The call to prayer continued to echo through the streets, the lilting sound of the muezzin's voice reverberating off the walls of the buildings. A crowd of men had begun to make their way into the nearby mosque. Wadjda saw Abdullah among them, trailing behind his father and uncle, the one with the ridiculous moustache.

Impulsively, she put her fingers in her mouth and whistled. Abdullah had taught her how. On her walks home, she'd worked to perfect her skill. She knew Abdullah was proud of her impressive volume. "You can whistle as loud as a real fire-engine siren," he'd told her, eyes wide with admiration.

Sure enough, the shrill blast got his attention. Abdullah turned his head, and Wadjda gestured with her eyes towards the handlebars of the green bike, barely peeking out from under the black cloth. Using her hands, she gestured broadly to herself.

Abdullah smiled and shook his head. Pointing to the bicycle, he rubbed his fingers together – *silly, it'll take a whole lot of money to buy that thing!*

With a dramatic flourish, Wadjda pulled the forty Riyals from her pocket, fanned out the bills, and waved them defiantly at her friend. His eyes widened – as did his smile. Then Wadjda turned and strutted off proudly into the fading afternoon sunlight, her sneakers kicking up a glorious trail of dust behind her.

CHAPTER TWELVE

"Will you believe me, or do I have to swear? / No words can describe how much I love you, how beautiful life is with you," Wadjda's mother sang, her soft voice filling the kitchen. "For you are like gold."

The song was the most famous of Talal Maddah's many hits. As her mother crooned, Wadjda's hands burrowed deep into a bowl of dough, working the mixture into balls. She handed each one to her mother, who flattened it down.

They were making *margoog*, sheets of wholewheat dough spread across a bed of meat, beans, sweet potatoes and courgette, all bubbling in a sizzling tomato sauce. The meat would cook until it fell off the bone, dripping with juices.

Wadjda didn't like *margoog*, but it was her father's favourite – and one of the most complicated traditional dishes. It took almost a whole day to prepare. Why did Mother have to spend the whole day in the kitchen, working on something that would be eaten in minutes? *It makes no sense*, Wadjda thought. When she grew up, she promised herself, she wouldn't waste her precious time making *margoog*.

Still, she was happy her mother was singing, and Wadjda cut the dough carefully, making sure it lined up perfectly in the pot. Her mother moved from the counter to the stove, her voice rising playfully.

"See, I put my heart on my hand, and hold it out to you / It is the most precious thing I own." Her voice was lovely, just like Talal Maddah's. Wadjda looked at her, feeling a rush of awe. Her mother was so beautiful. As she cooked, the soft light of sunset reflected off her eyes, making them sparkle. Tonight, she glowed like a star.

"Don't you wish you were a singer, *Ummi*? You have the most beautiful voice ever!" The words spilled from Wadjda's mouth before she could stop them. Blushing, she looked down at the counter, awkwardly patting flour off her hands.

From the corner of her eye, she saw her mother raise her hands to her face in feigned shock.

"Never! I seek refuge with God from what you've said!" Though she was smiling, she added sternly, "Remember, Wadjda, a woman's voice must not carry beyond the front door. It's important you don't forget that."

This bit of wisdom imparted, Mother went back to singing. Now she performed even more dramatically, moving her arms to the rhythm and playfully imitating the moves of the Kingdom's most famous female singers.

"*Ya lillah danah la danah*," she sang. "They say lovers' hearts melt from longing, but our oaths give us a heaven of love and tenderness."

Unable to resist, Wadjda joined in. Her voice was high and nervous, but somehow it blended seamlessly with her mother's.

"*Ya lillah danah la danah* / They say lovers' hearts melt from longing, but our oaths give us a heaven of love and tenderness."

They began to giggle, their laughter blending like their voices. Then they went back to their duties, working hard to bring the meal together.

After a few moments of quiet, Wadjda decided to take advantage of her mother's good mood.

"So I've saved up eighty-seven Riyals already," she blurted. "I only need seven hundred and thirteen more to get the bicyc–"

"*Oof!* Again?!" Her mother cut her off before she could finish. "I thought you understood, Wadjda. This subject is closed. You are not getting a bicycle. It is *haram*! Please, stop."

Forbidden. It is forbidden. The familiar words fell on Wadjda like a hammer. She bowed her head and bit her tongue. For several minutes, they worked without speaking, her mother rolling the dough, Wadjda cutting it into pieces.

Well, that ruined the moment. It was tough to keep her

mother happy on the best days, and here she'd bumbled in and ruined one of the few they'd had in the last week. Wadjda racked her brain, trying to find a subject that would win her back over. It came in a flash – the one topic her mother couldn't resist. Clothes.

"Ms Hussa says I need to wear the full *abayah* to school from now on." She kept her voice casual, looking away and trying not to smile.

"Wow, the *abayah raas*!" Her mother immediately took the bait, just as Wadjda had known she would. "Someone's becoming a woman. And so fast! Almost overnight. Hmm, maybe it's time we marry you off? What do you think about that?"

"Ha-ha. That's not funny." Then the memory hit Wadjda anew, and she scowled. "Ugh, *Ummi*, Ms Hussa is so mean to me. She waits at the door, watching us, and when I walk by she pounces like a cat. Everything I do is wrong to her. Sometimes I wish she would die."

"Shh! How can you say such a thing? That's far too harsh." Wadjda heard real concern in her mother's voice. "You mustn't wish death on anyone, Wadjda. And to talk that way about Ms Hussa, of all people . . . Her life hasn't been easy."

"Oh, I know!" Wadjda was so excited by the possibility of gossip that she spoke without thinking. "I've heard the story about the 'thief', the one who jumped over the fence of the house to see her –"

Her mother's lips twitched. Though she turned back to the dough and vegetables, her face showed she was enjoying the gossip as well. The scandalous story of the so-called thief had haunted her mother's one-time classmate throughout their teenage years.

Arranging the last bit of dough in the pan, she washed her hands and motioned for Wadjda to follow her into her bedroom.

"Come with me," she said, smiling at her daughter.

CHAPTER THIRTEEN

On the other side of the wardrobe door, Wadjda heard the metallic scrape of hangers sliding along the steel bar. When her mother emerged, she was dragging an *abayah raas* behind her. Its dark folds seemed to go on forever. Lifting the hanger high to pull its full length free of the wardrobe, Mother handed it to Wadjda.

"Try this," she said with a laugh. "It might be a little long, but you can always carry it like this."

Her mother bunched up her dress in her hands and paced the room, like a princess lifting her ball gown to cross a puddle of water. Smiling in spite of herself, Wadjda slid the massively oversized garment over her small, thin frame.

"Just like Ms Hussa!" She giggled, bunching the cloth in her fists and attempting her best impression of the principal's elegant strut. Then, throwing up her hands, she gave her mother a look of playful shock and murmured, "Oh no! A thief!"

Wiggling her rear end, she pretended to scamper away. This time her mother failed to suppress her amusement.

"Shame on you, talking that way," she said, trying to keep a straight face. "We don't know! It could have been a thief."

They burst into hysterical laughter together.

As they caught their breath, Wadjda felt the mood in the room change. Her mother crossed her arms and looked out of the window, fixing her eyes on a spot in the distance. Impulsively, Wadjda reached up and pulled down the full *abayah* and veil. Standing in the middle of the room, completely cloaked in black, she looked like a phantom, some sort of shadowy figure from the underworld.

Her mother was still looking out of the window. Wadjda stumbled forward to stand beside her. Without looking down at her daughter, her mother reached out and absentmindedly adjusted Wadjda's veil.

"Your uncle's wedding is coming up." She spoke abruptly, as if this was what she'd been thinking about the whole afternoon. "I have to buy something very nice to wear. You know, so that all the other women see what they're up against."

A wave of compassion swept through Wadjda's body. She bunched up the sleeves of the *abayah raas* and twined her fingers together. The tense atmosphere at wedding parties was way too familiar – Wadjda knew what was coming. Although the wedding wouldn't take place for some time, she could already feel stress radiating off her mother.

Weddings took place in two segregated realms: one for men, and one for women. The two parties couldn't be more different. In their area, the men would drink coffee and tea and ... what?

Well, basically, Wadjda thought, *they stare at one another*. Over and over, the men would exchange awkward greetings. They were like goldfish swimming in a bowl, seeing other fish for the first time, blowing bubbles – then forgetting and doing the whole thing over again a few seconds later. The tribal world had never taken the art of conversation very seriously. From what Wadjda had seen, men's talk rarely extended beyond "Hello" and "How are you?".

In contrast to the men's snore-fest, the women knew how to party. Weddings were the only opportunity women had to dress seductively, and they took advantage. Funny, Wadjda thought, cos they were just showing off for other women! Dresses were skin-tight and left little to the imagination – especially in the cleavage area. *Totally embarrassing!*

The *tagaga*, or wedding singer, knew how desperate the women were to let loose, so she made things even wilder. Her music offered a soundtrack guaranteed to get the ladies on their feet. In addition to singing, the *tagaga* played the *duff*, a large tambourine-like drum, patting it heavily with her palms in a rhythmic beat that pushed everyone to dance faster, faster! Sometimes women would pretend they were possessed by demons. That way, they could go out on the dance floor and shake their heads like crazy, writhe their bodies, wiggle their butts. *Just be super ridiculous, really*, Wadjda thought. It looked fun.

But, among the joy, the women were watching one another. Potential young brides glided around the dance floor with grace and fake modesty. And women whose husbands had decided to take on new, younger wives did a special dance to show that they were still around, even though they'd been relegated to "second wife" status. Their husbands might have decided to marry again – it was not uncommon for men to have multiple wives – but still they wanted to intimidate potential rivals.

The second wives had to keep up a proud face in public, even if the idea of their husbands marrying another woman hurt them deeply. To maintain their dignity, they would allow themselves to be swept up by the music and dance without fear. It was a declaration to the world that they were strong.

Yet, they were like wounded birds, too. The memory of a pigeon that had flown into the glass of her classroom window came to Wadjda's mind. She'd stood in the courtyard and watched the delicate creature struggle on the ground. Its wings were hurt, but it was determined to fly again. Though it was too injured to take flight, it would not accept it.

The second wives were like that. Beautiful, hurt and too proud to acknowledge their pain. When they danced, everyone at the party stopped to watch. Unlike the other events in the women's room, their dance brought collective sympathy and understanding.

Wadjda thought again of the strangeness between her parents. She shivered. She didn't want her mother to have to dance the dance of the second wives, not yet, not ever.

As if she could hear her daughter's thoughts, her mother stood back from the window and ran her eyes up and down Wadjda's form. Head bowed, arms outstretched, Wadjda turned to face her. Black fabric cascaded across her body, spilling on to the floor like a puddle of oil, leaving no trace of the girl beneath. Her mother smiled sadly. It was as if she was seeing her mischievous runt transform into a woman, right before her eyes.

Before either of them could speak, the phone in the kitchen rang. Mother rushed to answer it, leaving Wadjda alone.

Stumbling over the folds of the *abayah raas*, Wadjda moved to the door and stuck her head out, watching her mother snatch up the phone and hold it against her ear with one shoulder. With her free hand, she lifted the lid off the pot of *margoog* and stirred it slowly. As she listened to her friend, she absently lifted the spoon to her lips for a taste.

"I'm so sorry, Leila. Iqbal, you know, our driver? He's so rude! He shouted at poor Aiesha yesterday. Aiesha, who never raises her voice! She cried the whole way home. Three hours of tears. Can you imagine?"

The conversation continued, but Wadjda decided it wasn't worth eavesdropping any further. Leila was trying to find a driver, and Wadjda's mother had no way of helping her. All she could do was lend a sympathetic ear.

This is going to be a long one, Wadjda thought. *Poor* Ummi.

Removing the *abayah raas*, she flopped down on the floor and went back to her new favourite hobby: counting money. The *abayah raas* she threw across the bed. It was so big that if she'd spread it all the way out, it could have been mistaken for a sheet. The thought of wearing it to school was awful.

To distract herself, Wadjda ran her finger down from the top of the 800 Riyals column. She stopped at 25 and crossed it out. Then she sorted once more through the new stack of banknotes.

Forty-five, fifty, fifty-five, sixty, sixty-five, seventy, seventy-five, eighty, eighty-one, eighty-two, eighty-three, eighty-four, eighty-five, eighty-six . . . eighty-seven Riyals.

Perfect. Just like I thought. Wadjda nodded in approval and added the new figure to the bottom of the column.

In the kitchen, she heard her mother beginning to protest, to refuse her friend's pleas for help. Her voice was kind, but also firm.

"Leila, dear, we're completely full. Honestly, you'd be better off with another driver." A moment of silence. "If you're lucky, you'll get someone better than Iqbal!"

Wadjda raised the money to her lips, gave it an enthusiastic *smack* of a kiss, and put it carefully in a drawer.

On second thought...

She buried it in the very back, hiding it behind a pile of socks and underwear.

"Really? Abeer? Mariam's daughter?" Her mother sounded invigorated – like she'd been hit with a jolt of electricity. "How did she even end up in a car with him? Who is he?"

The words sank in slowly, and Wadjda felt her whole body go cold. It was like she'd been plunged into a pool of ice and was freezing from the outside in. Breathlessly, she tallied up the different Abeers her mother and Leila knew. Wadjda had a cousin named Abeer, but her aunt's name was Sara, not Mariam.

Please, please don't let it be that *Abeer*, she thought, digging her nails into her palms.

"Of course," her mother was saying. Leila must have told her the boy's name. Her mother laughed. "He's a playboy, just like his father." She laughed again.

In her bedroom, Wadjda grimaced, trying not to imagine the whole terrible scene – and her role in it.

"You have to admit, his father's good-looking," her mother said with a giggle.

Wadjda moved to her desk chair. Perching on the edge, she craned her body towards the door, hoping to hear any bit of information that would place this story far from her, her school and stupid Abeer – who'd probably been caught red-handed with the note Wadjda had delivered.

"The religious police? Mariam must be dying!" The shock and delight of having a genuine scandal to talk about had transformed her mother. "Come now, they should have married her off a long time ago. Pretty girls are curses on a family."

Wadjda drew herself up into a ball. If only she could shrink away further and disappear into nothing. Trying to assess the magnitude of what was to come felt overwhelming. She heard the front door open and buried her head in her arms, wishing there were some sort of escape hatch through which she could bolt to freedom.

"I have to go, Leila," she heard her mother say happily. "Our father's home!" This was, Wadjda knew, the way wives referred to their husbands – as "our father". "Keep me in the loop on this Abeer scandal. *Yalla*, bye."

A second later, the door to Wadjda's room swung open.

Her mother stuck her head in, her eyes darting about distractedly. Already, she'd removed the casual bandanna she wore to cook and started to fix her hair.

At the desk, Wadjda tried to look busy – and tried *not* to think about Abeer.

"Go and say hello to your father while I get dinner ready." Her mother was clearly distracted. Her eyes kept darting towards the front door, but something in Wadjda's shallow breathing alerted her to trouble. She looked more closely at her daughter and asked, "What's wrong? Are you OK?"

Wadjda looked back at her like a deer caught in the headlights. Her mother smiled ruefully and went back to fixing her hair. Tucking the glossy strands behind her ears, she said, "Don't worry, Wadjda. We won't marry you off . . . Not just yet!"

adjda walked slowly into the *majlis*, the formal living room her mother reserved for her father and his guests. It felt like a foreign space in her cosy home, and it made her even more nervous.

It's only a matter of time before Father, and everyone else, figures out what I did, she thought. The scene she imagined made her legs shake even more. The Abeer scandal would be huge.

In the *majlis*, her father sat on the floor in front of the large flat-screen HDTV, leaning against a multicoloured cushion, playing a video game on his beloved Xbox. His *ghutra* and *iqal* were folded up next to him. Wadjda's eyes went instantly to his brand-new mobile phone, tossed casually on top of the pile. It was his third in as many months. *Probably shoots laser beams out of the bottom or something*, she thought, lips twisting wryly.

On her father's right, a string of light blue prayer beads lay within arm's reach. Usually, the sight of this familiar object made Wadjda smile. It meant her father was home. But today even that joy was temporarily banished.

All she could think about was taking Abeer's note to the boy. How could she have been so stupid? Such a mess for forty Riyals.

Enough. Lingering by the door made her look suspicious, like a bad guy in an old movie. Wadjda squared her shoulders and stepped forward. At the sound of her footsteps, her father turned and smiled at her.

If he only knew! In her defence, Wadjda thought, she'd wanted to help Abeer. The problem was that she'd taken her money – and the boy's. It put her in a bad position.

She plopped down on the end of the couch, choosing the side closest to her father. For a few minutes, she watched the game, but it was boring – the usual slashing and shouting and killing. Casually, like she was yawning, she reached over to the side table and turned her framed Certificate of Excellence in Maths to face him. Sensing her movement, he glanced over quickly and took it in.

Then his eyes darted back to the TV.

"I'm losing. I should have stayed with my usual fighter." He leaned his whole body into the swing of his character's sword, gesturing wildly with the controller. On the screen a haggard warrior slumped over, as if exhausted by the battle.

"You're doomed," Wadjda said, bored. "The other guy jumps way faster."

Her father took a deep breath and looked up at her with mock annoyance. Then, shaking his head, he went back to his virtual warfare.

"So is that a real certificate," he asked, lifting the controller and twisting it to the right, "or a fake one like you made last year?"

Wadjda could hear the laughter in his voice, and smiled in spite of herself.

"Are you kidding? I'm great at maths. Do you want to hear –" Wadjda paused, sounding out the convoluted name in her head – "Py-thag-o-rean's Theory? It's a miracle – a proof of God! If you add up the angles right, all the things come out the same!"

She settled back on to the couch and crossed her arms triumphantly.

"Sounds like you know what you're talking about." Her father tossed a smile in her direction – and kept playing the game, face focused and intent.

Wadjda waited and watched for several minutes. On the screen, swords swished. Fake blood spurted. Her father's warrior leaped, hurdling over a giant pile of bricks. Then, all at once, she couldn't stand it any more. She took a deep breath, gathered her courage and blurted out, "I'm saving up to buy a bicycle!"

Her father leaned in, guiding his warrior in a

backflip, muttering something under his breath. Had he even heard her? If so, he'd apparently decided not to acknowledge it.

Dramatic music announced the end of the round. He dropped the controller in defeat, letting the expensive electronic pad clunk to the ground. As his attention finally left the TV, slight annoyance dawned on his face.

"Where's the *margoog*?" he asked. "Why hasn't your mother finished the cooking?"

Wadjda just shrugged. Her father shrugged back teasingly, then reached over and began rubbing the prayer beads between his fingers. Idly, Wadjda drew a cushion on to her lap and traced the fabric with her fingers. Unlike the rest of their house, everything in the *majlis* felt shiny and new.

Silence had so filled the space that Wadjda and her father were both startled when her mother pushed the door open. Her arms were full of plates and silverware. She leaned over and began to set the dishes on a little mat on the floor beside Father. Her eyes stayed on the ground for a tantalizing moment. Then she looked up and smiled.

In her presence, Wadjda's father seemed to come to life. Mother was dressed up and looking her best – and her best was very good. *That's her favourite Zara shirt*, Wadjda thought. It was made of soft brown fabric and patterned with dusty-rose-coloured flowers. With it, her mother wore tight black trousers that flattered her perfect figure.

"Wadjda, look! A movie star!" Her father beamed with pride and leaned back, suddenly at ease. "I've never seen anyone like her. Look at this hair, like a beautiful black silk waterfall!"

Her mother tossed that perfect hair back over her shoulders and looked up at him from beneath her eyelashes. She was pleased, Wadjda saw, and unable to hide it.

"A movie star, huh? Flatterer!" There was the tiniest pause. When she spoke again, the teasing note was gone. Now her voice sounded bitter. "I wonder why your mother's asking all over town for you, then, trying to find your new bride."

The words seemed to hang in the air. Wadjda looked down at the floor, tracing the intricate red and white patterns on the carpet with her eyes. In silence, her mother finished putting the plates and forks into place. Her father stared at her, as if willing her to lift her head. Finally, her mother did. She gave him a pained look.

Seeing her sorrow hurt Wadjda's heart. Ever since Father's mother had brought up the subject of another wife, tension had filled the house. Though she tried to ignore it, here it was again, expanding like a balloon until it touched the walls and sucked up all the oxygen, leaving no room for Wadjda to breathe.

Slowly, her father reached out and put his hand on her mother's. Wadjda's heart skipped with fear. What if her mother didn't want him to?

Still the same heavy silence. For a second, her mother didn't move – and then she looked up at her husband with tender eyes. Playfully, she pulled her hand away. Again, she tossed her hair over her shoulder. This time it was a sassy gesture, but still elegant. Father burst into laughter and pulled her towards him, grinning.

Their voices dropped, quiet, teasing each other. Though Wadjda couldn't hear what they were saying, the relief she felt at seeing them hold each other was huge. It was like a massive stone that had lodged between her shoulder blades was being lifted. She set the pillow she'd been clutching to the side, smiling.

"I'm not sure my mother's working *that* hard on her search!" Her father raised his voice again, lightening the mood. "Sit and play a match with me!"

Her mother laughed and wiggled her shoulders, gently freeing herself from his embrace.

"I can't, silly. I don't know how." Still smiling, she straightened her clothes and got up to get the rest of the food.

"Let me play!" Wadjda jumped down off the couch and snatched at the other controller. "I'll take the old guy!"

Her parents looked at each other and burst out laughing.

"You really think you can take me on?" her father asked.

"Oh yeah! Prepare to die!"

With that, she pulled the game controller close to her chest and started playing. True to her word, she really was good – her warrior could chop and leap with the best of them. In a few minutes, she'd caught up to her father's score. He watched her, smiling, at once taken aback and impressed by his daughter's endless array of unexpected skills.

CHAPTER FIFTEEN

Chocolate bars, mix tapes, football-team bracelets and shiny charms poured out of Wadjda's backpack on to Ms Hussa's desk in an avalanche. The principal gave the backpack one last shake, glaring down at the candy and jewellery like they'd personally insulted her.

Wadjda shivered. The AC was on, maybe the only AC in the whole school that worked. *Figures*, she thought. The icy principal likes her office icy cold. A single beam of sunlight cut through a small crack in the curtains. It shone down, a spotlight illuminating the illicit goods piled on the desk. Above their heads loomed pictures of Saudi Arabia's king and crown prince. Their grim expressions made it look like the candy upset them, too. But not as much as it upset Ms Hussa.

Silence stretched between them. Ms Hussa's scowl deepened. Wadjda looked away, squirming in her seat. The rock Father had given her was also on the desk. Wadjda could hardly look at it. She closed her eyes for just a second, wishing with all her might that Ms Hussa wouldn't take that, of all the things, away.

"Disgusting," the principal said. She sorted the items using only her fingertips, as if one of them might give her a disease. Finally, she picked up a tape and relaxed back in her chair to study it. Her steely focus made her look as if she were analysing a possible murder weapon at a crime scene.

"Tapes full of love songs, bracelets, all of this –" She struggled for words, but settled for a sweep of her hands over the desk. The gesture seemed to encompass everything Wadjda had done wrong in her whole life. "You know none of this is allowed in school!"

She stared at Wadjda intently. It felt like being pinned down by two lasers.

The seconds ticked past. Time seemed to move at a painfully slow speed. At last, Ms Hussa reached into a drawer and withdrew a folder. She slapped it open and started signing papers as she talked, the scratch of her pen very loud in the cold, still office air.

"Abeer was always a good girl." She flipped over a second document and signed the back. Her pen strokes were harsh slashes on the page.

At that moment, Wadjda knew Abeer had given her up. *Of course.* She must have broken under the pressure and talked. *It was inevitable*, Wadjda thought. Who wouldn't fear the punishments doled out to girls Abeer's age who got caught with boys? The lucky ones were forced to marry immediately. Those who were less lucky were lashed in public, often before a crowd. Wadjda shivered again. This time it had nothing to do with the AC's frigid blast. If she were Abeer, she might have turned Wadjda in, too. But just how much did Ms Hussa know?

The principal looked up from her papers sharply, as if she'd heard Wadjda's thoughts. But all she said was, "Do you happen to know how Abeer ended up out there, alone, with a strange boy? She knew it was against the rules. When the religious police caught her . . . it looked bad for her, and bad for our school."

Wadjda remained silent, trying not to let her face betray her emotions. If she blinked or twitched or made any movement at all, it might somehow acknowledge guilt.

When she didn't answer, Ms Hussa returned to her paperwork. She continued talking, though. Her voice dripped with cool indifference. It was scarier than yelling.

"Thank God they found someone to marry her off to. Her family certainly wouldn't have let her come back to school after such a disaster."

With that, she stopped signing papers, closed the folder and folded her hands on her desk. Again, she locked eyes with Wadjda, who did her best to look back at her like this was a normal, everyday thing – as if she weren't about to get suspended, expelled or worse. From the look on her face, you'd never have known that her heart was beating out of her chest, that her head felt like it was about to explode, that her mouth was so dry she couldn't even swallow.

At the thought, Wadjda tried to swallow, but it didn't work. She started coughing, bent over double in her chair. When she managed to get her breath and look up again, Ms Hussa hadn't moved.

"Did you arrange this rendezvous for Abeer and her lover?" she barked.

"No, of course not!" The words slipped out instinctively, like breathing. Wadjda barely had time to think about them.

"Don't lie. I know you took part in this." Ms Hussa narrowed her eyes and leaned over the pile of contraband on her desk. "I just don't know how." She sat back again and steepled her fingers. "So. What shall we do with you now? Expel you?"

Before Wadjda could reply, the door opened and Ms Jamila, the school secretary, entered. Wadjda almost smiled, but caught herself at the last minute. Ms Hussa might get even angrier if the smallest hint of happiness showed on Wadjda's face.

It was hard to keep looking sullen, though. Seeing Ms Jamila was a huge relief. She was a young, practical teacher who'd recently been promoted to the position of Ms Hussa's administrative assistant. Wadjda liked her. Ms Jamila didn't go out of her way to cause trouble for the girls – but she didn't go out of her way to defend them, either.

Ms Jamila looked at Wadjda now, one swift dart of her eyes. Ms Hussa caught the look and raised her eyebrows in annoyance.

"What?" she snapped. "I asked not to be interrupted."

Thank goodness someone else had arrived to deflect the worst of Ms Hussa's fury! Wadjda needed that space, that bit of breathing room, to collect her thoughts.

Taking a deep breath, she pushed her feet against the floor to keep them from shaking. Then she wiggled her toes, pressing them against the canvas of her Chucks. It was a familiar gesture, and it helped calm her down. But it also highlighted the way her beat-up sneakers stood out among the perfect order of Ms Hussa's office.

"Well?" Ms Hussa said, sounding even crosser.

Awkwardly, Ms Jamila raised the folder in her left hand. "The proposal for the Quran Recitation Competition," she said. "For the Religious Club?"

The second part came out like a question, but not an apology. From all appearances, Ms Jamila was accustomed to dealing with her boss's temper. She handed Ms Hussa the papers, saying, "We just need your signature to request an increase in the prize money."

As Ms Hussa turned her attention towards the forms, Wadjda looked again at her father's rock. It seemed so lonely, sitting all by itself on top of her notebooks. She wouldn't let it go. She couldn't. So much was bound up in that chip of stone. All her father's weeks away, all the talks they didn't have, all the things Wadjda did that he didn't know or care about. But all the things they had in common, too – their loud laughs, their love of pranks and games, their keen eyes and good aim. It was just a rock, but it meant too much to let Ms Hussa take it away.

Just like that, swift as a snake's strike, Wadjda's hand shot on to the desk. She scooped up the black stone and slipped it into her pocket, all without lifting her body from her chair.

Had the principal seen? Had she got away with it?

Ms Hussa shifted her eyes back to Wadjda. Wadjda counted in her head: *one, two, three . . .*

"Go to class, Wadjda," Ms Hussa said, gesturing towards the door with a swipe of her hand. "We'll deal with all this . . ." Her eyes dropped to the mess on her desk. "Later."

Was this good or bad? Slowly, Wadjda pulled her notebooks and schoolwork out from under her confiscated merchandise and put them in her backpack. The bracelets, tapes and candy, easily fifty Riyals' worth of goods, seemed to look back at her longingly. *All that money*, she thought.

All those sales – lost forever. A vision flashed in her mind: the green bicycle, pedalling away into the distance, some anonymous kid perched on its seat. And there was nothing she could do to bring it back.

At the same time, she hadn't been expelled – yet.

Slinging her bag over her shoulder, Wadjda turned to go. She shuddered as she passed the stiff furniture, all straight lines and sharp edges, and dodged the rows of locked cabinets stacked against the walls. What dark secrets did they hold? Everything in Ms Hussa's office seemed ominous, threatening. Her shoes squeaked as she crossed the black marble floor, and she winced, waiting for the principal's response.

It came – right on cue.

"And, Wadjda," Ms Hussa yelled, "from now on, you'll wear normal black shoes like all the other girls! That's an order."

Wadjda nodded, opening her eyes wide and dipping her chin so she looked extra obedient. Was the terrible conversation really over? Could she have dodged Ms Hussa's wrath so easily? Maybe Abeer hadn't given her up after all! The possibility was too wonderful to contemplate.

And maybe too good to be true. As she walked away, she heard Ms Hussa's voice drifting through the doorway. "Call Wadjda's mother. See if she can come in for a meeting tomorrow. We have to decide what to do about that girl, once and for all."

Again, Wadjda's heart sank, falling deep, deep into her stomach. The recess bell rang and girls flooded the hallways, almost trampling her as they stampeded out of the door to the playground. For once, Wadjda didn't race to join them. She stood where she was, letting a rush of girls in grey flow past her on either side, wondering if this time she had finally gone too far.

CHAPTER SIXTEEN

The school day felt endless. Thoughts of how her mother would react when Ms Hussa asked for another meeting tied Wadjda's stomach in knots. Beneath her desk, her black Converse sneakers swayed nervously, twitching back and forth, back and forth above the cheap linoleum tiles of her classroom.

I have to find a way to get new shoes, she thought, sinking lower in her seat. *Boring black ones, like everyone else's.*

But how? Her mother didn't have enough money to buy Wadjda a proper uniform with the mandated shiny black shoes for the start of each term. Wadjda had got used to making do. Usually, having her own style made her feel special. But now? Fixing this one would be hard. She sighed.

From her post at the chalkboard, Ms Noof stared down the class. She was chewing gum, which the girls weren't allowed to do in school. Wadjda suppressed a flash of anger at the sight. Ms Noof wasn't wearing proper shoes, either. Her flip-flop sandals were visible underneath her long black skirt and oversized blue blouse. She pushed the sleeves up so they wouldn't get dusty from the chalk.

There was nothing to be gained from letting Ms Noof annoy her, so Wadjda fixed her eyes on the board until the letters blurred into nothing. Her mind started to roam, and soon she was lost in her own world, far away from the hot confined classroom.

In this inner world, Ms Hussa had a change of heart. She came into the classroom with Wadjda's tapes and bracelets and candy in her hands, and handed them back to her. She even gave her a little extra money to put towards the bike. Then she told her she could leave early. *Go, have fun*, she said. *Don't worry about the shoes. Go visit your bicycle.*

The bicycle! At the thought, Wadjda tugged out her science notebook and turned to the last page. She'd drawn herself, riding through the streets of Riyadh. Hiding her smile, she began shading in the buildings on either side of the picture with gentle pencil strokes.

Only the distinctive sound of Ms Hussa's high heels clicking closer and closer down the hallway made her raise her head.

She wasn't alone. The sound energized all the girls, setting their bottomless appetite for gossip afire. Behind her, Wadjda heard Yasmeen whispering to Noura.

"Funny she's the one punishing Abeer. I mean, we all know the story about the thief at Ms Hussa's house . . ." She broke off in giggles, barely able to contain herself.

"Not a thief!" Noura whispered back. "Her lover! Her father just *thought* it was a thief. That's why he called the police!"

Salma bristled. She was one of the teacher's pets, short, with a square face, bad skin, and bushy eyebrows – the opposite of Ms Hussa in all ways. But Wadjda knew Salma thought the principal was perfect, and she hated any gossip about Ms Hussa.

The thought of a brewing fight made Wadjda brighten. Though the gossipy girls were being loud, there was no way Ms Noof would interfere. Every day, her lessons droned on for a solid hour. It was like a train of sound. No questions or answers could make it jump the track. She probably wouldn't stop even if one of the girls got up and ran out of the classroom, screaming. Most days, Wadjda was seriously tempted to try.

Now, Salma narrowed her eyebrows at Noura and Yasmeen and gave them a fearsome scowl. Putting a finger to her lips, she whispered, "Shut your mouths! If Ms Hussa said it was a thief, it was a thief!"

"Of course you'd think that, Salma." Noura rolled her eyes. "The only man who would ever speak to you would be a thief. No one else would want to!"

Salma looked down at her desk, her face pale like she'd been slapped. Wadjda saw her eyes fill with tears.

Yasmeen and Noura giggled – then straightened abruptly and folded their hands in their laps as the principal entered the room. Even Ms Noof straightened up. Her movements became noticeably faster and, Wadjda noted, she swallowed her gum.

"Girls, our principal is here to explain the Quran Recitation Competition rules – and make a special announcement," Ms Noof said. "Then we'll pass round a sign-up sheet."

She gave a piece of paper to a girl in the front row and moved out of the way to make room for Ms Hussa. Wadjda subtly turned a page in her notebook to hide her bicycle drawing. As if attuned to the tiniest act of rebellion, Ms Hussa's eyes went straight to her.

Unsure what to do, Wadjda tried to look extra studious, holding her pencil over the page like she was ready to take notes. The principal *humph*ed and turned her gaze to the rest of the class. For greater dramatic effect, she let the awkward silence in the room build before beginning her announcement. It worked. At her first words, students gasped.

"Girls, we have increased the amount of money that will be given as a prize. The winner will now receive one thousand Riyals instead of eight hundred. Of course, you'll have to learn all the long *suras*."

Wadjda raised her eyebrows. That was a huge amount of prize money. It would cover her bike and leave her with cash left over! Quickly, she flipped through the Quran on her desk, trying to tally up the number of pages she'd have to learn. The *Surat al Baqara* meant the first four chapters, and the first four chapters were *long*.

"You must learn the verses and the proper recitation," Ms Hussa was saying. "Then you must study the associated vocabulary, and be prepared to account for all the reasons why we know the verses descended from heaven itself." She said the next words with careful emphasis. "Correct tone, rhythm and pacing are very important."

The sign-up sheet was making its way round the room. Wadjda saw the list of names growing longer. *Of course Salma signed up*, she thought, resisting the urge to roll her eyes. *That know-it-all probably would've done it even without the prize money*.

Noura and Yasmeen put their names down, too. They weren't great students, but they were pretty, and when they spoke in class their lilting tones made it sound like they were singing. *Noura's probably sure she'll win*, Wadjda thought. Surreptitiously, she lifted the page in her notebook and sneaked a look at the picture of her bike.

"We want to hear the beauty of the Quran sing out through your young voices," Ms Hussa said.

The sign-up sheet fell on to Wadjda's desk. The thick white paper obscured the faint outline of her drawing. It was like a sign, a roadblock. *You have to go through me, Wadjda*, it said.

Fine. Here goes nothing! In bold black strokes, Wadjda added her name to the list of competitors. She made the letters a little bigger than the others, just in case.

Class ended, and Wadjda sprang to her feet, gathering her things more efficiently than even Salma. Squaring her shoulders and tucking her *abayah raas* under her arm, she walked as fast as she could to Ms Hussa's office. In a few brief moments, Ms Hussa would stride outside to begin her school gate inspections. Wadjda had to act fast.

"May I see Ms Hussa for a quick chat?" she asked Ms Jamila.

From her shocked face, Wadjda guessed Ms Jamila was surprised to see her back so soon – and voluntarily, at that! Still, her tone was sweet and easy.

"Of course, Wadjda. Go check and see if she's busy." She motioned encouragingly towards the principal's door and watched in bemusement as Wadjda walked over, took a deep breath and knocked. The door creaked open, and some of Wadjda's old fear returned. The sound was like something from a horror movie! But she knew exactly what monster lurked within.

"Well? Go on!" Ms Jamila made shooing motions with her hands.

So Wadjda did.

Inside, she stood in front of the giant desk for what felt like a long time. The dark wood seemed to suck up all the light in the room. Ms Hussa had her head buried in yet another file, and she did not look up. She flipped page after page, making notes, adding her signature at various points. Finally, Ms Hussa raised her head and arched an eyebrow, acknowledging Wadjda's presence.

"Well?" she said, as if *she'd* been the one waiting for Wadjda to speak.

Wadjda crossed one foot over the other, trying to cover her black high-tops.

"I thought about what you said," she blurted. "I was wrong, and I'm ready to change."

Both Ms Hussa's eyebrows lifted, as if to say, *Really?* But the look of doubt remained on her face.

"I want to join the Religious Club!" Wadjda declared. She fought to make sure her voice didn't shake. To convince Ms Hussa, she needed to sound strong and sure.

Ms Hussa's facial expression still didn't change, but her

eyes narrowed slightly. Despite her outward calm, Wadjda felt like she could practically hear the principal's brain buzzing and whirring as she tried to make sense of this strange new information.

"What, you're becoming a *sheikha* all of a sudden?"

"Maybe I'll learn something," Wadjda said slowly. "You know . . . to put me on the righteous path." Seeing that her words weren't having the dramatic impact she'd hoped for, she decided to add more fuel to the fire. "You'll see," she said, making her back oh-so-straight and tall. "I can be different."

Ms Hussa peered at her, clearly suspicious, but also intrigued.

"Yes," she said slowly. "We'll see."

CHAPTER SEVENTEEN

Winding her way through the backstreets on her way home, Wadjda felt lifted, like she was walking on air. A deep sense of determination hummed in her heart and powered her steps. Her enormous new *abayah raas* flowed out behind her like a superhero's cape as she marched forward, heading straight to the toyshop.

Outside, she stood face-to-handlebars with the bicycle, taking in the totality of its awesome presence. The bike had started to feel like a person to Wadjda, something more alive and present than spokes and wheels and chrome. It was a friend, a companion on an adventure. But it was a door, too, an opening that would take her to all the places she'd dreamed of going.

Beep! A passing car tooted its horn furiously. The sound snapped Wadjda back to reality. With a sigh, she pushed open the door. The little bell jangled, announcing her presence. Fixing a smile on her face, Wadjda stepped into the toyshop. The owner looked up from a stack of receipts and stared at her over his reading glasses. His eyes were curious.

Today, the old man's *ghutra* was pushed to the back,

exposing more of his forehead and giving him a relaxed, casual look. *This guy's stylish*, Wadjda thought. *He's got flair*. Was that a good thing, though? She frowned, toeing her shoe against the ground. She had flair, too, or at least she thought she did. But all her purple shoelaces and cool sneakers had ever brought her was trouble.

Still considering, she slipped into one of the aisles and pretended to be examining the dusty toys. Every so often, she sneaked a look back at the owner.

A traditional pot of Saudi blond coffee sat on his desk. The shopkeeper poured himself a little cup, drank it, and then deliberately set both coffee and coffeepot down. Keeping his eyes on Wadjda, he flipped the record on the player beside him. It was an easy, practised motion, like he did it so many times a day he didn't even think about it any more. The needle crackled and hissed as it tripped across the grooves of the old record, and a rush of sound filled the shop, the familiar sounds of a faraway time playing out in crackles and spurts. Terrible sound quality! Wadjda had to resist the urge to put her hands to her ears.

"You know they've invented this new thing called a tape player?" she yelled over at him. *Now's as good a time as any to break the ice*, she told herself. To have any hope of convincing the owner to sell her the bike, she needed him on her side.

The old man sniffed, but didn't answer her question.

"Do you ever plan to buy anything?" he grumbled. Wadjda smiled back innocently. So far, he didn't seem super friendly. But he wasn't asking her to leave or chasing her away, either. And every so often his eyes would twinkle – with amusement? Kindness? – in a way that encouraged her to keep going.

"How would I know?" she said. "People need to browse, don't they?"

With that, she turned her back to him and strode nonchalantly through the shop. As she paced, she pretended to look at the dolls and rubber balls and stacks of board games. But her eyes kept slipping back to the window – and the spectacular bicycle, sitting front and centre outside. It shone like a beacon in the afternoon sunlight.

Tearing her eyes away, she looked up and saw the owner still staring at her, still peering suspiciously over the top of his glasses. Gathering the stack of receipts, he tapped them into an organized pile, neatly squaring the edges. And still his eyes didn't leave Wadjda. He was making her nervous! Determined to escape his gaze, she sneaked off to one of the back sections: *Computer Games*.

Idly, she turned over a large box. *Learn Quran the Easy Way* was emblazed on its side in bright red letters. Was this what she needed to win the competition? Mental images of the girls in her class ran through Wadjda's mind. To beat the best students, like Salma, and the best speakers, like Noura, she was going to need a leg up.

"You won't find any tapes back there." The owner yelled casually, without looking her way. "This is a modern shop, you see. We only have CDs."

This time, Wadjda saw it for sure: a twinkle in his eye. As she watched, a smile creased his wrinkled face, making his eyes go crinkly at the corners. OK, it looked kind of mocking. But a smile was a smile – and a smile was the sign she'd been waiting for.

Yes! she thought. She beamed back at him, a giant grin that showed all her teeth. Her joy was real, nothing fake about it. For there was no doubt in her mind now: he would sell her the bicycle.

"Thank you very much!" she chirped, her voice light and happy, like the song of a bird. Still smiling, she made her way towards the exit, fixing her veil as she went. "See you tomorrow!"

This was his heads-up. He should know that he'd be seeing a lot more of her – right up to the moment when she set eight hundred Riyals down on his counter and pedalled her bicycle home.

The shop was stuffy and thick with afternoon heat, so Wadjda left the door open. As she passed the bicycle, she ran her fingers through the ribbons on the handlebars, letting them play across her skin like water. The gesture seemed to spur something in the shop owner. He poked his head out of the door and called, "Can you even ride?"

"Ride?" Wadjda raised her eyebrows and folded her arms challengingly. With her feet planted on the ground, she felt like a strong tree. "I race the wind."

A triumphant note to leave on! Wadjda could have clapped her hands together for joy. Head held high, she spun –

And tripped on the dragging hem of her enormous *abayah raas*. She stumbled forward, bent at the waist, taking fast steps to keep from falling face first into the dirt.

So much for that, she thought, feeling herself blush beet red beneath the protective covering of her veil.

Behind her, the owner was laughing. Not loudly. But his shoulders were shaking, and his lips were pressed together, as if to hide a smile. When he caught her looking, he *harrumph*ed and went back inside. A second later, the music from his beat-up record player got louder, as if he'd cranked the volume. Wadjda smiled.

The shop owner may have been trying to hide it, but Wadjda knew she had an ally now. All of a sudden, her quest to buy the bicycle felt so much more possible.

CHAPTER EIGHTEEN

Was there a class in the history of school that made it easy to stay awake?

Wadjda leaned her sweaty cheek into her even sweatier palm. Her body felt like it was swaying slowly, back and forth. The AC hissed above her. The fan turned, lifting hot air so heavy it felt like a physical weight. All Wadjda wanted was to tip over on to her desk, close her eyes and sleep for a thousand years.

At the front of the room, the teacher cleared the blackboard, wiping away the equations and figures from their maths lesson. As the complex problems disappeared, so, Wadjda thought, did all sense of logic. In the absence of maths, nothing in school made sense to her. It was a lot of words, blowing around the room like sand.

Today, their teacher was collecting ideas for the Religious Club's bulletin board. Though she was the club's newest and supposedly most enthusiastic member, Wadjda's eyelids kept slipping shut. With each comforting flash of darkness, sleep seemed more tempting. At this point, Wadjda's arm was barely able to hold the weight of her head.

Stay awake, stay awake, stay awake. Wadjda recited the words like a mantra. Dragging herself upright, she started pinching the palm of her right hand with her fingernails. Determined, she stared at the blackboard – and even gave a small smile to the teacher, who didn't seem to notice Wadjda's new keenness.

"Let's compile all the stories we know about torment in the grave and make a pamphlet for the whole school. Any ideas about what we should include?"

Noura raised her hand eagerly. The teacher nodded, giving her the floor.

"I want to tell the story of the giant snake from hell," Noura blurted. "There's a girl who didn't pray on time. After she died, the giant snake was sent to torment her!"

"Good, Noura. Thank you." The teacher wrote "giant snake from hell" on the top line of her chart.

Were they really going to do this for a whole hour? Wadjda gazed idly out into the corridor. Was that? . . . She frowned. Yes, definitely the faint tapping of high heels, in the distance but coming closer. The hair on the back of Wadjda's neck stood up.

"What other ideas do we have?" the teacher was asking.

Sitting up in her seat, Wadjda tried to concentrate. She had to think of a good story. Torment in the grave . . . If the Prophet Mohammad put a fresh twig on a grave, it was said to ease the dead person's suffering, right? Wadjda furrowed her brow, trying to decide if that would be a good addition to the pamphlet.

In the hallway, the sound of clicking heels grew closer. And then Wadjda's worst nightmare was there, coming true right in front of her. Her mother, walking with Ms Hussa towards her office.

Wadjda's whole body went rigid as she watched them disappear down the hall. Her mother was nervously fixing her hair and adjusting her blouse, holding her black *abayah* at her side as she walked behind the principal.

Forget the torment of the grave, Wadjda thought, slumping back in her seat. She was about to experience torment right here on earth.

CHAPTER NINETEEN

Crash!

A plate smashed to the ground and broke with a resounding clatter. Smaller crashes followed as the pieces ricocheted off the kitchen cupboards and table legs.

In her bedroom, Wadjda sat up like a shot. She could hear her mother cursing her as she cleaned – or broke – the pile of dinner dishes from the previous night.

"Always trying to get money. Sneaking, lying, breaking the rules – and for what?" Mother's voice, usually low and beautiful, was a screechy scream. Each word trembled with rage. "To buy a bicycle? I swear, Wadjda, you'll never have that thing, not as long as I'm alive! Do you think I'll just wait around until you get expelled?"

Wadjda sneaked to the door and oh-so-carefully peeked round the corner. When she made out her mother's figure, she sank back against the wall and buried her head in her hands. Mother was still in her work clothes. That meant things were *bad*. She never cleaned the house wearing her good blouses and skirts. They were far too valuable. Each month, she saved just enough money to buy one or two

147

things at Zara. Each night, she took great care washing and ironing them so that they'd last longer. Looking good at work was one of her mother's top priorities, and with the mess she was making in the kitchen her favourite red silk shirt was going to get ruined.

Smash! Wadjda heard another plate shatter. She covered her ears, desperate to block out the sound. When that didn't work, she flung herself across the room and slapped at the dial on her radio, hoping music would cover the sound of her own sobs. The song that came on was a new R & B hit by Beyoncé, the notes low and pulsing.

Swiping at her nose with the back of her hand, Wadjda cranked the volume all the way up, desperate to tune out her mother's vicious scolding.

"Turn off that damn radio! Recording those evil songs?" Now her mother sounded even angrier. "You're no better than Abeer! And what happened to her? I'll tell you: she's staying at home until her parents marry her off. That's what I'm going to do with you, too! No school for you tomorrow! You're not leaving this house."

Wadjda turned off the radio and fell back on to her bed. The tears were rolling down faster now, but she swallowed every sob that rose in her throat. Scrubbing at her cheeks, she fought to gather her courage. Then she crept to the door again, wondering why the kitchen had gone strangely silent.

The moonlight beamed in through the dirty window. It silhouetted her mother, who stood very still, surveying the broken glass scattered across the floor. As Wadjda watched, her mother pulled her dishevelled hair away from her face, gathering it back strand by strand. For a long time, she stood there, one hand holding her hair, one palm pressing against her forehead. Water roared out of the tap in the sink beside her. Several minutes passed before Mother turned it off. All the rage had left her body. Now she just seemed terribly tired.

As Wadjda watched, her mother searched slowly through the cabinet under the sink for a dustpan and brush. Dropping to her knees, she swept up the mess, dumping the pan full of broken glass into the bin. The shards made a loud clatter against the sides of the plastic container.

Padding silently on the balls of her feet, Wadjda crept out further into the hall. Her mother was in the living room now, pacing back and forth. Wadjda could hear her nervous footsteps, a fast patter that muffled suddenly when she stepped on to the rug. Once, twice, she reached for the phone, only to pull away. Then, abruptly, she snatched up the handle, punched in a number and waited.

The ringing sound on the other end of the line was very loud in the quiet house. All at once, it stopped. But before her mother could say anything more than "Hello" Wadjda heard a muffled, squawky sound. The voice on the other end hadn't wasted any time in speaking!

Mother's breath grew faster as the squawking continued. Here and there, Wadjda could make out a word, a sentence. She'd know that broken Arabic anywhere. *Iqbal.*

Her mother tightened her grip on the receiver. In her mind's eye, Wadjda imagined it shattering into a thousand pieces, broken by the force of her mother's anger.

"I know, Iqbal, I know. You waited a long time, yes. But my daughter had a problem at school." Wadjda could tell her mother was working hard to keep her voice calm. "I didn't have time to tell you I was leaving early."

Clearly Iqbal wasn't buying it. Her mother paced the floor in tight circles. Then she pulled the phone from her ear – "selfish, stupid," Wadjda heard Iqbal saying – and held it out to the side, giving herself a small break from his rant.

"Well, you're paid for the trip whether I'm there or not!" she broke in, her fury growing. "Fine. Don't come tomorrow, if that's how you feel."

Iqbal's voice rose on the other end of the line. He was shouting so loudly that Wadjda could make out every word. Her jaw dropped. He was calling her mother such awful things! She wanted to dive into his stupid van and give him a good strong kick.

"How dare you speak to me that way?" Her mother's face was red with rage. "Do you think you're the only driver in town? Just watch! I'll find someone else!"

Slamming down the phone, she fell back on to the couch. Wadjda watched her mother's chest rise and fall, heard her breath stutter as she tried not to cry. In silence, she crept back to her room, perched on the edge of her bed and drew her knee up to her chin. With a black marker, she began to colour in the white toe and sole of her shoe. Her pen marks were thick and careful. Once the whole thing was black, she went over it again and again, making the colour as dark as possible.

Still no sound from the living room. Wadjda put the marker aside. One by one, she tugged the faded purple laces through the eyelets and set them down on her desk. In their place, she strung the black twine that she'd used for her bracelets.

There was a gentle thump from the hall – the sound of the front door opening. Father must be home. Wadjda froze and tried to listen. Would her name come up right away? She rushed to finish lacing the twine and darted back to her position by the door.

The tense, hissed tones hit her ears like a slap. The fight was getting louder. Soon, Mother's and Father's voices would carry into the yard. Wadjda hoped none of the neighbours would hear.

"I can't afford a private driver for a week!" her mother was yelling. "Why don't you help me? Why can't you pay for something, for once?"

"How?" her father shouted back. "With what? You want me to steal, is that it?"

"You find money whenever you need a new mobile phone, don't you?"

Her throat felt hot and scratchy again, but there'd been too much crying tonight. Pressing her lips tightly together, Wadjda put on her shoes. Though the sneakers hugged her feet just right, like always, they looked wrong. Coloured black, they'd be lost in a crowd. They'd make her look like everyone else.

"And what about the dowry money? Surely my handsome groom could spend a little of that wealth!" Her mother's voice dipped meanly on the words *handsome groom*.

"Do you think it's easy for me?" Her father's voice was even louder and angrier than her mother's. "You think I want to support two families? But I don't have a choice!

I'm the town joke. And somehow I have to get that son you can't give me!"

Drawers banged open and slammed shut. Wadjda swallowed even harder.

"Forget it! You think I need this nonsense? You think I like your complaining? Don't count on a visit next week! Don't even think about it!"

"I don't care!" Her mother's voice was a burst of raw emotion, like nothing Wadjda had ever heard. "You think I don't know how much time you spend at your mother's? That every night you're discussing potential brides?"

The front door slammed so hard that the pencils on Wadjda's desk rattled. Then there was silence.

Wadjda stayed awake for a long time that night, her stomach filled with a heavy, indigestible sadness. In her mind's eye, all she could see was the chart she'd made to track her savings for the bicycle.

Somehow, she thought, *I have to fix this*.

CHAPTER TWENTY

The morning brought sun like a hammer, its hot rays slamming against the cardboard over the window and forcing Wadjda out of bed. She woke knowing she couldn't spend the whole day in her room. Grounded or not, after the chaos of the previous night, she needed to escape.

Delicately, she tiptoed around, neatening the sheets, pulling on jeans and shoes. She was careful not to make any noise that would draw her mother's attention. From grim experience, she knew how these days went. Mother would camp out on the couch all day, watching TV, or she'd lie in bed, staring at the ceiling. Now and then, she'd sneak on to the roof for a cigarette. But then she'd be back, on the couch or in her bed, her dark eyes seeming to follow Wadjda around the apartment.

Wadjda's shoes were laced. She was ready. With the utmost care, she put her hand against the bedroom door, giving it tiny nudges with her finger. Finally, it opened enough for her to look across the hall.

Her mother was in her room, sitting up in bed, hair all over the place, a look of exhaustion on her face. In her left hand, she held the phone. Her whole body leaned into it, listening nervously. The voice on the other end must have said something bad, because her mother started rubbing her temples with her fingers.

She probably didn't sleep last night, Wadjda thought. Again, guilt twisted in her stomach. *And it's all my fault.*

Her eyes went to her father's side of the bed. The sheets were neat, undisturbed.

"Can you count it as emergency leave?" Mother offered, breaking off whatever was being said on the other end of the line. "I still have some days, I think? You know how hard I've been working, covering for everyone. And I wouldn't have missed today if it weren't for that driver! I'll open up for the entire month if I have to, I promise."

Her voice trembled as she spoke, and Wadjda saw desperation on her face. Then, suddenly, her whole body seemed to relax. Her eyes closed, and Wadjda saw her lips move, as if in silent thanks.

"OK," she said. The relief in her tone was almost painful. "Thank you. Thank you so much. See you tomorrow."

As she hung up, though, she shook her head. It was a hopeless gesture, and it hit Wadjda right in the heart. Last night's wasn't the first fight she'd overheard between her parents. So she knew what her mother was thinking. While she'd managed to buy herself one more day, she still had no driver – and no way of getting one. Father was gone. The money was gone. Mother had exhausted all her options. And if she didn't make it into work tomorrow she'd almost certainly lose her job.

Wadjda remembered the long months of her mother's job hunt well – it had taken forever to find a school that would hire her. "They're overflowing with applications," Mother had said, slumping over the kitchen table, folding the most recent rejection letter between her fingers. "Most won't even take mine."

In the end, she'd been hired by her current school, in a remote area very distant from their house. The commute was horrible – an endless drive of almost a hundred miles along a desolate road. Her mother worked at a remote desert village school near the Empty Quarter, the vast sea of shifting sand dunes that surrounded Riyadh. To reach it, she spent two hours each morning stuffed into a minivan with six other teachers. And then another two hours on the way home.

"It's the only option," she told Wadjda tersely when she accepted the offer. "We need the money."

Once, Wadjda remembered, Iqbal's battered old car had got a flat tyre a few miles away from the school. Her mother and the other six teachers had to walk. They'd made the trip alone, because Iqbal refused to leave his car. Wadjda could picture them, walking along the side of the road, seven indistinguishable figures backlit by the early-morning light. Her beautiful mother one more drifting shape in a dark *abayah*.

Her mother had tried to sing, hoping to make the journey less stressful, but it hadn't worked. One of the teachers had got angry at her, hissing furiously about how they should recite the Quran silently in their hearts. "That way," her mother told Wadjda, "God would protect us." She rolled her eyes, making a joke of it.

But no one walked on the highways surrounding Riyadh – to do so was a death wish. Cars drove on the medians and shoulders, and didn't watch out for people on foot. And even when her mother wasn't walking her long commute was dangerous. On an almost daily basis, newspapers reported horrifying stories of people killed on that desolate road. Cars were old, with tyres that burst or shredded because the drivers went at such colossal speeds. The drivers were bad, poorly trained or self-taught. Some packed extra women into their cars to make more money. The seat belts, like the AC, were almost always broken. With every trip Wadjda's mother took to earn her living, the threat of deadly accidents loomed.

And yet, Wadjda thought, as awful as the trip was, she'd do almost anything to bring that horrible Iqbal back to her mother now.

As she watched, Mother fell back into bed and rolled towards the window. She pulled the sheets over her head, hiding herself from the world. Gingerly, Wadjda tugged her door shut. *Somehow*, she thought, *I'm going to put everything right again*.

She walked to her desk and turned on her radio, spinning the volume dial all the way down. A pleasant low hum murmured out. Next, Wadjda snapped on the light above her desk, which added to the illusion of an occupied room.

Should she stuff pillows under her blanket, in the shape of a body? Wadjda paused at the end of the bed, pursing her lips. She'd seen kids do that in the movies when they were sneaking out, but honestly it seemed like a waste of time. She knew that her mother wouldn't be checking on her today. When things got this bad, Mother drifted off into her own world. Wadjda couldn't just walk out of the front door, but she didn't have to act like a superspy, either. It was a matter of finding the right moment and moving fast.

Music buzzed from the radio. The heat beat against the window. Wadjda watched the dust rise and fall through the sunbeams as the AC dribbled cool air into her room. Finally, Mother moved from her bed to the living room, where – sure enough – she fell on to the couch and turned on the TV. A Turkish soap opera blared to life, a handsome man and a beautiful woman, arguing. Wadjda didn't know why her mother watched this stuff when she lived it in real life.

Still, with the added noise, Wadjda was able to creak her door open, slide her body out and let it latch shut again without drawing her mother's attention. The worn soles of her sneakers made her steps virtually soundless as she tiptoed past her mother and slipped into the stairwell that led to the roof. She climbed noiselessly and swiftly, feeling her heart beat faster, like a hummingbird's wings fluttering in her chest.

One last step, and sunlight hit her full in the face. Wadjda closed the stairwell door behind her. Stepping forward, she leaned against the waist-high wall that ran along the flat surface of their roof. From here, she could look out across the entire city. Riyadh spread before her like a painting, penned in at the top by a thick blanket of yellow smog. Blocky old apartment complexes huddled next to sleek new construction. The stadium, which looked like an alien spacecraft, stood out, its reddish colour dampened to ochre by the smudgy air. Each street, each roof garden was a story, a mystery. And it kept going, on and on as far as Wadjda could see. Almost as far as she could dream.

Though her parents' argument still tugged at her mind, Wadjda felt some of the tension in her shoulders ebb away. She hung her hands, shook them out and rolled her neck from side to side. She loved being up here, above it all, wearing whatever she wanted and feeling the breeze against her face. Below, the burning concrete streets stifled the wind to nothing. Up here, it teased Wadjda, whispered, *I am ready for that race.*

The space held many memories, too – most of them very good. On winter nights, her mother used to wash the roof. When it was dry, she'd lay out three mattresses, side by side: Mother, Father, and Wadjda in the middle.

It had been a long time since they'd had one of their sleepovers, Wadjda thought now, watching a car speed by on the street below. A lot of their neighbours still did it, though. Maybe sleeping in the open air gave Saudis a taste of the ancient, nomadic desert life they used to have, before oil and the massive concrete buildings, paid for by oil, took over their land.

I loved those nights, Wadjda thought, leaning her face into the wind. When she was very small, her father would hug her and whisper old folk stories in her ear. Since the night breezes could be chilly, her mother boiled hot milk with ginger and honey to warm them up. They'd snuggle together, all three of them, a small cluster of warmth in the vast desert night. When it was clear, Wadjda and her father would count the stars as they sipped their hot drinks. This, despite her mother's giggling objections. Wadjda could practically see her, her big eyes free from the worry she now wore like a cloak. She'd burrow her head into her husband's side, smiling.

"Shh," she'd whisper. "You know the old women say counting stars gives you warts!"

Every time her mother said this, her father would double over, laughing. "Silly beliefs," he'd murmur, pressing his cheek against hers. "How can you possibly believe them?"

Just in case, Wadjda always checked her hands and feet in the morning light. She never found any warts. Since then, she'd been suspicious of all the old wives' tales that guided her mother's thoughts and behaviour. Like so much of the adult world, Wadjda thought, the ancient warnings seemed designed to keep her from doing things that were fun and interesting, the things that made her feel most alive.

Since those long-ago winter campouts, the roof had become Wadjda's special place. This was where she went to escape it all. And when she said "escape", she meant it literally. Another grin broke out on Wadjda's face. The promise of action cleared away the memories like a broom sweeping out dirt. She tightened her *abayah* round her waist and kicked her leg over the wall. As the muscle memory that comes with much practice kicked in, she lowered herself down the pipe that ran along the front of the house. Though it was only a two-storey villa, when Wadjda looked down at the concrete patio below, it seemed a lot higher up.

As she shimmied past the living-room window, her foot slipped on a loose piece of concrete. Gasping, Wadjda kicked down, trying to find a stable footing on the house's crumbling side. For a moment, she had her balance, and then the chunk of concrete ripped free of the wall completely. Gasping, her palms slick with sweat, Wadjda pulled herself hard against the pipe, scrabbling her toes back and forth. Her precious black rock fell from her pocket and bounced across the courtyard – a series of loud *snicks* as it clacked against tile.

Breathless, Wadjda darted an eye to the window. To her horror, she saw her mother rushing over, hastily covering herself as she moved from the couch. Wadjda pulled herself tighter against the wall and froze. If she didn't move, if she didn't look, there was the slightest chance she'd go undiscovered.

An agonizing moment of silence passed. Then Wadjda heard the rattle of curtains on the rod. Cautiously, she lifted her head. Her mother had drawn the shades. *Safe*, Wadjda thought. Hopefully her luck would improve from here.

She lowered herself the rest of the way down, scooped up her rock and moved to the gate. Propping it open with her foot, she popped a piece of gum in her mouth and chewed till it was good and sticky. Then she plastered it carefully to the lock, ensuring that it wouldn't close completely and catch her out.

Donning her *abayah* – the regular one today, thank goodness – and veil, she ran out into the street, moving fast and true like an arrow shot from a bow.

CHAPTER TWENTY-ONE

A safe distance from the gate of the boys' school, Wadjda waited, her body practically thrumming with nervousness. She'd hidden behind a wall, tucked into a shadowed door frame near one of the building's corners. She didn't want to look suspicious, but she didn't want anyone to see her this close to the boys' school, either.

She wasn't being cautious because she was worried about her reputation. *Ha!* Wadjda snorted at the thought. At her school, all the whining and hand-wringing about immorality bored her to tears. And she wasn't worried about her mother's threats to marry her off, not really. It was just that she had a mission to accomplish. She couldn't get side-tracked by curious onlookers.

The final bell was about to ring. Why hadn't Abdullah shown up? Wadjda poked her head round the corner. Lots of figures were passing by, and a mess of cars had parked against the wall, waiting to offer rides. But still no sign of her friend's familiar skinny form.

Hmm. Wadjda ducked back into her doorway and closed her eyes, thinking hard. Was this really a good idea?

She wasn't sure. But though she'd prefer to carry off her mission solo she knew she needed help. And Abdullah was the only one she could count on to go with her. If he would just show up already!

Another peek round the corner. Nothing. Maybe he'd already slipped out for the day? Wadjda grimaced. While girls in Riyadh had to go through a virtual army inspection to get in and out of school, boys pretty much came and went as they pleased.

Aha! Inspiration came in a flash. Behind the boys' school was an abandoned shopping mall. Abdullah loved to hang out there, throwing rocks at the already-broken windows, riding bikes with the other boys, just generally acting tough. Keeping her head low and her veil raised over her face, Wadjda sprinted round the corner, down an alley and across the street. Putting her back against the mall's dirty wall, she caught her breath and waited.

Sure enough, there was Abdullah, tossing rocks and shouting playful insults at his friends. Smirking, Wadjda scooped up a stone and threw it in his direction. Her aim was good, but not good enough. The rock narrowly missed, *ping*ing against one of the wheels of his bike. Abdullah whirled, eyes darting across the barren car park. When he saw Wadjda, his face shifted from anger to shock. He looked nervously at his friends, but they were busy aiming stones at one of the few unbroken panes of glass on the vast wall above them.

Still chicken, Wadjda thought, rolling her eyes. *Doesn't want to be seen with me.*

She lifted another rock and waved it at her friend, as if to say, *This time I won't miss!* Without waiting any longer, Abdullah rolled his bike over to her hiding place.

"Do you know how to get to Adira?" she asked.

Abdullah stared at her, baffled. Seemingly without thinking, he reached up and adjusted his *taqia*, patting it down with his fingers. The delicate white fabric was lovely, Wadjda thought, and the weaving was perfect, like a sturdy spider web. It even had a flash of silver thread round the edges. It looked beautiful, sitting just so on her friend's head. She wanted to tell him that, but didn't. Somehow, it felt too weird.

The silence stretched between them. Then Abdullah dropped his hands back to his sides, nodded and tilted his chin towards the west edge of the car park. They set off together without further explanation.

Wadjda stood on the pegs of Abdullah's bicycle, balancing on either side of the back tyre as he pedalled them along. Before getting on, she'd rolled up the edge of her *abayah* and tucked it under her body to keep it from getting tangled in the spokes. She couldn't have it getting dirty – she'd learned her lesson with her veil.

Standing on the pegs wasn't a bad way to ride. Abdullah was a steady cyclist, and it was much faster than walking. But it wasn't very comfortable, either. They flew past the toyshop, and Wadjda thought she saw the green bicycle glimmering in the distance. She sighed and looked down, watching Abdullah's feet spin the pedals.

If I had my own bicycle, I'd have done this on my own, she thought. *I wouldn't have needed anyone's help.*

At this time of day, the streets of Riyadh were a clogged mess. As he manoeuvred the bicycle through the cars backed up on the roads, Abdullah looked back over his shoulder at Wadjda. He tried to say something, but she couldn't hear. He tried again, shouting to be heard over the grumble of idling engines.

"You have to get off if we see someone we know! And cover your face. I don't want people to talk about me. I'll say you're my sister."

"No one will believe it," Wadjda shouted back. "I'm way too cute to be related to you!"

"Yeah, right," Abdullah sounded annoyed, like he wanted her to be more grateful for his help. *Fat chance*, Wadjda thought. He was lucky she was letting him come along. "And isn't the principal going to call your mother? You're skipping school!"

"I'm taking a personal leave day," Wadjda said. "The school knows."

She could have said more, could have told him the whole awful story. About Ms Hussa finding her backpack and confiscating the bracelets and mix tapes, about her parents' fight, her mother threatening to marry her off or lock her in the house forever. But in the end she stayed quiet. Her family's drama was no one's business but theirs.

They approached a busy road, and Abdullah stopped so Wadjda could get off and walk alongside him. To avoid attention, she was trying unusually hard to be demure, but it was no use. Her veil kept falling off. Try as she might, she couldn't master the stupid thing. And every time it slipped down Abdullah shot her a worried look. Wadjda tugged the cloth back into place for the fifty millionth time and sighed heavily.

The walk was hot and tedious, but soon they were a safe distance away from any onlookers. Grinning, Wadjda jumped back on the pegs, and they continued across town to an older part of the city.

The Adira section of Riyadh was completely new to Wadjda. It looked nothing like her neighbourhood, with its rows of villas and strong protective walls. Here, dilapidated buildings slumped against one another. Many looked like they might fall over at any moment. Small shelters were built at their bases, crowding the narrow alleys. Everywhere, sheets of ragged cloth had been pinned up against the brutal sun. The area was crowded with groups of foreign workers, smoking and laughing as they passed by.

Every so often, one of them glanced Wadjda's way. Each time, fear crawled up her spine. She remembered the workers on top of the building. Now they'd entered a neighbourhood entirely populated by single men. Wadjda pulled her *abayah* tight round her, covering her jeans and favourite T-shirt. Though everything in her was screaming, *leave, leave*, she kept her eyes resolutely forward.

I have to do this, she thought again and again. *My mother needs me.*

Down one of the alleys, an older Indian man sat on the steps in front of a tiny convenience store. Sun-faded packages of crisps and candy and gluey-looking soda bottles were stacked on the shelves inside. Abdullah nodded towards him and raised his eyebrows at Wadjda. Wadjda nodded back. Gathering her courage, she approached. The man kept staring into the distance. Wadjda gave him a slight smile and a wave, looking back over her shoulder at Abdullah.

"Hey, hi there," she said. "Do you know where Iqbal the driver lives?"

The old man looked at her suspiciously. There was a long pause, long enough that Wadjda began to wonder if he spoke any Arabic at all. Should she ask in an easier way, using the simpler Arabic she was accustomed to speaking with Iqbal?

"Do you know how many 'Iqbal the drivers' there are around here, little girl?" the man said finally in broken Arabic. Taking a drag from his cigarette, he blew out the smoke in a steady stream.

Wadjda shrugged, muttered, "Thanks," and turned back to Abdullah. Together, they wheeled his bicycle forward, determined to explore Adira's backstreets together.

It wasn't a pleasant search. The lanes and alleys were dusty and dirty. Rubbish lay heaped in sprawling piles. Here and there a stray cat or dog picked at an old packet of food. Side by side, keeping close, Abdullah and Wadjda passed from one street to the next. It was almost lunchtime, and several workers hurried by carrying big sheets of *tamees* bread.

Wadjda smiled. She loved *tamees* bread. Her father used to bring it to work every Friday morning, to eat before prayer. Along with a huge plate of *Yemeni glaba foul*, cooked beans with tomato and olive oil, topped with light hummus, it was one of his favourite meals – and Wadjda's, too. But at this moment she couldn't think of food. Her stomach ached too much from nerves.

Finally, Wadjda spotted a minivan with taped-on headlights parked next to a shabby house. The bus looked familiar – she could swear she recognized that big dent on the left fender, and the scratched-up bumper! Breathless with anticipation, she pointed it out to Abdullah, and they ran to take a closer look. Wadjda stepped up to the passenger-side window, cupped her hands over her eyes and peered inside. Sure enough, there was the picture of the little girl on the dashboard. Definitely Iqbal's!

Whirling, Wadjda flashed Abdullah a triumphant "yes", raising both thumbs high. She felt like an explorer who'd hacked her way through a thick jungle to a lost city full of treasures. "This is the building!" she cried. "Let's go."

Abdullah tried to go first, but Wadjda stayed close to his side, and they pushed open the crumbling wooden door together. Stepping inside, they found themselves in the middle of an empty courtyard. Makeshift drying racks, each strewn with frayed work clothes, stood in front of a series of doors. Beside each door, men's shoes and sandals were heaped in jumbled piles.

Leaving Abdullah to wait, Wadjda flitted from door to door. Iqbal's distinctive sandals, the toe straps wrapped in dingy orange tape, were in front of a room on the far side. She motioned for Abdullah to knock, but he shook his head and moved back behind his bicycle, which he still hadn't drawn all the way into the courtyard.

"This is your war, Wadjda!" he whispered. "I don't want any part of your crazy schemes!"

"Fine!" Wadjda hissed back. For a second, she frowned at him, but, no, getting mad was a waste of time. She needed to gather her courage to confront Iqbal.

Taking a deep breath, she faced the door and knocked. The sound was more confident than she felt, a loud *BAM BAM BAM*. She waited several moments for a response, her heart beating faster and faster. It seemed to echo the knocks on the door: *BOOM BOOM BOOM*.

No answer. Wadjda looked back at Abdullah, who seemed determined to ignore her. Slouching against his bicycle, he was playing with his *taqia*. He'd made his face look bored and distracted, like he was pretending not to have a care in the world. Wadjda twisted her lips, frowning. *Stupid boy*. Probably thought she hadn't thanked him enough or something.

"Are you going to help or not?" she whisper-hissed across the courtyard.

"You want my help all the time, Wadjda! And you act

like I have to just jump up and run when you come calling! No thanks from you, no nothing."

Wadjda rolled her eyes; she'd been right. This made Abdullah even angrier, and for a moment she felt bad – he *had* come all the way to Adira with her. But before she could say anything more Abdullah said fiercely, "You can do it yourself this time!" and Wadjda snapped her lips shut. *No more niceness for you, Abdullah!*

Turning, she knocked again, even louder. What if Iqbal wasn't home? Secretly, Wadjda kind of hoped that was the case. But before she could turn away, shrug her shoulders and chirp, "Oh well, guess we should go," there was a metallic *click*. The door swung open, and Iqbal stumbled out, rubbing sleep from his eyes.

When he saw Wadjda, every trace of tiredness vanished. Iqbal's eyes popped open wide, like someone had squeezed him round the middle and surprised him.

"You!" he shrieked, a look of fury on his face. "What do you want?"

"You can't do this!" Wadjda shot back. In a second, all her nerves were gone. She felt like a blazing torch, one giant fiery purpose. Iqbal didn't know it, but she was ready to fight. "You can't just stop driving my mother in the middle of the semester!"

The driver gave a dismissive wave and tried to close the door. Quick as a flash, Wadjda drove her foot into the space between door and frame, stopping him.

"Don't you dare close the door on me! You were already paid, remember?"

"Get out of here, little girl! You have no business being out of your house. Does your mother know you're here?" Iqbal's face was twisted and ugly. Looming above Wadjda, he seemed scarier than he did during their regular morning stand-offs. "Maybe I should go see her, hmm? Tell her what you're doing?"

Wadjda backed away in despair. She had no idea what to do – if Iqbal made good on his threats, she'd be in even *more* trouble.

Then, suddenly, Abdullah was there. He jumped in front of Wadjda and put *his* foot up against the door. Wadjda's jaw dropped.

"Where's your *iqamah*?" Abdullah asked assertively. The *iqamah*, or residency card, was a necessity for all foreigners living in Riyadh. At the sound of its name, Iqbal's already tense face went even tighter. His menacing gaze shifted to Abdullah.

"Go away!" he shouted.

"It's a good job you've got," Abdullah said, trying to sound tough. "No problems, lots of money . . ." Wadjda blinked. His tone was grown-up, pragmatic. He sounded like an old man discussing a business transaction. "Just go back to picking up Wadjda's mother, and we can all forget about this incident."

Iqbal wasn't taking the bait. He snorted and turned, giving up on his attempts to close the door. Cold sweat sprang up on Wadjda's palms. Could they come so close and lose him now?

In front of her, Abdullah raised his voice. His tone was forceful, each word a challenge. "Do you know who my uncle is? The one with the moustache? Have you seen his election posters? I'm sure he'd be interested in investigating your legal status."

The words worked like magic. As the driver stared down at the tiny troublemakers, his shoulders slumped. Bitterness stole across his face. Sensing his newfound power, Abdullah stood his ground.

Behind him, Wadjda folded her arms and raised her chin, waiting for Iqbal to answer. *We've won*, she thought. Her mother was saved.

CHAPTER TWENTY-TWO

Her *abayah* fell open, and Wadjda threw her head back, letting the fresh air wash over her face. Outside the sweltering courtyard and cramped backstreets of Adira, the city seemed clean and open, the endless journey home a walk in the park. Laughing boldly, Wadjda dashed after Abdullah, who rode ahead, swerving jubilantly back and forth across the street on his bicycle.

Finally, breathless, Wadjda stopped. She planted her feet and crossed her arms, her pose a perfect mimicry of Abdullah's as he'd confronted Iqbal.

"Come, come, surely you know my uncle?" she said in a deep voice. "The one with the giant moustache?"

Abdullah laughed, dismounting and straightening his white *thobe*.

"Laugh all you want. He did know him! That moustache is a registered trademark!"

Wadjda thought Abdullah looked happier than she'd ever seen him. In Iqbal's courtyard, he'd been like a knight in a storybook, full of chivalry and courage. They'd both been! At the thought, Wadjda laughed, too, happy and relieved.

Things had worked out. And she had a true friend in Abdullah, someone who was willing to follow her into danger and stand by her side. The thought sent a gush of pride welling through her.

They set off again, walking together, cutting down alleys in an attempt to avoid the main road. The area was residential now – blocks of houses and small corner shops. Wadjda felt fingers tug at her *abayah*. She looked over and saw Abdullah pointing at a house further down the street. It was busy with men, who came and went through the front gate in a steady stream.

One man, older, a full moustache bristling on his upper lip, stopped at the door. He wore his white *ghutra* without an *iqal*, the black belt men used to fasten down their head coverings.

"Why . . ." Wadjda started, gesturing towards the man. He was wearing his *ghutra* in the style of the *Haya'*, or commission, men. The Commission for the Promotion of Virtue and the Prevention of Vice, to be exact. Which meant she and Abdullah needed to slip away unnoticed. The man might be religious police, and if he caught them hanging out on the street she'd be in serious trouble. "Uh-oh," Wadjda breathed.

Beside her, Abdullah sighed and shook his head. "Don't worry. He's busy. See how he's greeting the people? There was a death in the family." Turning his bicycle, he gestured to a cross street that led away from the house. "We should go this way."

Wadjda's eyes were wide with surprise. "A death! Really? Do you know what happened?"

"Their son died fighting in Iraq. From a bomb."

Wadjda's eyes went wide. "That must have hurt so bad!"

"No." Abdullah shook his head, correcting her. "If you die for God, it's like the prick of a needle – hardly any pain. Then you fly up to heaven and you have seventy women, all yours!"

"Really?" Wadjda giggled in spite of herself. Abdullah, talking about seventy women! Ridiculous. He hid from his friends every time he even talked to a girl. Honestly, the whole idea sounded silly, like when her mother told her the Tooth Fairy would give her more money for extra-clean teeth.

"Really," Abdullah said, wheeling his bicycle forward, wounded by her giggles.

Wadjda ran to catch up, thoughts tumbling through her mind. Soon, they reached a small grocery store. Abdullah leaned his bike against the wall, his annoyance forgotten.

"Stay with the bicycle," he said. "Make sure no one steals it. I'm going to get us some ice cream to celebrate."

"Yeah, yeah," Wadjda said. She ran her hands along

his bike, enjoying the feel of the cool metal bars, the slightly cracked leather seat. "Hey, buy the one with the sweepstakes entry!" she shouted, remembering right as Abdullah opened the door.

"Ew! That one tastes like mud."

"Yeah, but we might win!" Wadjda's eyes sparkled. "Just think – twenty thousand Riyals!"

Abdullah shook his head and disappeared into the shop. Wadjda looked down at the bicycle, itching to hop on and ride. By the time her friend came out, she'd be all the way down the block! But that would upset him, and he'd helped her so much today.

With a sigh, Wadjda leaned against the bicycle. She put her right arm casually between the handlebars, stuck her left foot back against the crossbar and propped her hand on her hip. It was a pose she'd seen an old American movie star, Marlon Brando, make in a movie about motorcyclists. The movie had aired three nights in a row on TV. In it, a group of men rode across America, entering contests on their bikes and fighting rival gangs. Wadjda watched it every single time. Now she tried to imitate Marlon's bored, cool expression as she watched Riyadh's late afternoon traffic flow by.

Abdullah came out of the shop, already-melting ice creams in hand, and smiled.

They'd nearly reached home when the two friends parted ways. Wadjda made the rest of the trip alone. Several streets from her house, she passed a hole-in-the-wall shop that developed pictures. The window display was vivid and busy, packed full of T-shirts, notebooks, pillows, mugs and other trinkets, all personalized with family photos.

Most of them were so cheesy! Wadjda laughed aloud at a pillow near the front. It showed a man standing in front of a country farm backdrop – fake red windmill, fake black-and-white cows, fake green grass. For extra pizzazz, an airbrushed, multicoloured butterfly had been added to the top. It was almost the same size as the man's arm!

Still laughing, Wadjda slipped inside and examined some of the other items on the counter. Then inspiration hit. She fumbled through her wallet, pulled out a photo and held it up: a veiled woman, her face hidden, tenderly holding a smiling baby girl in her slender, henna-decorated hands.

"Can you put this picture on a mug?" she asked.

CHAPTER TWENTY-THREE

Wadjda creaked open the front gate and pulled her gum out of the slot. Long strands of goo trailed after, sticking to her fingers and making a gummy mess. *Ew.* Wadjda tossed the wad into the bushes and rubbed her hands together to get rid of the residue. She let the gate snap closed behind her, and then, moving stealthily as a street cat, she crept to the front window and lifted her head just high enough to look through.

Inside, her mother lay on the couch, eyes still fixed on the TV. Holding back a sigh, Wadjda hunkered down, knees pressed to her chest. It might be a long wait.

Her eyes drifted up to the roof. Though it was tempting, she knew there was no way she could shimmy back up.

Things weren't all bad, though. Even in that tiny glimpse through the window, Wadjda had seen contentment on her mother's face. Mother seemed carefree, as if a weight had been lifted off her shoulders. Iqbal must have called and apologized, or at least offered to drive her again.

Victory! Wadjda would have loved to hear that conversation. Just thinking about it made her grin.

She sneaked another peek over the sill. This time, she saw her mother looking around furtively as she pulled out a pack of cigarettes. Wadjda ducked down again, to be safe, but she knew she wasn't in any danger. Her mother always made that face before she smoked, like she thought it was some big secret.

Ha! Wadjda's lips twisted wryly. She'd known Mother was a smoker for years – ever since she started finding discarded ashtrays on the roof. It had to stay secret, though, so Wadjda made sure not to let on. In the Kingdom, only sleazy women smoked – actresses or tacky fashion models, the ones who appeared in foreign magazines. Their tight outfits, with exposed arms and bare midriffs, had to be blacked out with a marker by the censors before they were put on the racks. *What a crazy job*, Wadjda thought. To have to go through *every* copy, blacking out all the legs and shoulders and cleavage! If anyone ever found out Wadjda's mother smoked like them . . .

Wadjda shook her head at the thought. It would be a huge scandal. Her father would be so angry. And she didn't like to think about what her grandmother would do!

But this was why Wadjda kept her mother's secret. She thought smoking was maybe the only rebellious thing her mother could do. The only way her mother could feel free. Sometimes, when Wadjda was lying in bed and smelled the gross smell of smoke, it made her think of how she felt when she ran through the streets, arms and legs pumping.

Besides, from listening to gossip and smelling people's clothes and breath, Wadjda knew her mother wasn't alone. Many Saudi women secretly smoked – but only in complete privacy. They could never risk the awful consequences of getting caught.

Inside, Mother pulled out a cigarette and lighter, rose from the couch, and made her way upstairs. As soon as she stood, Wadjda started crawling towards the front door. In time with the beating of her heart, she started counting: *one, two, three . . .*

When she was sure her mother was out of sight, she closed her eyes and twisted the knob. It opened quietly . . . *four, five, six . . .*

By the count of ten, without ever making a sound, Wadjda was safely inside. To everyone but Iqbal and Abdullah, it was like she'd never left. In her room, she fell back on to her bed, exhaustion dragging her body down into the mattress. Pride stirred inside her, along with relief – and a touch of gratitude. She'd been able to take care of her mother, to save her job without sacrificing her pride. Sure, the whole mess was kind of her fault, but it had all worked out in the end.

And there was still so much to do! Before she got *too* lost in patting herself on the back, Wadjda rose, determined. Her *abayah* went back under her schoolbag. With a towel, she wiped her face, mopping away the sweat. Then her eyes went to her savings chart, and she darted across the room to count her money.

Slowly, she ran each bill through her fingers, straightening the wrinkles, smoothing the imperfections. It was silly, but Wadjda found herself hoping that if she were careful enough, there'd be more than the last time she'd counted. Somehow ...

"Forty, fifty, five-five, sixty Riyals," she whispered.

Her door opened. Wadjda's head shot up instinctively. A second later, her mother poked her head inside. Though she was trying to look stern, her inner happiness shone through her eyes. It was like trying to put a basket over a light bulb.

Wadjda smiled – and then gulped. *Oops.* She'd been grounded all day. She was supposed to be apologetic! Trying to make her face look both innocent and repentant, she lowered her head and stared up at her mother. Peeking out from beneath her eyelashes, she looked like a sad puppy.

Without turning her head, she blindly shoved the money under her chart with her right hand.

"Had enough?" her mother asked.

Still doing her best to look defeated, Wadjda nodded.

I accept my punishment, her wide eyes said. *It was all my fault.*

"Tomorrow you can return to school," her mother said, "but you're staying in that Religious Club for the rest of the school year, Wadjda, like you told the principal."

Wadjda nodded again, bowing her head even lower. Her mother smiled. It was clear from her face that she thought she'd found more than just a suitable punishment for her daughter. She had put Wadjda on the track to redemption. As she closed the door and walked down the hallway, Wadjda heard her singing softly to herself.

The Religious Club was a small price to pay for this truce! Wadjda started to do a little whistling of her own. She pulled the bills back out and kept counting. After her impulsive stop at the photography shop, though, she had less, not more. In her mind's eye, the green bicycle seemed to slip further away, falling back into the distance.

"Fifty-seven, fifty-eight, fifty-nine, sixty, sixty-one . . ." She searched the drawer, scouring the corners for any remaining bills, and sighed. "Sixty-two Riyals."

The last note went on the pile, and Wadjda gave the diminished stack a gentle pat. Then she picked up the mug she'd purchased and stared at it. Some details had been lost: her mother was nothing but a black blob. Still, the image exuded unmistakable love. The way her mother was holding baby Wadjda, the gentle, protective curve of her hands . . .

Wadjda smiled, put the mug in her bag and went out to the living room.

CHAPTER TWENTY-FOUR

The TV was on, but muted. Silent figures danced across the screen – two men in an office building, a boy playing with his friends in the street. Wadjda plopped down on the floor in front of the TV, dropping her heavy bag of schoolbooks off to the side. She thought idly about doing her homework, but she was already a day behind. Even thinking about the amount of catching up she'd have to do tomorrow made her tired.

Instead, she sprawled back on the floor, spread her arms to either side and lay for a while, daydreaming. Every so often, her eyes drifted to the TV. The show had gone to commercial, an ad for the movie coming up next: *The Matrix*. Though the movie was a million years old, like everything else on Saudi TV, Wadjda liked Keanu Reeves's sunglasses. They made him look cool. If only she had those to sell at school!

On the other side of the room, Wadjda's mother had settled back on to the couch, but she seemed bored, too. Her hair was pinned up, a few curls dangling down to brush her neck. It was a fancier style than her usual one. She had beautiful eye make-up on, too.

As Wadjda watched, Mother picked up the phone and held the receiver to her ear. As she waited for an answer, her gaze moved to Wadjda, and a flash of annoyance lit her face. With her eyes, she motioned threateningly to the schoolbag.

Fine. Wadjda sighed and pulled out a book. She tried to read, but the words blurred before her eyes. She tried to take notes, but it felt like dragging an iron rod across the page. Sticking her pencil in her mouth, she chewed on the eraser. After a few seconds, she gave up entirely and rolled on to her back, twirling the pencil between her fingers.

Mother was pacing back and forth, the receiver still in her hand. The phone rang and rang – and then Wadjda heard a voice. Father! Her mother smiled a slow smile. It looked sweet. And very flirty.

"Come on, don't you miss us?" she said into the phone. Her voice was low and teasing. "It's been almost two weeks since you stayed for the night. And I didn't hear from you at all yesterday. Are you punishing us, or have you already found someone new?"

Though her mother's sappy giggling made Wadjda roll her eyes, hearing her parents talking again after their awful fight sent happiness zinging from her head to her toes. She stared down at the richly patterned carpet, trying to hide her smile.

"If I'm the original brand, why do you look for imitations?" her mother trilled into the phone, quoting the lyrics of a famous song. On graceful feet, she padded into the other room, dropping her voice lower still.

This was the moment! Wadjda pulled the mug from her bag, tore a piece of paper from her notebook and shook red, green and blue crayons free of their box. Carefully, she wrote out a famous poem, making each word a different colour. She wrote slowly, to ensure her handwriting was its absolute neatest.

"Mother, Mother," she whispered as she wrote. "I can't believe I love her so much / I miss her all the time / I want to kiss her hand / My mother is full of tenderness / A true gift from God."

Folding the note into quarters, she slipped it into the mug and set her gift on the table. Then she rushed back to her homework. Through the doorway, she saw her mother pacing the kitchen, the phone still pressed to her ear. Apparently she and Father had finished talking, because Mother was dialling another number. When she spoke, she sounded much happier and more at ease.

"Leila, how are you?" A pause. "Wonderful. Listen, Leila, remember how I collected money for you from the other girls? Well, I've had it for some time now – aren't you coming to pick it up?"

She stopped, almost dropping the phone. Wadjda started at her sudden movement.

"Really!" her mother exclaimed. "You're working at the hospital across the road? For how long now? What did your husband say? Doesn't he mind you working with men?!" She paced the floor, listening intently, then said, "It's like two blocks from my house. What? Now? Yes, great – we're home."

She hung up and stared off into space. Absently, she rubbed her fingernail against her bottom lip, a gesture she made when she was thinking. Then, as Wadjda watched, she left the kitchen and walked down the hall. Wadjda scrambled to her feet and crept to the door, watching her.

Her mother was bent over the dresser in her room. She opened the top drawer and pulled out a wad of money. Wadjda's eyes widened. It was huge! The bundled Riyals made a giant fistful in her mother's hand.

Saving money wasn't easy for her mother – or any of her mother's friends. To Wadjda, it seemed like Saudis were people who liked to spend whatever they earned right away. They'd say, "Spend what you have in your pocket, and what God destines for you will come." Of course, Wadjda thought, watching her mother flip through the stack of notes, what's destined doesn't always seem to happen.

That's why she was working so hard for her bicycle. And it was why women like her mother used the system of the *Jamaaea*. Nine or ten women would chip in part of their salaries to a collective pot. Each month, they'd take turns holding on to the full stash. It was a creative way to force themselves to save. The pressure of commitment to people they knew kept everyone on the straight and narrow. This month, it was Leila's turn to collect the pot.

The *Jamaaea*. Wadjda sighed and shook her head. Nope. That wasn't for her. She was going to shake things up, do something seriously different. Provided she could escape Ms Hussa's iron fist, she would work hard and save all she needed, all by herself.

Brrrring! As one, mother's and daughter's heads lifted at the sound of the doorbell. Sensing motion in the doorway, Mother turned to meet Wadjda's curious stare. Frowning – she was always yelling at Wadjda for the way she crept around the house – she moved to close the door to her room.

"Go see who it is," she called as the latch clicked shut.

Why not? Better than homework! Rubbing her hands together to remove smudges of crayon, Wadjda dashed into the narrow hall, enjoying the skid of her stocking feet on the tiles. Sliding to a stop, she pulled open the door and saw Abdullah, shifting awkwardly from foot to foot, a roll of extension cord coiled over his shoulder.

For a few moments, they stared at each other. It was weird to see Abdullah again, so soon after he'd offered his help. It made Wadjda feel kind of shy. She wondered if she might be blushing. *Fat chance!* She leaned against the doorjamb, trying to act cool and indifferent.

"Hello," she said in her most neutral tone. "What do you want?"

Abdullah shuffled his feet and darted a glance behind him, as if checking for pursuers. "My uncle wants me to string these lights all the way down the street. Can I attach them to your roof?" He sounded sheepish. Then, as if he could hear his voice and didn't like it, he said with more conviction, "And, by the way, you're welcome for all the help, Wadjda. Too bad you never said thank you!"

"Ask the neighbours about your lights. In this house, we don't care about your uncle or his moustache." Wadjda bit her lip, searching for what to say next. Abdullah looked so insulted – and hurt. She wanted to thank him, but the words of gratitude seemed to pile up behind her lips, refusing to come free. What she said instead was, "And thanks for what, exactly?"

He made a sour face at her. "Thanks for taking you all the way to Adira and fixing the situation with your driver! He's taking your mother again, right? And, as for the lights, your neighbours don't have a pole to hang them on. Yours is the only roof that'll do."

He raised his eyebrows expectantly, as if sure he'd won. But Wadjda wasn't paying attention. She was looking past him, at his bicycle, which was weighed down with rolls of lights, electrical wires and bunches of small green flags.

"Hold on," she said. Before he could respond, she slammed the door and ran to her mother's room. The door was open again, the room empty.

Wadjda sprinted back to the living room. "Hey, Mother!" she shouted. "Abdullah Al Hanofi wants to use our roof to string up lights for the election, so his uncle – the uncle with the giant moustache – will win."

She skidded into the doorway, flinging a hand to either side, catching the frame and letting her grip on the wood pull her to a stop. Breathless, she saw her mother standing by the coffee table, holding the mug. She was beaming at Wadjda. Wadjda smiled back shyly.

"Thank you, sweetie. You were such a cute baby." The corners of her mother's eyes crinkled. "And you are so sweet now – when you want to be."

She stepped forward. For a moment, Wadjda thought her mother might hug her. Instead, she chucked Wadjda affectionately under the chin.

"As for the boy, tell him to go away. His uncle isn't even part of our tribe! We will not vote for him, and we certainly won't help him with his lights."

Abdullah stood on the front step of the house, fidgeting impatiently. The coil of wire dragged and rubbed against his shoulder. He was hot, sweaty and frustrated.

How could Wadjda not be more grateful? Unbelievable. After everything he'd done for her! He'd missed the last class of the day, risked his friends seeing him with a girl and travelled into a horrible part of Riyadh to strong-arm a bunch of scary people. All of that, and still she acted as if nothing out of the ordinary had happened!

He stood beneath the hot sun, seething. Finally the door opened, and Wadjda leaned out. There was something cool and calculating in her eyes. It made Abdullah nervous.

"I'll let you on to the roof," she said casually. "*If* you bring your bicycle."

CHAPTER TWENTY-FIVE

Time seemed to stand still. Defiantly, Wadjda looked at Abdullah. He stared back, equally defiant. It was a showdown for the ages, with neither prepared to yield.

The rumble-rattle of a car clanking up to the gate caught them both by surprise. Their eyes met, and Wadjda nodded decisively. They'd pause their fight for now.

As one, they turned to see a minibus full of foreign, mostly Filipino, nurses jerk to a stop in front of the house. A fully covered Saudi woman jumped out. The minibus idled in place as she hurried up the stairs towards Wadjda, accidentally bumping Abdullah, who tried to move out of her way. Overburdened by the heavy coil of wire, he almost fell to the ground, catching himself at the last second. The woman didn't seem to notice.

"Hey, Wadjda, it's me, Leila! How are you?" Leila's voice was clean and bright, like sunshine on a lemon tree. She removed her veil, exposing her smiling face. "Wow, you look so grown-up and cute!"

Wadjda smiled proudly, glancing at Abdullah to make sure he'd heard. But Abdullah was still too annoyed with

Wadjda to sit around and watch her be praised. Waving indifferently, he jumped on his bicycle and pedalled away, swerving round the minibus, which sat outside the gate in a growing cloud of exhaust and dust.

"Can you call your mother?" Leila asked, darting a look over her shoulder. "I have to hurry – I'm so sorry, but the bus is waiting."

Wadjda felt a warm presence at her back. Inhaling deeply, she breathed in the sweet and spicy smell of her mother's perfume. Mother wasn't veiled, so she was careful to stand out of view of the front gate, hiding her face from any strangers who might be passing.

"Traitor! I can't believe you're working so close by and you didn't even tell me!" She pulled Leila deeper into the courtyard, giving her a kiss on either cheek. As an afterthought, she tugged Wadjda after them and slammed the gate shut.

"Working at the hospital's great," Leila said with a laugh. "I wasn't sure about it, you know, but I couldn't find a driver, and . . . And I'm happy there! It's only been a few days, but it pays more, they provide transportation, and I don't have to endure someone like Iqbal for hours every day!"

It is cool to hear Leila so happy, Wadjda thought. For

the first time in ages, her face wasn't tight and strained. The lines around her mouth had faded, and she seemed younger – more like her real age.

Though they'd taught at different schools, Mother and Leila had shared rides on and off for most of the past four years. They'd become good friends during the long commutes, and Wadjda was accustomed to the nightly sound of their rambling phone calls. From these conversations, she knew Leila and Mother were the only ones who secretly passed fashion magazines – sometimes even romance novels! – back and forth under their *abayahs*. The other teachers were far too conservative to follow the fashions of Western women, and God forbid they read about men and women hugging and kissing!

"I miss you," Wadjda's mother said now. "You're well free of drivers like Iqbal!"

"And that drive," Leila said, shaking her head at the memory. "The heat!"

Both women laughed bitterly. Then Wadjda's mother pressed a large stack of notes into Leila's hand. Leila smiled widely as she tucked the cash into her purse.

"Thank you, dear," she said. "When's it your turn?"

"Next month. I want to buy a nice dress for her uncle's wedding." Mother gestured at Wadjda, who was kicking her favourite rock around the courtyard and not-so-subtly eavesdropping. "All the other potential wives will be attending," she added, trying to sound casual.

Leila laughed. "God be with the one he chooses! You might rip her heart out that night!"

Wadjda laughed, but her mother shot a laser glare in her direction, so she closed her mouth and kept kicking the rock. If she didn't watch it, her mother would send her inside and she'd miss the rest of the gossip.

"Is he going to drive you to the wedding? I mean, so he sees you before you go to the women's reception," Leila asked.

"No, his mother is taking us in a cab." Mild annoyance crept into her mother's voice.

Outside the gate, the minibus honked its horn. Leila and Mother looked back, startled.

"Ugh, I have to go. Before I forget, they're hiring at the hospital. Think about it. It's closer than that school of yours, and if you work there we can chat all day."

"My husband would kill me. He's so jealous. He can't stand the thought of other men looking at me." Her mother shook her head ruefully. "Forget working with them!"

"Oh, stop," Leila said with a laugh. "You blame everything on him. Enough! If you change your mind, call me. I'll keep an application at reception for you."

She took Wadjda's mother's hand in hers, gave it a firm squeeze and left. Her mother followed for a moment, careful to stay out of sight as she watched the minibus jolt away down the street. Wadjda saw the envy in her eyes.

She wishes she had Leila's courage, Wadjda thought sadly. *But she's too scared.*

Sighing, Wadjda pulled back her leg and kicked her rock as hard as she could. Her mother wouldn't do anything that might cast her further out of the mainstream. Working at the hospital was a big step. Too big.

CHAPTER TWENTY-SIX

The ceiling fan turned slowly, adding its thumping pulse to the otherwise soundless space. On the wall, beneath a large sign reading INTERIOR MOSQUE, hung posters with instructions on how to wash for and perform ritual prayer. The drawings were detailed, boxes and boxes of tiny figures carrying out the intricate rites.

By the door, Wadjda's coloured-black shoes sat atop a jumbled pile, all her classmates' shoes thrown hastily to the side as the girls entered. At this time of day, when the Religious Club met, the classroom doubled as a mosque. Shoes could not be worn inside, and heads had to be covered. There were no desks, so the girls sat cross-legged in a circle on a red Oriental carpet.

Sitting here among the chastest of the chaste, Wadjda felt out of place, like a wolf in sheep's clothing. But she had no choice. The combined power of her mother and Ms Hussa was too great. So she sat patiently, focused on the teacher, Ms Noof. Behind her head was a big poster showing a young girl praying. The girl's face was blurred out, and Wadjda thought she looked like a ghost.

Someone thrust a Quran into her hand. Wadjda looked up, startled. It was Salma, of course. Ms Noof had asked her favourite student to take copies of the Holy Book from a small shelf in the corner and give one to each girl.

Despite the seriousness of the club, Ms Noof was chewing yet another stick of gum. Like her students, she sat cross-legged, watching as Salma completed her task.

"Let's start our programme." She eyed the new students suspiciously – two other girls in addition to Wadjda. "Before we start, I know some of you may have got your period. Remember, you are not allowed to touch the Quran during that special time."

There was an eruption of giggles, quickly stifled behind hands. Wadjda felt her cheeks go hot. To bring up such a shocking subject in school! She hadn't spoken the words herself, nor did she have her period, but she still found herself embarrassed.

"Shush!" Ms Noof waved her hands irritably. "*Tahara*, this is the term for being clean and pure. It is one of the most important things we will study. A woman is not *tahara* during her period days. During that time –" she said each word with deliberate emphasis – "Do. Not. Touch the Book directly." You must hold it using a piece of tissue. Remember, this is no laughing matter."

Her eyes swept the room, moving from girl to girl.

"You are young ladies now. Your bodies are fragile, like flowers. Danger lurks round every corner. For example." Her gaze settled on Wadjda. "You could damage your virginity riding a horse or dancing ballet like those heretics in the West."

Wadjda squirmed uncomfortably. Her cheeks were so hot she felt sure she could start a fire with them. The rest of the girls continued to giggle.

"All right, let's read," Ms Noof said abruptly. Across the room, Wadjda saw Yasmeen flipping delicately through the pages, using a tissue to shield her hands.

Again, Wadjda felt her teacher's grouchy stare. Ms Noof smiled sarcastically at her and waved a heavy hand. "We'll start with this enthusiastic new face. Wadjda. Open to page fifty and read the first verse."

Wadjda took a deep breath and flipped to the right page in her Quran. She didn't read aloud in class if she could help it. Her school wasn't a world of which she was a part. She knew she held herself apart and didn't really try – but why bother? The system was against her. It always had been, from the day Ms Hussa and her classmates had figured out she didn't fit in. Why bother trying to change that?

But now she *was* trying, and it was as if all her fears had been realized. The sound of her voice, alone in the air, made her feel sick to her stomach. Her voice cracked and trembled out into the classroom.

"O mankind! Be dutiful to your Lord, who created you from a single person, and from . . ." Wadjda stopped. Reading quickly and accurately was a struggle, especially when it felt like a hand was squeezing her throat.

"From him He created . . ." Ms Noof prompted impatiently.

Wadjda repeated the line from her teacher in halts and starts, and then brought her eyes back to the page. Words stumbled from her mouth in an uncomfortable rhythm.

"He created his wife, Hawwa, and, uh, from them both –"

Ms Noof blew out her breath in a huff. "Enough. Stop, please." She scanned the room for a better candidate. "Noura, continue."

Noura, with her perfect diction and pretty voice, was guaranteed to get them through at least one verse. Yet, the teacher still seemed annoyed. She crossed her arms and rolled her head from side to side, brow furrowed.

Ignoring Ms Noof's grumpy demeanour, Noura began, her voice pure and perfect. She enunciated every word, letting it trip delicately off her tongue.

"He created many men and women. Fear Allah, through whom you demand your mutual rights, and thy wombs.

Surely, Allah is ever Allah, Watcher over you," she recited.

"Beautiful as always, Noura," Ms Noof grumbled. She didn't sound like she meant it, but Noura beamed anyway, smiling at the other girls like she'd just won a beauty contest.

Wadjda looked back at Noura, feeling extreme jealousy through her whole body. She could never read like Noura had, not in a million years.

But, if she wanted to win, she was going to have to learn.

CHAPTER TWENTY-SEVEN

ead this! Recite that! Memorize this! *Ugh!*

All the new work for Religious Club had left Wadjda bored and exhausted. It was break time, and she wandered the school courtyard aimlessly, looking for a quiet, shady place to hide. Somewhere she could close her eyes and imagine herself free, pedalling through Riyadh on her green bicycle. Somewhere far from the girls who made fun of her, who thought she couldn't keep up or follow along or read the text right.

At the back wall, Fatin and Fatima were in their usual spot – and, of course, looking at football magazines and slipping off their shoes to paint their toenails. When they saw Wadjda, they beamed at her. But once again Wadjda was too tired to muster more than a shadow of a smile, one that didn't touch her eyes.

"Where's the nail polish?" Wadjda heard Fatima whisper.

Fatin bent low, running her hand underneath the bench. "I don't know! I hid it here the other day."

Wadjda approached casually, ready to tell them she'd

scooped up their contraband treasure and hidden it so the principal wouldn't see. But then she caught her breath and ducked out of the way, concealing herself in the shadow of the wall.

As she watched in horror, Ms Hussa swooped down on the two older girls like an avenging angel. For once, Fatin and Fatima were taken completely by surprise. They fumbled to cover their bare feet. Eyes wide and panicked, they pushed the forbidden magazines under each other's clothes. Fatin shoved one behind Fatima's back. Fatima slipped a second magazine under Fatin's legs.

"What are you doing here?" Ms Hussa shouted, her eyes darting between the two girls. "Why were your hands under her skirt?"

Fatin and Fatima froze. It was as if fear had turned them to stone. In her hiding place, Wadjda stood motionless as well, watching.

"That's all we need," Ms Hussa said in disgust. "Two girls, hiding in shadows, putting their hands all over each other! Tell me what that means?" Fatin and Fatima recoiled from each other, mortified. Unmoved, Ms Hussa stared down at them coolly. "I'm fed up with you two. Just saying 'sorry' isn't going to cut it this time. In my office. Now!"

Still too scared to move, Wadjda watched the principal

march Fatin and Fatima inside. Seeing her idols caught and shamed was a harsh dose of reality, like a splash of icy water to the face. If they could be punished, she thought, then no one was safe.

After sitting anxiously through her final class, Wadjda rushed out of the room like a shot fired from a cannon. She had to track down Fatin and Fatima! Frantic, she scanned the crowds of girls pouring out of the high-school classes.

Nothing, nothing – and then there they were. Fatin and Fatima walked fast, heads down, in an obvious hurry to get away. Each girl had her veil pulled up to hide her face, but Wadjda saw the anger in both girls' eyes.

The crowd bumped past Wadjda on all sides, a steady stream of black. At the front of the line, like a crest on a wave, Fatin and Fatima surged forward and disappeared. When they had vanished fully, Wadjda let out her breath in a *whoosh*. With slow hands and a sad heart, she tugged on her *abayah*.

There's no way to salvage such a crummy day, she thought. *But maybe the toyshop will help.*

And it did. As she walked, she felt her anger and fatigue start to swell into something else – a feeling of growing determination. The giggles of her classmates rose up in her ears. Noura's little smirk swam before her eyes. And each time Wadjda fought back the sounds and images she felt herself grow stronger.

She'd beat them all in that competition, she told herself, beat everyone who thought she couldn't win. She'd do it for all the school kids in Riyadh who spent their days getting humiliated or mocked. Then, triumphant, she'd ride off on her bicycle and leave everyone behind her, gaping helplessly in defeat.

With each step Wadjda felt more powerful. She walked faster. Her feet lifted further and further off the ground. Soon she was practically running. Her hand gripped her veil, ensuring it wouldn't fall or tangle and slow her down. The store drew closer, and Wadjda smiled. She knew what she had to do.

As usual, the owner was in his own world, listening to old records and sipping traditional coffee. His head jerked up when he saw Wadjda. His surprise when she walked right past the green bicycle was obvious. Wadjda might have laughed if she hadn't been so focused. But her mission called. Without pause, she disappeared into the back aisle. A second later, she re-emerged, carrying *Learn Quran the Easy Way*. She slid the game box on to the counter and looked up at the owner. He raised an eyebrow.

"It's for school," she said. "How much?"

The old man flipped it over and examined the barcode. "Only eighty Riyals," he said. "Cheaper than a bicycle."

"How about sixty-two?" Wadjda said politely, holding up her remaining funds. With trembling hands, she spread everything she'd saved out on the counter.

This was her biggest gamble ever.

CHAPTER TWENTY-EIGHT

The wind blew, brushing cool air across her skin. Riyadh spread out beneath her, a patchwork of buildings, of cars and buses, of stories and secrets. High above it all, safely hidden on the roof of her house, Wadjda sat triumphantly astride Abdullah's bicycle.

It hadn't been easy to push the heavy bike up the stairs, but Abdullah was desperate. He wanted to impress his uncle and do a good job with his task. In addition to having a well-placed pole that would support many wires and cords, Wadjda's house was strategically located above the empty plot of land where the election tent would be built. There was no better place to hang lights for the event.

"So I guess," Abdullah said, panting, as they tugged the bike round a tight corner, "letting you ride while I work is a small price to pay."

From her spot on the steps above, Wadjda blew her sweaty hair back from her face and smiled down at him. Abdullah was all big talk. She knew he liked hanging out with her. Tucked away on the roof, no boys would make fun of him for playing with a girl. Pretending to let him have his way was a small price for her to pay, too.

They dragged the bike up another few steps. Looking down, Wadjda noticed that Abdullah was wearing the same beautiful *taqia* he'd had on the day they went to Adira. This, too, made her smile.

Now he was hard at work, and she was riding. Cautiously, her toes skimming across the roof's small amount of flat surface, Wadjda pushed the old bicycle forward. In spite of herself, she was terrified of falling. At the same time, she felt that same rush of determination, telling her to keep going, to try to turn in circles. Awkwardly she pedalled and weaved, barely keeping her balance for the few seconds her feet were off the ground.

Across from her, Abdullah fastened a hook to the outside wall. To his left, a crude mass of metal hung off the edge. *It looks*, he thought, *like a crazy metallic nest tangled together by defective robot rats*.

"What *is* that?" he asked, inspecting the twisted lump inquisitively.

Wadjda's head shot up, and she planted her feet on the ground.

"What do you think?" she shot back, offended. "It's an antenna, stupid. I can get signals from way beyond _your_ world on that thing. How do you think I make my Awesome Mix Tapes, anyway?"

"With all the people shouting in the background?" Abdullah said smugly, going back to work. "And the static? 'Awesome' indeed! Listen, my uncle likes the Quran radio station now. He wants to talk about his campaign there. They have all these famous readers – they recite the Quran beautifully! It makes your heart melt, my uncle says."

Wadjda put her hand over her own heart, as if to show Abdullah what she was speaking was the truth. "He should hear my mother sing!" she said. "Talk about heart melting. She should have a channel all her own."

Abdullah sniffed. _Whatever_, Wadjda thought, and stretched out a hand, pressing it against the railing, using the pressure to push herself along. As she moved jerkily forward on the bike, her eyes drifted to the campaign tent. In front was a poster of Abdullah's uncle, but he looked wrong somehow, like another person. This serious-faced candidate had no moustache, just a long, carefully grown-out beard. Was it even the same guy?

"Why does your uncle look so different?" she asked, wrinkling her nose.

"Didn't you hear?" Abdullah bent a cord and wrapped it round the pole. "Men shouldn't shave their beards! It's _haram_! What do they teach you at school, anyway?"

"You know, we learn about our periods, post-delivery discharge . . ." Wadjda said sarcastically. Abdullah practically turned purple with embarrassment. Wadjda burst into a fit of laughter as he sheepishly pretended to busy himself with work.

Another turn round the roof. Wadjda's feet stayed mostly on the ground. The bike tyres wobbled precariously every time she tried to pedal. Turning in a slow circle, she balanced as best she could and gave the bike's bell a *brriiinnng*! The bright trilling rang out proudly, seeming to grow louder as it rebounded off the exterior walls.

"Everyone in the neighbourhood's going to hear you," Abdullah cautioned.

"Who cares?" Wadjda depressed the bell's lever with her left-hand thumb. *Brriiinnng, brriiinnng!* "Look, I'm a natural!"

Still laughing, she planted her feet, gave herself a big push – then swerved the front wheel and fell hard to the ground. Abdullah jerked his head up, concerned, ready to ask if she was all right. But when he saw she was fine he snickered instead.

"A natural? Yeah, right. All this fuss over a bicycle, and you don't even know how to ride."

"How would I?" Wadjda asked defensively. She rotated her wrist, wincing, and shook out her stinging hip. "Where would I ride a bicycle?"

Frustration twisted her face. Abdullah saw her pressing her lips together so tightly they almost turned white. The sight tugged at his heart. Impulsively, he dropped his tools and jumped up to stand behind her.

"Go ahead," he said, holding the bicycle steady.

Wadjda smiled enormously, showing all her teeth. The expression banished any tension or anger, made her eyes dance with light.

"Ready?" Abdullah asked. She nodded, and he pushed her, trotting alongside as she pedalled.

Together, they swept the bicycle round the roof, turning low circles at the edges, laughing and squealing with delight. Neither Abdullah nor Wadjda could think of a better place to learn to ride, could imagine a city with better weather or bluer skies. For one suspended moment, they were free, two kids playing high above the world.

The palm trees swayed in the late-afternoon breeze. The sun shone down, but its rays were cooler now. They were advancing deeper into the year.

CHAPTER TWENTY-NINE

That night, before switching off the light, Wadjda reached over from her bed and flicked on the radio. Scrolling through the channels, she lingered on a song she liked, tapping her fingers against the radio, humming the words under her breath. Then she remembered her mission. Methodically, she spun the dial until she found what she was really looking for.

"You are listening to the one and only Quran station. Tune in all day, every day, to hear your favourite readers. Now, Al Hudafi will recite *Surat Al-Baqarah*," the DJ announced.

Slumping back against her pillow, Wadjda laced her fingers behind her head and stared up at the ceiling. The voice on the radio rang out through the room.

"In the name of Allah, the Beneficent, the Merciful. *Alif Lam Mim*. This Book, there is no doubt in it, is a guide to those who guard against evil."

As if in afterthought, Wadjda took her Quran from the desk, flipped to the right page and tried to follow along.

The male reader was moving very fast, though, and she soon fell behind. Sighing, Wadjda set the Quran back down, making sure to keep it open to the right spot. There was just so much to memorize. Could she ever read with this man's ease?

Wadjda turned her head towards her desk. Her gaze fell on the video game she'd bought, and she smiled.

Footsteps sounded in the hallway. The door clicked open. Mother poked her head round the jamb, her half smile disappearing when her eyes fell on Wadjda's desk. As fast as she could, she reached over and closed the Quran.

"Don't ever, ever leave the Holy Book open!" she scolded. "Satan will spit in it!"

Yet another old wives' tale. But this time, instead of arguing or rolling her eyes, Wadjda nodded in agreement.

"Yes, *Ummi*. I'm sorry."

"Good girl." Her mother was smiling again. "Come, sit with me for a while."

Pleased by the unexpected invitation, Wadjda clicked off the radio, grabbed the video game and followed her mother down the hall. A great day was continuing to get better, she thought.

In the living room, her mother perched on the couch, counting *oud* pieces – small sticks of scented wood imported specially from India. *Oud* was very expensive.

Only a few ounces were worth as much as Wadjda's dream bicycle.

Wadjda knew the price well, because she'd been with her mother when she bought it. The salesman was a squat, fat man who sat brooding over his wares like a toad. As he and Mother bargained, his eyes fixed on her hands, the only exposed flesh he could spot. However she moved, whatever she said, his gaze never wavered. Wadjda could tell Mother felt horribly uncomfortable. At one point she tucked her hands inside her *abayah* sleeves to hide them from view. And she paid the salesman's full, ridiculous price, just so she could leave.

I wish I could have done the bargaining, Wadjda thought. *I'd have saved a fortune!*

Still, the *oud* would make the whole house smell wonderful, like a thick, luxurious fog had rolled through, leaving a perfumed charcoal mist that stung your nostrils when you breathed in. When it burned, Wadjda and her mother could pretend theirs was a rich person's home, a place for people who could afford whatever luxuries they wanted.

Humming softly, Mother arranged a small *mubkharah* on the coffee table. The *mubkharah* was a tiny burner that used real coal. Wadjda took a deep breath. Was there a special occasion? she wondered. Why was Mother burning the *oud* now?

She'd have to wait to find out. Wadjda plopped herself in front of the TV and started fiddling with the wires. After ten minutes, she threw the cords down on the carpet. She sighed once, then again, louder. Frowning and frustrated, she looked up, wondering if her mother had noticed her struggle.

"I'll never win the Quran competition," she said, poking at the wires. "This game doesn't work on our 'state-of-the-art' TV, so how can I practise?"

She tried to sound casual, to hint that there must be a better option – which, of course, there was. But her mother just looked at her, perplexed. Then she got Wadjda's meaning. Her eyes darted to the *majlis* door.

"Don't even think about it. Your father will go crazy if you mess up his TV."

Wadjda sighed. Father had recently got a giant flat-screen, something like fifty inches, so he could play his video games in style. The ancient, boxy TV in the living room couldn't compete. Its picture was grainy and obscured by rolling lines of static. It didn't have the right inputs for a DVD player, much less a video game.

I could probably rig something up, Wadjda thought, examining the back of the TV more closely. *But it would be so much easier to use Father's.*

Whatever she did, she had to act fast. Getting the game up and running was a key part of her new plan to win the competition. She closed her eyes, imagined circling the roof on Abdullah's bicycle. Only in this daydream, it wasn't his clanking old bike but the sleek green bicycle she loved so dearly.

Figure something out, Wadjda, she told herself. *Or else!*

CHAPTER THIRTY

She'd survived the first few meetings. Her nerves were settling down. And maybe, just maybe, Wadjda was getting the hang of Religious Club.

At every meeting, she was one of the first to arrive. For a whole hour, she sat up, back straight, eyes lowered to the Quran. She nodded every once in a while, pretending to listen to her teacher's passionate diatribes. Sure, she never knew exactly what Ms Noof was talking about, most likely the million different ways you could go to Hell. But the look on Wadjda's face always made it seem like the most fascinating thing in the world.

Today, her pretend focus caught up with her. Several minutes into a rant, Ms Noof stopped speaking and looked out at the circle of girls. "Wadjda, what do you think?" she said, zeroing in on the only girl who looked remotely interested.

Um . . . Wadjda felt a giant lump lodge in her throat. "I . . . I . . ."

Focus, she told herself. *Take a few minutes to gather your thoughts.*

Across the circle, Noura elbowed Yasmeen and rolled her eyes.

That was all the motivation Wadjda needed. That now-familiar sense of determination flowed into her. She squared her small shoulders.

"I think this competition is very hard for me," she said.

Noura and the other girls looked taken aback by her confident tone. But not *that* taken aback. *Yeah, we know*, she saw Salma mouth to the girl beside her. Two or three others couldn't help but giggle.

Ms Noof waved an impatient hand, silencing them. "Go on, Wadjda," she said.

"Yes, it's hard. But I . . . I heard on the Quran channel yesterday that if recitation is easy for you," Wadjda said slowly, "then you get only one reward from God. If it's hard for you to read and remember, you get two rewards. One for reading the Quran, and one for the great trouble you go through."

For the first time in all their meetings, Ms Noof didn't look annoyed. Her gaze was full of something else: pride. A gleaming look, like she had somehow contributed to Wadjda's incredible breakthrough.

"Thank you for sharing this with us," she said. "Girls, I want all of you to listen to Wadjda. She is a great example of a person who tries hard, a person devoted to God."

Noura and her cronies looked dumbfounded. Yasmeen's jaw actually dropped.

"Thank you," Wadjda said shyly, relishing her new role as teacher's pet. Though she kept her face modest, she stole a peek to either side. Had Salma heard? Could she believe that Wadjda had won Ms Noof's favour, even temporarily?

It was hard to keep her face still, but Wadjda made herself read the same sentence over and over until her smile faded. Even when her face was composed, she continued to bask in the glory of the moment. It felt good to be the star pupil. Maybe she should try it more often.

Ms Jamila appeared in the doorway, stuck her head in and motioned for Ms Noof.

"Excuse me a moment, girls." The teacher dragged herself to her feet and lumbered over to the doorway. Ms Jamila met her eagerly, and they gossiped and giggled for a minute. It seemed Ms Jamila was admiring Ms Noof's blouse. She kept reaching out and feeling the fabric of the sleeve. And Ms Noof was praising Ms Jamila's new veil! For another few seconds, they traded compliments.

Watching them, Wadjda had a strange thought. Maybe her teachers could actually be normal people? Was it possible? Could they laugh and smile and talk about clothes and friends – everyday life stuff – at least once in a while?

"Wadjda," Ms Noof called. "Ms Hussa needs to see you. Go to her room now."

Oh no. Wadjda felt her stomach sink, her mouth go dry. She fought to swallow.

"Oh, and, Wadjda?" Ms Noof gave her another smile. "I told Ms Jamila to tell Ms Hussa how well you're doing."

This was comforting – but just a little. Wadjda's moment of glory had apparently passed. Her classmates were back to giggling . . . and she was back to her usual trek down the endless corridor to the principal's office.

CHAPTER THIRTY-ONE

Why did I wear jeans? Today of all days? Stupid, stupid!

Wadjda stood in front of the principal's desk, fidgeting, struggling to pull her uniform down over her jeans and coloured-in shoes. The position was all too familiar. Only this time she had no idea why she was there. She'd all but stopped selling stuff, she'd shown up to school on time almost every day, and she'd been careful to wear the *abayah raas* in just the right way. The Wadjda of the last weeks was a girl transformed.

And maybe it was working? She sneaked a glance at Ms Hussa. The principal wasn't giving her that familiar evil eye yet. In fact, she looked totally relaxed, lounging in her chair and staring into space.

Yes. Something was definitely different.

"Wadjda," Ms Hussa said abruptly, turning to look at her.

Wadjda blinked. Was she – was that . . . a smile?

"I have to say, I didn't believe it when Ms Jamila told me. But apparently you really are doing well in Religious Club. If this is a permanent change, I'll be very impressed."

Behind her back, Wadjda's fingers were knotted together

so tightly they hurt. But she put on a polite face and tried not to squirm.

"Thank you, Ms Hussa," she whispered.

The principal stood and started thumbing through a cabinet. When she found the file she was looking for, she pulled it out and checked the papers inside, confirming its contents. Then she fixed Wadjda with a longer stare, one Wadjda didn't understand.

There was a moment of silence, broken by a *swish* of paper as Ms Hussa tossed the file on to her desk. There was meaning in her actions, but, try as she might, Wadjda couldn't make it out. The file felt like something of which she should be aware, like it was meant for her to take. But what if she was wrong?

In the end, she didn't move. Ms Hussa returned to her seat and picked up the file, tapping it against the desk's smooth surface. *Tik-tik-tik.*

"You may not believe it," she said, looking at Wadjda out of the corner of her eye, "but I was reckless at your age, too. And look at me now!"

Again she tapped the file against the desk. *Tik-tik-tik.*

"If you keep going the way you're going, I believe you may be able to win this competition." Without taking her eyes off Wadjda, she leaned over and pressed a button on the intercom. "Ms Jamila? Please come by later and pick up the Quran competition file. All the questions are complete. Thank you."

She sat back in her chair and pushed the folder to the front of her desk, towards Wadjda. Wadjda's eyes widened as she stared down at it.

"I'll bet the other girls would die to know what's in there." Ms Hussa said. Her intense eyes never left Wadjda's face.

A sharp rapping sounded. Someone was knocking on the door. Wadjda jumped, startled. At her desk, Ms Hussa sat perfectly still, her face calm. "Come in," she called.

The door swung open, and Fatin and Fatima entered. Wadjda's heart began to pound, hammering against her ribs.

"Close the door, please," Ms Hussa said. Fatin did as she asked, then turned and stood defiantly next to Fatima.

Wadjda's mind was really racing now. The two older girls stood between her and the door. Why hadn't Ms Hussa asked her to leave? She shuffled her feet, scuffing her squeaky sneaker soles against the cool marble floor. Her palms were sweaty.

For a moment, there was silence. Fatin and Fatima kept their eyes straight ahead. Ms Hussa stared at them. Everyone in the room seemed to be looking through Wadjda.

"So. You still claim you weren't doing anything out there, behind the school?"

"We were reading magazines. That's all," Fatima returned. "Nothing like what you said!" She motioned towards Wadjda. "Ask *her*!"

Tik-tik-tik went the folder on the desk. Then Ms Hussa pressed her fingers down on to it and dragged it in a slow circle. As she did, she looked at Wadjda and raised her eyebrows.

"Well?"

Wadjda felt as if she were standing at the base of a hill. A big boulder was tumbling down towards her at top speed. If she didn't jump out of the way, it would crush her. But she was surrounded on all sides by a deep pit filled with crocodiles. The hungry beasts seethed beneath her, jaws snapping hungrily.

Rock or crocodiles? Which to choose?

She looked at Fatin and Fatima, panic squeezing her throat. They looked back at her confidently. Fatin almost looked cocky. They were so sure she would back them up.

Rock or crocodiles?

Wadjda turned and looked at Ms Hussa. She looked at the folder in her hands. Then she dropped her head and closed her eyes.

"I'm not sure," she said quietly. "I was standing far away."

At the same time, Fatin's and Fatima's jaws dropped. They exchanged a glance. Fatima had gone very pale. Fatin

227

stared at Wadjda in disbelief. Wadjda kept her eyes pinned to the floor, avoiding their gaze.

"I see," Ms Hussa said. "So we may never know if your biggest crime was just 'painting your toenails', as you'd claimed earlier today." She paused, smirking. "A stupid lie. You didn't have any nail polish."

The words hit Wadjda like a slap. The principal didn't notice. Flashing a satisfied smile, she said, "Wadjda, thank you very much. You may return to class." A beat, and then she picked up the folder from her desk. "Please give this to my secretary," she said, staring intently at Wadjda. "And close the door behind you."

With trembling hands, Wadjda took the folder. She clenched it tight, sure her damp palms would leave smudgy fingerprints on the pristine paper.

Fatin and Fatima moved out of the way, clearing a path for her exit. Wadjda had never realized how much they towered over her. They were so tall! Like two stern-faced statues, glaring down at her tiny figure as it passed between them.

In the loneliness of the corridor, Wadjda stood motionless, trying to catch her breath. The folder in her hands felt heavy, like it was full of lead weights. She opened it slightly, just enough to see the top sheet of paper inside: "Competition Questions".

The principal's words echoed in her mind: *I believe you may be able to win this competition.*

Wadjda flipped the front cover all the way back. She was about to start reading when the conversation in Ms Hussa's office got louder.

"It's only a few words," Ms Hussa was saying. "Sign it, and we'll forget this ugly mess."

"No!" Fatin shot back. She sounded like she was almost in tears. "It's a lie! We weren't touching each other!"

The cool wall rose to meet Wadjda's back. She slumped against it, staring up at the ceiling. Though she'd escaped Ms Hussa's office, she still couldn't breathe. Now her throat was choked with tears.

The bell rang. The noise of chattering girls and slamming doors began to fill the hallway. Wadjda looked down at the folder, then back towards the principal's office. With the clamour that had sprung up, she could no longer hear the argument inside. But it didn't matter. Her mind was made up.

Before she could think better of it, Wadjda slapped the folder shut, dragged herself to Ms Jamila's desk, and dropped the folder into her in-box.

If I win, I'm doing it my way, she thought, and walked away without looking back.

CHAPTER THIRTY-TWO

"*Allahu Akbar Allahu Akbar!*"

The haunting lilt of the dawn *adthan*, or call to prayer, echoed through the streets and into Wadjda's dark bedroom. "*Al Salatu Khairun Min Al Naum*," the muezzin called, which meant, "Prayer is better than sleeping." It was a line unique to the dawn call.

Wadjda's mother was already awake, sitting on the side of her daughter's bed. She reached over and touched Wadjda's shoulder tenderly.

"Wake up, little troublemaker," she whispered.

Wadjda lifted her head, rubbing her eyes. It had taken her a long time to fall asleep the previous night. Too many thoughts and feelings were stampeding through her head, sending her emotions into a churning mess.

Her mother ran her hands through Wadjda's hair, working the tangles free. Still Wadjda lay silently, staring at the bottle of blue nail polish. It sat on the desk, right next to her money-saving chart. It reminded her of the tiny rebellions she'd relished with her old friends, with Fatin and Fatima, even with Abeer.

"*Ummi*," she said. "Do you think Abeer is OK?"

Her voice trailed off as her eyes sought her mother's.

"After what happened?" The last words were a whisper.

Her mother smiled.

"Of course, darling. Abeer's engagement was the best day of her life. She's a very lucky girl. She couldn't be happier not having to go to school any more!"

Wadjda bit her lip, uncertain. The bottle of nail polish kept drawing her eyes. It seemed in that moment like a tiny blue finger, pointing at her, accusing her of –

The call rang out again, and Wadjda turned her head away.

In the bathroom, Wadjda's mother used the tap in the shower to perform *wudu*, the required washing before prayer. The showerhead was detachable, and connected to the pipes by a long length of metallic hose. This made it easy to wash her arms and feet without having to get too far into the shower.

Behind her, Wadjda leaned over the sink. She sniffled up water to clean out her nose, cupped water in her hands to splash her face and industriously rubbed water behind her ears. There was a lot about *wudu* on the Quran radio station.

"I saw girls riding bicycles on TV, *Ummi*," she said,

bending to dab water on her feet. "Why don't you give me the money to buy one? I know you can. I saw all the money in your drawer!"

"Here, girls don't ride bicycles," her mother said. She turned the showerhead, spraying her feet, and stepped out of the stall on to the tiled floor. "You won't be able to have children if you ride a bicycle!"

Another ridiculous answer! Every time Wadjda brought up the bicycle, her mother seemed to have a new silly reason to say no. This time, though, Wadjda had a retort. In the midst of her frustration, she blurted without thinking, "You've never ridden a bicycle, and you still can't have any more children!"

The words fell into the room like a cupboard's worth of crystal goblets smashing on the floor. Her mother dropped her towel. Deep anguish filled her face, a darkness that shadowed her eyes and turned down the corners of her mouth.

Wadjda went white. Only now did she realize the significance of her words. Now, when it was too late to take them back.

"How could you say such a thing?" Her mother's voice broke. "I almost died having you!"

Snatching up the towel, she threw it on the rack and stormed out, slamming the door behind her. Crushed, hating herself for hurting her mother, Wadjda dropped her head on to her crossed elbows. In the bathroom mirror, she watched drops of water run down her reflected face and drip off her nose into the sink. From this angle, they looked like tears.

By the time Wadjda came out to join her in prayer, her mother was already wrapped in a bright red covering. The beautiful cloth flowed down her body and on to the floor. Tucking her own covering under her chin, Wadjda stood tentatively next to her mother. Without speaking, they pulled two prayer rugs out of a small, beautifully decorated wooden box.

Wadjda's mother twisted her lips. The box had been a wedding gift from Wadjda's grandmother, brought specially from the holy city of Mecca. Wadjda knew her mother was trying to sell it, which was a sore point between her and her mother-in-law.

"If we need money," her mother would say, "what can I do?"

They laid their prayer rugs out, side by side, and lined up to pray. Again, Wadjda positioned herself as close as possible to her mother. She heard the steady *drip, drip, drip* of water from the bathroom tap. The sound blended with the voice of the imam, echoing from the loudspeakers of the nearby mosque.

"*Qad qamat al-salah*," the voice called out. Mother shifted her weight and raised her hands up near her ears. Wadjda looked down at the floor, instinctually following her movements.

"*Allahu Akbar*," her mother whispered. Wadjda moved her lips silently, reciting the prayer along with her.

CHAPTER THIRTY-THREE

Hands full of supplies, Wadjda's mother rushed out of the front gate of their house, followed closely by Wadjda, who was also loaded down with stacks of schoolbooks and papers. Her mother was fully veiled, shrouded in black. Only her eyes were visible.

Despite her tremendous hurry, she came to an abrupt stop when she looked up and saw the string of lights attached to the roof. "What –" she whispered, and looked accusingly at Wadjda, who blushed. *Caught red-handed!*

Luckily, Iqbal was waiting. He gave a long blaring blast of the horn and poked his head out of the window. But when he saw Wadjda he pulled his head back inside again. Thankfully, her mother didn't notice. Muttering under her breath, she pulled open the van's sliding door and threw her things on to the seat. Turning, she snatched the unwieldy stack of papers from Wadjda's arms.

"We'll talk about that later," she said, gesturing towards the lights. Wadjda looked away sheepishly as her mother climbed into the van and slammed the door shut.

Iqbal lurched the van forward, casting up a sooty cloud

of exhaust. He shot Wadjda another glare through the passenger-side window as he drove by.

This I can handle! Laughing, she placed her pointer finger across the bottom of her nose, like a moustache, to remind him of Abdullah's threat. Mouthing curses at her through the dirty glass, Iqbal pushed the car to a higher gear. The van jolted away down the street, a little moving tornado of dust and grey smoke.

Wadjda's day at school was a blur of forgettable, boring, unremarkable nothingness. Before she knew it, Wadjda was dragging herself back through the front door, dropping her bag in the hallway and wandering mindlessly into her mother's room. Now that she wasn't selling things, she had more time after school. The long afternoons left her feeling restless. And she kept thinking about the *Jamaaea*.

Sighing, she opened the drawers of her mother's dresser, one by one, inhaling the familiar sweet and spicy scent. Finally, she opened the top drawer and moved aside a layer of clothes. There it was. Revealed, the wad of money seemed even bigger. Wadjda's eyes widened as she stared down at it. Gingerly, she pulled out the stack of notes, barely held together by a straining rubber band, and flipped through it, counting each bill silently. For a while, she held the cash in her hand, feeling its weight. To think of all the things those Riyals could buy!

Her eyes wandered to her mother's almost-empty wardrobe, and the corners of her mouth turned down in a frown. With a sense of finality, she put the massive stack of bills back. She carefully folded the clothes over it, closed the drawer and left the room.

In the living room, restlessness tugged at her heart. She'd been so good lately! Not looking at the competition questions. Not taking the money. Surely she'd earned some sort of licence for mischief! Like using her father's brand-new TV. A smile lit Wadjda's face at the thought. She knew she wouldn't break anything, so it was more or less a victimless crime. Besides, it was for studying! Practically a noble thing to do.

On swift feet she flew to the kitchen, opened a small box hidden underneath the cabinets next to the oven and pulled out a ring holding the different house keys. Without hesitation, she walked to the *majlis* door and started testing them. One after another, she jammed the keys into the lock and gave a twist, hoping for the right fit.

The keys clanked and jangled. Just when she thought she'd gone through them all twice, she felt one slip into place. The lock clicked open. *Yes!* Wadjda pumped her fist in the air, grinning. From there, it was a matter of seconds.

She brought in her game system and hooked it up to father's brand-new TV.

The picture was enormous, crisp and clean. When the game's cheesy graphics scrolled across the screen, they looked old-fashioned and fuzzy. The TV was so nice that it made the cheap animation look like junk. Still, it was way better than the living room.

"Choose the correct answer," the game commanded. The first question popped up. "Who are the Sabians?"

"The what?" Wadjda said aloud. Randomly, she hit a button. It was a complete guess. She had no idea who or what the Sabians were.

"Incorrect!" the game said. Its tone was robotic, but somehow angry. "Try again. Who are the Sabians?"

"OK, mister. I'll show you. Except, um . . ." She still had no idea who the Sabians were. Desperate, Wadjda scanned the multiple-choice answers on the screen and hit another button.

"Incorrect! Try again," the game said in the same mean robot voice. "Who are the Sabians?"

Frustrated, Wadjda threw the controller on the floor, where it bounced against the carpet.

"How am I supposed to know?" she screamed defensively at the TV.

At that moment, the doorbell rang. Relieved to have an excuse – any excuse! – to abandon the game, Wadjda sprinted over to see who it was.

But if I'm going to win, she told herself, *I have to figure out who the heck the Sabians are – and fast!*

CHAPTER THIRTY-FOUR

The sound of panting filled the stairwell. Both Wadjda and Abdullah were breathing heavily as they heaved his bicycle up towards the roof. Abdullah was a welcome distraction to the long, languishing afternoon. Well, at least his bicycle was. The Sabians could wait.

"I don't care if they memorize everything," Wadjda said, forcing the words out between puffs of breath. "I'll be better! I'll beat them all!" She paused, letting the bicycle rest against the wall. Her voice grew stronger. "Seriously, I'm getting good!"

Not wanting to argue, and unsure what exactly Wadjda was talking about, Abdullah nodded his silent approval. Today, he was having a harder time with the stairs. It was his boots. They were too heavy. He dragged his feet as he pushed himself and the bicycle upward, its wheels bumping forward one step at a time.

At last, they lowered the bike on to the cement surface of the roof. Still panting, Abdullah went to work on the lights. Wadjda leaned over, struggling to catch her breath – and blinked, surprised. The bicycle was standing on its own!

Suspicious, she paced a tight circle round it. Training wheels had been bolted on to the back tire! Her eyes filled with fury. Whirling, she shot Abdullah a look of death.

"What is this?" She gave one little wheel a kick.

"It will help you learn," Abdullah said defensively. "Look, I need to work on the lights. I can't be pushing you around all day."

Wadjda marched over to where he was working and planted her hands on her hips, glaring down at him.

"So I can't recite, and I can't ride, is that right? I hate you! And, and . . ." But the words wouldn't come. Nearly paralysed with anger, she kicked Abdullah's toolbox away. Hammers and screwdrivers clattered out on to the roof, and Wadjda collapsed on to the concrete, head buried in her arms, crying.

Abdullah looked at the scattered tools and sighed. Without saying a word, he grabbed a wrench. Still in silence, he walked over to the bicycle and cranked the bolts off the training wheels. First one, then the other. When he was finished, he walked over and dropped them on the ground beside Wadjda. First one, then the other. *Clunk, clunk.*

Finished, he sat beside her and stared off across the city. It was smoggy today. The furthest buildings were invisible, and even the nearby ones were made fuzzy and indistinct by haze.

"I took them off," he said softly. "You'll learn how to ride, and you'll read well, too. It's only a matter of time."

Wadjda didn't move. Her shoulders shook with silent sobs. Desperate, Abdullah reached into his pocket and fumbled around, pulling out a few crumpled bills.

"I'll give you five Riyals if you stop crying."

He held the money out in her direction. Keeping one hand over her eyes, Wadjda reached out and snatched it. She put it in her pocket, raised her head and wiped her nose.

Across the roof, the new ribbons on Abdullah's handlebars swayed in the breeze. For a moment, Wadjda watched them lift and dance. Then she turned back to Abdullah and smiled.

The two of them sat next to each other on the old concrete roof, not speaking, enjoying the silence. The sunset *adthan* started, calling for prayer, signalling the end of their day. For the moment, they smiled at each other, content.

But still, Wadjda knew, there was work to do.

CHAPTER THIRTY-FIVE

Iqbal's battered car jolted into potholes and juddered over speed bumps, making its shaky way forward through the neighbourhood. In the back, Wadjda and her mother sat, neither one speaking. Every so often, Wadjda's mother adjusted her *niqab*, pulling the veil tight round her head. But every new vibration and bump shook the fabric off again.

They stopped at a traffic light across from the toyshop, and Wadjda leaned over to see if she could spot her green bicycle. It should be there, waiting for her.

Instead, to her shock, she saw the shopkeeper talking to a man and his son. They were standing by her bicycle, staring right at it! Now the owner reached out, put his hand on the crossbar and gestured to the seat. Though Wadjda couldn't hear what they were saying, a feeling in her gut told her they were bargaining.

No, no, no! Wadjda pressed her face against the dirty window, squinting, trying to get a better look. At that moment, the owner raised his head and spotted her, saw her wide eyes staring longingly through the glass. Wadjda saw his own eyes widen in recognition. But then he looked away, smiled and kept talking to the potential buyer.

The man and his son wore crisp, shiny *thobes*. *They must have a lot of money*, Wadjda thought, *to afford that kind of fabric*. The man's white *ghutra* and neat black *iqal* resembled the ones her father kept for special occasions. The bike's eight-hundred-Riyal price tag was probably no big deal to them.

Iqbal shifted into gear, and the car rattled off down the street. For a desperate moment, Wadjda considered opening the door and jumping out, but good sense prevailed, and instead she squirmed uncomfortably in her seat. She wanted to chase away the man and his annoying son, to yell at the owner for even showing her bicycle to anyone else! Confused, her mother glanced over at her, and then peered out of the window to see what had put her daughter in such a state. Behind them, the green bicycle sparkled in the sun.

A moment later, they rounded a corner, turning on to a big main street. Wadjda could no longer see the toyshop in the rear window. Fuming, she fell back into her seat, caught the hem of her *abayah* in her hands and began twisting it into knots.

"Madame, only one hour," Iqbal called from the driver's seat in his usual broken Arabic. "I have no time to wait for you. You are late, I go. You find taxi."

"We understand, Iqbal," Mother said. "Enough."

To stop him from talking to her, she pulled out her phone and pretended to text. Wadjda's eyes roamed the interior of the car, looking for something to take her mind off the bicycle. She paused on the little girl's picture, taped – as always – to the dashboard. Wadjda folded her arms across the top of the front passenger seat and pushed her veil up out of her face, trying to get a better look. The girl in the picture had big dark eyes, a mole on one cheek and a sweet smile, with one tooth missing.

"Who's the little girl, Iqbal?" Wadjda asked.

"This is my daughter," he said, meeting her eyes in the rear-view mirror. "I didn't see her for three years now."

He shook his head, sad but smiling, and adjusted the picture to give Wadjda a better view.

"She goes to school." He paused, and then added, "I didn't go to school."

There was so much pride in his voice. It touched Wadjda, but she didn't show it. This was Iqbal, after all. Sarcasm was always the better option.

"Obviously you didn't go to school, because you don't have any manners," she said, trying to tease him. In the rear-view mirror, Iqbal saw the gleam in her eye.

"You, too, have no manners," he retorted, half smiling. Wadjda gave him a grin, showing her teeth, and stuck out her tongue. Her mother pulled her back into her seat, clucking impatiently. She needed nothing more than her eyes to show Wadjda that it was time to knock it off.

The car bounced and swerved as it sped across the empty desert. In the last week, the weather had cooled even more. Days like this one were almost pleasant. But it was also the time of year when the blasting storms, or *huboob*, rolled through, covering everything in sand. The *huboob* always seemed magical to Wadjda. Often, it moved into Riyadh like a rounded wall, the front edges of its sandy cloud reaching into every nook and cranny like the inquisitive fingers of a giant.

Would it come tonight? Wadjda wondered, pressing her face back against the window. Already visibility was limited. Gusts of sand, driven by the wind, covered the road ahead of them. But it wasn't a real storm, not yet.

CHAPTER THIRTY-SIX

The mall was bright, cool and crowded, its arched hallways full of people rushing in every direction, trying to get their shopping done before the stores closed for dusk prayer. All the female shoppers looked the same, distinguishable only by the make and size of their handbags. The men looked more or less the same, too. Every one of them seemed to be wearing a white *thobe* and red-checked *ghutra*. And every person in the mall had the same harried look in his or her eyes – including Wadjda's mother.

The second floor, where they were heading, was especially crowded with figures dressed in black or white. *It looks like a giant chessboard*, Wadjda thought. But the pieces were shifting too fast for her to keep track of them. Her mother walked ahead, moving quickly, not looking at the masses of laughing, chatting people.

Behind her, Wadjda lingered, moving aimlessly. At a kiosk selling accessories and small pieces of jewellery, she stopped. Heading straight to the salesperson, she pointed accusingly at the rack of bracelets. They looked just like the ones she wove, but without the homemade touch that made hers special. The sign above read, ONLY 20 RIYALS!

"I make better bracelets than these," Wadjda said, winding one of the poor imitations between her fingers. "How much will you pay me to make you some? Ten Riyals apiece?"

"No thanks," the guy behind the counter said, laughing. "I buy them from China, little girl. For ten Riyals, I can get ten thousand."

"China won't do the national colours!" Wadjda countered. *My custom bracelets are a far superior product*, she thought, examining the one in her hand closely. This twine was cheap. The colour would fade, or it would break, after only a few wears.

"You mean like this?" the salesman spun the rack, pointing to bracelets in several variations of Saudi green and white.

"Wadjda! Where are you? Wadjda!"

Oops. Standing on tiptoe, Wadjda searched the mall, striving to make out the source of her mother's voice. The shout came again, this time clearly from above. Wadjda looked up and saw her mother, already on the upper level, glaring down at her through the small slit that exposed her eyes. Waving off the ignorant shopkeeper, who had no idea how great a business deal he'd just blown, Wadjda raced to the escalator.

On the way, she passed a series of posters. The first advertised the most Islamic method of wearing the veil. The second was about the importance of acting decent in mixed-gender places, like the mall and the big open-air marketplace of the *souq*. Running around wasn't OK, apparently. *Too bad*, Wadjda thought, shuffling as fast as she could up the escalator.

When Wadjda caught up to her mother, she was dawdling in front of a dress shop at the far end of the corridor. A large assortment of gowns filled the window. They were in every colour of the rainbow, and most were embellished with crystals and beading. A beautiful red dress stood out among the others, and it was this fantastic creation that Wadjda's mother was staring at hungrily.

They walked inside, and her mother reached out to feel the fabric of the red dress. She caressed the silk, letting it run across her fingers. Something about the way she studied it broke Wadjda's heart. There was such yearning in that gaze. Or maybe it was the contrast between the bright red garment and her mother's featureless black *abayah*.

Suddenly, as if she'd snapped out of a trance, Mother dropped the sleeve of the red dress and walked over to the salesman.

"May I see the red dress in the window, please?" she asked. From her body language, Wadjda could tell she felt uneasy talking to this strange man. Her mother's shoulders were stiff, and she hung back cautiously, not coming close to the salesman as they talked.

Turning away, Wadjda plopped down on a chair near the entry and stared out at the action in the corridors. From the corner of her eye, she saw the salesman remove the dress from the mannequin in the window. Quickly, he covered the naked form with a cloth. Then, critically, he ran his eyes up and down the full length of her mother's body. His scrutiny made her blush. Wadjda saw the tops of her pink cheeks beneath her veil.

"It's a beautiful dress," he said, "but maybe a little big for you."

Her mother nervously tucked her hands into her *abayah*, like a turtle retreating back into its shell.

"What size is it?"

"Large," the salesman said. Wadjda's mother was petite, and he seemed confident that it would overwhelm her slender frame.

"That's all right." Her mother spoke fast, like she was hoping to end the conversation as soon as possible. "Can I try it?"

"Sure," the salesman shrugged. "You can use the women's bathroom." He pointed towards the public washroom at the very end of the corridor. "If it turns out to be big, we can tailor it for you. After you pay a deposit, of course."

Dressing rooms were not allowed in individual shops. It wasn't OK for women to take their clothes off in open, unprotected places – or so the reasoning went. Wadjda had heard that salesmen sometimes put up secret cameras or drilled holes in the walls so they could see naked women while they changed. To stay safe from prying eyes, women had to try on clothes in the public bathrooms instead.

In the small, cramped room, Wadjda perched uncomfortably on the hard edge of the sink while her mother changed in the stall. The bathroom had a squat toilet, nothing more than a hole in the ground with grooves on either side for the feet. The floor was wet from splashing water, so her mother changed gingerly, standing on tiptoes, trying not to let her clothes touch the floor. Positioning her body awkwardly near the door, she struggled to finish zipping the dress while holding its hem up between her legs.

"I know it's a lot of money," her mother whispered, "but I have to show your father that he can't do better than me."

My mother isn't really talking to me, Wadjda thought. *She's just trying to comfort herself.* Since no reply was needed, Wadjda kept playing with the soap dispenser: pushing the lever, filling her cupped palm with soap, then rinsing it off and watching bubbles foam up in the sink. It was boring, but at least it was something to do.

Despite all the distractions of the mall, her mind was still full of thoughts about her bicycle. That stupid rich kid was probably riding it around now, getting it all muddy.

And here she was, trapped and helpless, playing with *soap*, totally unable to stop him.

After what felt like forever, her mother opened the stall door and stepped out. She spun in a slow circle, showing off the dress. Even in the dank, smelly bathroom, with its flickering fluorescent lights, her beauty was undeniable. But Wadjda, leaning over the sink, holding her mother's *abayah* in her non-soapy hand, was still too preoccupied with thoughts of her bike to do more than give a half nod.

"Do you think your father will like it?" Mother asked, twirling round. Again, she spoke more to herself than to Wadjda. As the shopkeeper had predicted, the dress was way too big. She had to pull the sides tight round her waist to imitate a proper fit. Noticing this, Wadjda shrugged and held her hands out to either side, to show how huge the dress looked.

"Let's take it back to the salesman. I'll give him a deposit so he can start getting it fitted." Mother sounded annoyed that Wadjda wasn't being more supportive. "Then we have to go quickly, before Iqbal gets angry and leaves."

She raised the dress up to her ankles and went back into the stall. Wadjda jumped off the sink and handed her the *abayah*, passing the bundled cloth carefully over the door.

"Don't worry," she said quietly. "He won't leave."

Strangely, it was true. She trusted him.

CHAPTER THIRTY-SEVEN

The sun set over the city in a blaze of red and orange. The air pollution in Riyadh made the colours brighter and more intense than the pictures of sunsets Wadjda saw on TV. Each cloud glowed brightly, as though a spotlight shone directly on it from behind. They looked like individual flames burning amid the vast long fire of the sky.

Wadjda and Abdullah were back in their by-now-usual spots on the roof. The night before, a sandstorm had howled through. The city was still thick with dust, and little drifts of sand covered the grey concrete surface. A strong overnight wind had brushed across the drifts, drawing out trailing streaks of golden-brown dust in intricate twisting patterns. Wadjda steered the bicycle in a lopsided circle round each sand drift, using them as obstacles on her course.

She pedalled more steadily now, but her movements were still awkward. It looked as if she could come crashing down at any minute. The dust made the bike's worn tyres even more slippery and harder to balance on.

As Abdullah watched, Wadjda rode the edge of disaster,

253

always catching the bike and turning herself to a steadier position at the last possible moment.

"I think I'm done with my work now," he said. He sounded sad, weighed down by the knowledge that their afternoon play dates would soon come to an end.

On the far side of the roof, Wadjda swooped perilously into a turn. Abdullah looked over the edge of the wall, watching the strings of lights sway in the warm breeze.

"My mother saw the lights, but forgot to ask me about them," Wadjda called.

"She doesn't know?" Now Abdullah sounded panicked. "What about your father?"

Seeing him squirm made Wadjda smile. "I think they like your uncle. After he was on that radio programme, I mean!"

She swung the handlebars hard to the left, jerking the bicycle round in the least graceful turn Abdullah had ever seen. He opened his mouth to coach her –

"Aiiyyyeee!!!!" The scream sounded from the other side of the roof, cutting shrilly through the peacefulness of the rose-gold evening. Wadjda and Abdullah snapped their necks round, startled.

To their horror and disbelief, Wadjda's mother stood at the entrance to the roof, mouth agape, still dressed in her work clothes. She looked as stunned as Wadjda and Abdullah. Immediately, she spun, fumbling to put out the lit cigarette in her hand. At the same time, Wadjda swerved, tipped and crashed to the roof with a *thud*. The pain from the fall twisted her face into a grimace, and she looked up pleadingly at her mother.

"I'm bleeding!" she moaned. "Look!"

Wincing, she held out her fingers, which were smeared with red stains from her injury. Her mother's face went pale, and she collapsed back against the wall, gripping the railing to steady herself.

"You stupid girl," she shouted. "You think you can act like a boy?" She pressed her hand over her eyes. Then, thinking better of it, she parted her fingers slightly and peeked out between them. "Your honour! Oh my God, oh my God, what have you done? Where is the blood coming from? Where?"

"From my knee?" Wadjda wasn't sure what the big deal was, but her mother's hysteria was making it easier to calm down. *It didn't hurt that badly*, she thought, looking at the wide, shallow scrape on her right knee.

"What?" Her mother dropped her hand, sighing in relief. All the tension went out of her body as she slumped back against the wall. "Oh, thank God it's only your knee! I can't imagine what we'd do if the fall had harmed your virginity."

But, as her mother's fear dissipated, her anger returned.

255

She marched over to Wadjda and grabbed her by the shoulder. "Bicycles are dangerous for girls," she said, shaking a finger close to her daughter's face. "And you almost saw why! Can you imagine? Your life would be ruined, and –"

Cutting herself off, she turned and flashed a look of such fury at Abdullah that he snapped to attention like a young recruit being called out by a drill sergeant.

"And you!" she barked. "What were you thinking? I'll tell your uncle to teach you some manners. Get out of here!"

Abdullah ran left, then right, back to the left and almost to the wall before he realized the door was in the opposite direction. He looked like a panicked chicken, dashing about, unsure how to escape.

Sighing, Wadjda pointed subtly towards the stairway, hiding the gesture from her still-furious mother. Nodding, Abdullah grabbed his things and stumbled towards the exit. Before he reached it, though, Wadjda's mother pointed a trembling finger at the bicycle.

"And take that damn thing with you!" she called.

Spinning back round, Abdullah shoved his belongings under his left arm and lifted the bicycle on to his right shoulder. Turning, he ran towards the stairway, struggling to carry the bicycle alone. Even fitting it through the doorway was a challenge. Its weight kept tipping him forward. To Wadjda, it looked like the bicycle might pull him down the stairwell, like an anchor dragging itself down to the bottom of the sea.

When Abdullah finally disappeared round the corner, Wadjda's mother turned back to her. Some of the anger had left her voice.

"Shame on you, bringing a boy upstairs with no one home. What would your father do if he knew?" Before Wadjda could say anything, she answered her own question. "He'd kill you!"

Wadjda looked away, rubbing her sore knee – the bleeding had almost stopped – and patting the dust off her clothes. "Why are you home early, anyway?" she muttered, hoping to move past the subject of the bicycle.

Bending down, her mother knelt and put her face right up to Wadjda's. They were at the same eye level. Her gaze was threatening.

"Listen to me," she said. "Don't bring him up here ever again. I'm being serious now. Do you understand? I will tell his uncle, and he'll be in big trouble. If I weren't busy with your father's party, I'd have been really upset with you, too. We would have had a *long* talk about this."

Wadjda nodded sullenly. Her mother sighed and looked away, staring out at the horizon. The whole city glowed, the last blush of fading red sunlight sparkling amid the haze. It reflected off the endless windows on the buildings, thousands of tiny sunsets in miniature.

For a time, they were both silent. Then Wadjda's mother stood, shaking off the edges of her long black skirt to clean it of dust.

"Let's go downstairs," she said. "We need to start cooking. Your father's friends are coming over tonight."

She paused and fixed Wadjda with a meaningful look.

"You know how important that is," she said.

CHAPTER THIRTY-EIGHT

The kitchen was alive with the sound of bubbling pots and sizzling pans. Clouds of steam and smoke – and wafts of delicious cooking smells – filled the air.

Working side by side, Wadjda helped prepare the massive plates of food her mother would serve to the group of men in the *majlis*. As they moved from one dish to the next, the sounds of loud conversation and male laughter echoed through the house.

Wadjda was panting a little – this was hotter work than carrying the bicycle up all those stairs! Blowing out her breath to ruffle her bangs, she used her shirt sleeve to dry the sweat beading on her brow.

Beside her, Mother was spooning rice into an enormous serving tray. A large lamb thigh, which she had cooked for several hours to ensure maximum tenderness, sat prominently in the middle of the dish.

Her mother's face was strained. Lines had appeared on either side of her mouth, and she kept staring worriedly at the food. How to relieve the tension? Wadjda had an idea.

"*Ya Laylah Dannah, La Danah*," she sang coyly, hoping her mother would join in.

"Shh!" Mother snapped in an angry whisper. "Be quiet! Do you want them to hear you? Here, put this in the oven."

She shoved a stack of pitta bread into Wadjda's hands. Chastened, Wadjda stopped singing, lifted the low oven door with her foot and shoved the bread on to the middle rack.

Do this, do that, not good enough! It felt like her mother had been shouting at her for hours. The time that had passed since she and Abdullah got caught on the roof had been stressful. After the storm, the house was full of dust, so they had to clean everything, top to bottom. It was a regular ritual at this time of year. Their house was getting older. With no insulation on the doors or windows, dust permeated every seam. After a particularly fierce *huboob*, they would have to scoop sand out of the corners using buckets. It was almost like a snowstorm, but, instead of melting, the grit gradually built up in every nook and cranny.

During the cleaning, her mother was extra careful with the *majlis*, where the men would sit. She burned more *oud*, disregarding the expense, determined to perfume the room. The scented smoke seemed to settle into the cracks and crevices they'd just cleared of dust. Before her mother shut the door, hoping to better capture the smell, it sent Wadjda into a mild coughing fit.

Now, after hours in the kitchen, Mother lifted the large plate of rice and meat and walked to the *majlis* door. Setting the platter down gently on the floor, she straightened her hair and dress, and knocked. Father opened the door just wide enough to slip his body out sideways, shutting it immediately behind him. In the brief moment it was open, Wadjda's mother hid herself from view, stepping to the left and out of sight.

As he lifted the serving dish and inhaled the enticing scents of aromatic rice and meat, Wadjda saw her father smile an enormous smile.

"Wow! All this food!" He kissed Mother's forehead and looked her in the eye, beaming. "They'll be impressed. You make me so proud."

"Obviously not proud enough," she said sadly. But her eyes were flirtatious.

As he closed the door behind him, Mother came back into the kitchen and started fixing the next dish, *Jarish* – chunks of meat covered with gooey sheets of wheat and topped with fragrant fried onions and spices. It smelled delicious.

In the *majlis*, Wadjda could hear the men talking about the stock market. Many of them had lost most of their money through bad deals. This was common. When the market first took off, she remembered, half the people her family knew had invested their life savings. What they didn't know, and what was much discussed in the news these days, was that Saudi's rich and powerful classes were manipulating the stock market. When it eventually crashed, a lot of regular, hard-working people saw their dreams of fast cash disappear – along with everything else they owned.

Luckily, Wadjda thought, her father had never had enough money to buy stocks. What had seemed like a curse when she was small was now a blessing. His voice was calm, not nearly as agitated as the other guests in the discussion.

After the men had eaten their fill and ventured out into the night together, Wadjda and her mother went to get the dishes they'd left in the *majlis*. Everything was piled in a row along the long seating area on the floor.

Quickly tired of cleaning, Wadjda wandered about the room, enjoying the rare chance to explore and ask her mother questions. "What's this?" she said, lifting a large gold frame. It must have been a gift to her father, though she didn't know when he'd received it. The image inside resembled an enormous tree, but the branches were made of lines. On each line, a name was written in flowing cursive. Wadjda ran her fingers experimentally along one limb, tracing out the shape as it forked along.

"Your father's glorious family tree," Mother said cynically. She'd perched on the couch, and was nibbling bits of discarded food off the plates. "You won't find your name, though. It only lists the men."

Though she spoke in a matter-of-fact tone, bitterness and anger lurked behind her words. Wadjda blinked and set the family tree back down.

Across the room, her mother finished eating and rose, stacking the plates. When she moved a napkin aside, she discovered her husband's prayer beads beneath it. She picked them up and went to hang them on their customary hook by the front door.

Taking advantage of her absence, Wadjda pulled *Learn Quran the Easy Way* from its hiding place under the couch. In the process of cleaning, her mother had probably discovered she'd been using the TV. And, after being caught with Abdullah and his bicycle on the roof, she was already in an impossibly deep hole. Might as well get everything out in the open, she thought, and began hooking the game up to the TV.

When her mother came back in and saw what Wadjda was doing, she frowned. But she didn't stop her.

"Make sure you clean that up when you're done," was all she said. "I don't want to do anything that will get him upset with us again."

Wadjda nodded in quiet understanding. But the game took a while to load, and she soon tired of lying on the floor, waiting. Tossing the controller aside, she wandered back to the family tree and read the names aloud, tracing her fingers across the leaves.

"Khalid, Mansour, Mohammed, Omar . . ."

When she came to her father, she stopped. His name stood alone on the end of a branch, isolated and cut off. All around it were his brothers' names. Each sprouted many leaves, the names of boy after boy flowing out below them in a glorious cascade.

For a long while, Wadjda stared at the family tree. Then she reached over, tore a piece of blank paper from her notebook and grabbed a small piece of tape from her bag. In large block letters, she wrote her name on the paper and stuck it under her father's, helping his corner of the tree to grow.

CHAPTER THIRTY-NINE

While the other girls in Religion Club crowded round Salma, giggling and chattering like a flock of noisy pigeons, Wadjda sat off to the side, working. Her knees were drawn to her chest, her notebook perched atop them. Her energy was laser-focused. She was trying to memorize the verses they'd just been assigned, fighting fiercely to hold the jumble of words in her mind.

It wasn't easy. Salma was passing round a stack of photos. The girls laughed and reached for them, knocking one another's hands out of the way in their eagerness.

"Let me see! Let me see!" Noura snatched two of the pictures from the girl to her left. As she examined them, she gasped, covering her face in mock astonishment.

Ms Noof came in then, clumping heavily along on the worn floorboards. Spotting her, Wadjda pulled herself even further away from the group of girls. The other students didn't notice. They continued snapping up the photos hungrily, like a bunch of street cats fighting over pieces of food. Oblivious to her teacher's presence, Noura held up a picture.

"Is this your father?" she asked.

"That's Khalid, my husband!" Salma shot back, clearly offended.

"He looks like your grandfather." Noura laughed. "But I guess that's the best your family could do!"

All of the girls except Wadjda joined in, giggling madly. Salma snatched the photo back, humiliated, and held it to her chest.

Ms Noof cleared her throat with a loud *harrumph*. "What's going on in here?" she asked, giving her students a tired glare.

The girls fell silent.

"I told them they couldn't have pictures at school," Wadjda offered, looking pointedly at Noura.

"No, you didn't!" Noura snapped back. Putting on her best fake-nice face, she turned to the teacher and pointed at the stack of photographs in Salma's hand. "Ms Noof, Salma just got married. Look, she brought pictures!"

"Let me see," the teacher said, suddenly interested. Snatching the photos, she looked them over curiously. "Who's this, your mother? And is this your husband?"

As they talked, Wadjda's eyes drifted to the hallway – and she flinched back, startled. Fatin and Fatima were passing by, followed by two women who had to be their mothers. They were dressed in full *abayahs*, their heads turned away, so Wadjda couldn't make out their individual features. But the way they hovered close, looming over their daughters, made her sure they were related.

Then they turned their heads, bringing their faces into view. Wadjda's heart sank. Both women looked furious and scared. Their daughters had been charged with a devastating crime, and the knowledge had left their mothers frozen with fear. At that moment, Fatin was trying to explain something, but her mother silenced her with a glare.

Fatima, who was closest to the classroom, saw Wadjda watching sympathetically. But she didn't smile or nod. She just turned her head away, eyes bitter. Wadjda looked down at the floor, feeling shame rise up in her body, burning her cheeks red.

Behind her, the conversation had dwindled.

"OK, put these away," Ms Noof said, handing the photos back to Salma. "Wadjda's right. You're not allowed to show pictures at school."

Another blush heated Wadjda's cheeks at the reminder of this new, smaller lie.

"Let's get started," the teacher continued. "Myriam, read from page thirteen."

"I need a tissue," the girl whispered. Sighing in exasperation, Ms Noof waved her off and looked for a more suitable candidate.

"Read, Wadjda," she ordered. "*An-Nisa'*, the third verse."

Wadjda lifted her head and closed her Quran. "I'll do it without looking."

Her serious tone showed she meant business. Ms Noof blinked, genuinely surprised, but gestured for her to begin.

Showtime. Wadjda recited as fast as she could, the words leaving her mouth so quickly that she could barely catch her breath.

"And if you fear that you shall not be able to deal justly with the orphan girls, then marry women of your choice, two or three or four, but if you fear that you shall not be able to deal justly, then only one or that your right hands possess."

When she finished, she sucked in a deep gulp of air and sighed in satisfaction. She'd got every single word right.

"Very nice, Wadjda," her teacher said curtly. "You remembered it all. But you have to recite! You can't just go, *badababdababdaba*! These are sacred words."

She looked around the room for another candidate and fixed on Salma.

"How about our young bride? Let's hear that voice. Listen closely to her, Wadjda. You'll have to recite like *this* if you want to win."

"And if you fear that you shall not be able to deal justly

with the orphan girls, then marry women of your choice, two or three or four . . ." Salma recited reverently. Each word trembled on her tongue for a tantalizing moment before tripping out delicately into the world. Frustrated, Wadjda looked back at the empty hallway.

Fatin and Fatima had vanished. Salma's voice echoed through the room, but all Wadjda could think about was where they'd gone – and whether she could have stopped it.

CHAPTER FORTY

link! Smash! Clang! On the way home from school, Wadjda threw her rock at anything that dared cross her path. Every bottle was a target, every street sign a bull's-eye. Her anger and exasperation powered each throw, sent her rock hurtling straight and true.

At last, she found herself near the toyshop. But she was almost afraid to look. Would the green bicycle still be there? What would she do if it were gone? One tentative step forward, then another, and Wadjda drew her eyes up from the ground like a prisoner facing her executioner.

But the bicycle was there! A surge of energy flowed into her weary bones when she saw it in front of the shop, glimmering in the afternoon sun. For a few seconds, she revelled in her relief.

Then rage hit her. How dare the owner even consider selling it? It was *hers*! She marched into the shop, ready to tell him exactly what she thought about the whole ordeal.

"So who were you talking to about my bicycle?" she said, hands on her hips. "The other day? Outside? You know I saw you!"

"I don't. I don't even know what you're talking about," the owner sputtered, unsure why he was even engaging in such a ridiculous argument – or why he sounded so defensive.

"You know *exactly* what I'm talking about." Wadjda shifted her weight, planting each foot against the floor like a mighty warrior. "I don't want you showing my bicycle to anyone else."

The shopkeeper shook his head, as if he couldn't believe the ridiculousness of the whole situation. Undaunted, Wadjda reached into her pocket and pulled out a cassette tape.

"Here," she said, and held out her peace offering. "I made you a tape. It's a mix, actually. A bunch of songs to introduce you to the modern world."

Her eyes went pointedly to his scratchy record player. The shopkeeper took the tape from her, eyebrows arched practically to his *ghutra*. Clucking his tongue, he looked down at the weird song titles scrawled across the cover.

"Thank you for your generosity," he said sceptically.

Wadjda smiled and pointed at the bicycle once more, as if to emphasize the point of their discussion. The owner laughed, tossed the tape on the counter behind him and went back to reviewing his receipts.

Before Wadjda had even turned the corner to her street, she could see the election tent for Abdullah's uncle. It towered above the rooftops of the neighbouring houses and filled the huge empty plot across from their front door. The lights that Abdullah had strung reflected the late-afternoon sun. Guest workers bustled about, putting up poles and laying down red carpet. A big space near the centre had been cleared of debris and filled with tables, lined up from end to end. That would be the eating area, Wadjda knew, where whole grilled lambs would rest atop massive plates of rice.

Nearby was a big plasma-screen TV and a projector. Chairs had been arranged in a semicircle in front. On all sides, the strings of lights flowed down beautifully, making a triangular shape around the top of the building. Beneath them, Abdullah was busy encircling the area with a long piece of fabric, like a billowing cloth fence. As he unspooled the banner and wove it meticulously round a series of stakes, Wadjda saw his uncle's name emblazoned on the cloth in huge letters.

No big deal, right? Lifting her chin and staring straight ahead, Wadjda marched forward like she didn't see Abdullah – and wouldn't have cared if she had. Even when she walked right by him, she didn't say anything.

Sweating and tired, Abdullah leaned the cloth against a stake and yelled after her.

"What, *you're* the one who's upset now? Your mother almost broke my neck pushing me down the stairs!"

"My mother doesn't want me talking to you any more," Wadjda called primly. "Besides, I have to study."

Giving her *abayah* a toss, she continued walking towards her house. Hiding a grin, Abdullah grabbed the helmet he'd hung from his handlebars and ran after her.

"Since when do you listen to your mother?" he panted. "Oh, and here – I got you this." He tossed it casually, like it barely mattered. Like he hadn't put it right on the front of his bike, to be sure Wadjda saw it.

"It's a bicycle helmet," he added. "Like the ones kids wear on TV."

With a gasp of pleasure, Wadjda caught the helmet in her outstretched hands. Her whole face lit up. Abdullah couldn't hide his pleasure at seeing his gift's effect.

"Do you want to ride in the empty plot behind the tent?" he asked. "We have a few minutes before people come."

Wadjda nodded in excitement and followed him round the giant white pavilion, strapping the helmet to her head atop her veil. Then, her *abayah* flowing behind her like a true superhero's cape, she rode in circles through the empty plot of land. Every so often she'd laugh happily, tossing her head back, letting the sound roll out into the world.

Smiling to himself, Abdullah perched on a breezeblock, watching her circle round and round.

"Watch this!" she called excitedly.

Taking a deep breath, she lifted her hands off the handlebars, pedalling steadily to keep herself balanced, and waved triumphant circles in the air. Abdullah nodded in approval. "That's it!" he called.

The bicycle wavered, and Wadjda lowered her hands. But the experiment gave her confidence. She kept riding, letting go for longer and longer periods of time. Now she stretched her arms out to either side, making her *abayah* flow like wings.

Her joy forced words to Abdullah's lips that he'd meant to keep silent.

"The toyshop owner told Khalid and his father that the bicycle was already reserved," he yelled.

Wadjda's reaction wasn't at all what he'd expected. She hit the brakes hard, planted her feet on the ground and smiled triumphantly.

"Yes!" she shouted. "He must be holding it for me. I knew it!" She pumped her fist in the air with glee.

Across the street, curious passers-by stopped, dumbfounded, staring at this strange girl, standing astride a bicycle in a dusty plot, shouting at the top of her lungs. Abdullah squirmed and ducked his head, feeling more nervous with each passing car full of onlookers. But Wadjda ignored them. She knew that she was one step closer to her dream.

Pushing off again, she rode in larger circles, moving more confidently, enjoying the protection of the helmet and the rush of open air.

This will be even better on my bicycle, she thought.

CHAPTER FORTY-ONE

Later that night, slumped in front of her video game in Father's *majlis*, Wadjda still wore her helmet. New resolve lit her eyes, and she depressed the buttons on the controller with steady hands. So far she'd got every question right.

"What is *Al Mahrab*?" the robotic voice of the game asked.

"Oh, I know that one," Wadjda said confidently, and hit the button.

"Correct!" the voice cheered. *Even the robot announcer is tired of giving me a hard time*, Wadjda thought, smirking.

"Finally!" She threw herself back on the couch, raising her arms over her head in the universal sign for "Victory!" On the screen, her score flashed. A hundred per cent! Happy music played over the hi-tech speakers.

Still smiling, Wadjda looked at the family tree – and the smile fell from her face. Her name had been taken off. The scrap of paper lay crumpled on the table to the side. She picked it up, turning it over slowly in her hands.

That was when she heard her mother, on the phone in the other room, yelling.

"If you won't listen to me, I don't know why I should listen to you!"

Wadjda jumped to her feet and ran to the doorway. As she watched, her mother slammed the phone hard on to the nightstand, tugged on her *abayah* and started pulling her *niqab* over her face. Seeing her daughter peeping round the door, she yelled, "Get ready, Wadjda. We're going out!"

Quickly, Wadjda took off the bicycle helmet – she'd got lucky. Her mother was too preoccupied to notice. Moving as fast as she could, she sprinted to her room to get her *abayah*. Her mother had already left, hurtling through the front door like a human cyclone. Wadjda had to run to keep up.

No one spoke as they hurried down the street. The experience was impossibly strange, and Wadjda was starting to worry. Mother never walked anywhere. Where in the world were they going? And why was she so angry?

A passing car slowed to a crawl beside them. Wadjda skittered back from the edge of the pavement, tucking her body into her mother's side.

The driver of the car lowered his window and began talking to her mother in a slimy voice. All Wadjda could make out was the word, "*Helwa, helwa,*" which he hissed over and over. Though Wadjda thought her mother was the most beautiful woman in the world, it sounded awful when this man said it. She looked up nervously, trying to read her mother's face. Mother was ignoring the man, keeping her eyes straight ahead. Still, she walked faster and faster – and then crossed to the other side of the street. Wadjda did the same, struggling to match her mother's fast pace.

No matter what they did, the guy wouldn't give up. Through the window, Wadjda saw his beady eyes fixed on her mother's cloaked form. When they switched pavements, he switched lanes, rolling the car along at a snail's pace right beside them.

Finally, her mother had enough. With shaking hands, she picked up a big chunk of rock and hefted it threateningly. She shouted as loud as she could, projecting her delicate voice into the street.

"If you don't leave us alone, I'll smash your headlights in!"

Her whole body was trembling now, but there was no doubt she was serious.

Despite her anger, the guy in the car started to laugh. He tossed a piece of paper out of the window. It landed at Wadjda's feet, and she saw a phone number written on it. Pressing down on the accelerator, he sped away, shouting, "Call me if you change your mind!"

Wadjda and her mother walked on in silence. Her mother moved more slowly, though. The fire that had possessed her and driven her out of the house seemed to be smothered, dying. With the loss of momentum, their pace dragged. Soon Wadjda was able to walk easily next to her mother. The new speed didn't make her feel better, though. If only she knew what was wrong!

After another few minutes, they reached their destination. Wadjda's eyes widened. They were at the hospital, the one just down the block! Her mind raced as she followed her mother through the automatic doors. What if someone was sick? Who could it be?

But then she remembered the conversation with Leila on the stoop. Had her mother listened? Maybe she was going to apply for a job! By the time they reached the lobby, Wadjda had started to get excited.

At her side, though, Mother looked nervous. She stood, shifting from foot to foot and drumming her fingers as she scanned the partitions and desks for a familiar face.

There! Leila was at the far end of the room, wearing a lab coat and sorting big binders of files on a shelf. To both Wadjda and her mother's shock, Leila wore only a *hijab*. Her face, even some of her hair, was revealed.

As they watched, a male doctor set a cup of coffee on the counter next to Leila. Wadjda felt her mother tense up. But there was no cause for alarm. Leila and the doctor were chatting, laughing and joking, even!

"Are you going to work here with Leila?" Wadjda whispered, tugging at her mother's *abayah*. "Those lab coats are cool, like the ones in *The Matrix*, only white!"

"Shh!" her mother snapped. "I . . . I just want to give her something, that's all."

But Leila had heard Wadjda's voice. She spotted them across the room, smiled and waved excitedly.

"Hey! You came. Wonderful." Once more, Wadjda found herself thinking how young Leila looked, how happy. "Wait one sec. Let me get the application."

"Leila, what happened?" Mother whispered. "Why are you showing your face?"

Leila smiled confidently, waving off the remark without comment. She went behind the desk and began shuffling through a file cabinet, searching for a job application. A minute later, the male doctor returned and started organizing his own set of files – on the table right in front of Wadjda and her mother. At first he was distracted by his work, but then he noticed the duo and smiled politely at them.

"How are you?" he asked Mother. She turned her head away without answering and tucked her hands into her *abayah*.

Undeterred, Wadjda looked at the man casually and said, "Hello."

The doctor smiled at her, grabbed a set of X-rays and went on his way. Mother, overcome by the whole situation and growing more uncomfortable with each passing moment, leaned over the counter, waving her hands furtively to get Leila's attention.

"Leila, dear, don't worry," she whispered. "I'm not here for an application. We were just passing by, and I thought . . . I thought we'd say hello."

Leila's eyes darted to Wadjda's face, and Wadjda scrambled to cover her surprise at her mother's lie.

"We'll leave you now to work," Mother said hurriedly. "You seem so busy."

"It's a good job, and the places are filling up quickly," Leila said. Wadjda almost winced at the sympathy in her voice. "You should –"

"It's good to see you, Leila," Mother interrupted. "I'll call you later."

With that, she took Wadjda's hand and led her towards the door. Wadjda looked back at Leila wistfully, then turned to gaze at her mother. In spite of herself, she tugged on her sleeve and whispered, "I thought you were going to –"

"Enough!" Mother said, and quickened her pace out of the door and away from the hospital.

CHAPTER FORTY-TWO

In the courtyard, the entire school had gathered for a special assembly. The girls stood in long rows, organized by class. The teachers walked among them, helping students find their places, straightening the shoulders of those who slouched. Each girl was carefully inspected. Was she wearing black shoes? Were her nails cut and without colour? Any make-up or accessories were forbidden. Wadjda saw a girl to her right surreptitiously tug a bracelet off her wrist and hide it beneath the sleeve of her uniform.

The few girls with long nails were pulled from the line, handed nail clippers and sent to the back. Under the watchful eye of a teacher, each one cut her nails into a large bin. This, Wadjda knew, was to ensure that the clippings were securely disposed of. Common Saudi belief held that if someone got hold of your discarded fingernails, or even a lock of your hair after it was cut, they could use it to cast a magic spell on you. The prospect was scary, Wadjda had to admit that.

After what felt like hours of waiting, Ms Hussa emerged

and made her way to the makeshift stage. With neat, deliberate motions, she picked up a megaphone and flicked it on. Sternly, she assessed the crowd, meeting each row of expectant eyes in turn. Aside from her watchdog duties at arrival and dismissal, she rarely made public appearances. The students responded with appropriate awe. Complete silence filled the courtyard.

"Girls, I would like you to listen well." Ms Hussa held the static-y megaphone a few centimetres from her lips, which made the words very loud and a little blurred. "We've discovered two girls doing something extremely inappropriate here in our school."

Her gaze swept back and forth across the student body. Her words echoed, bouncing off the walls on every side.

"In our own backyard." She paused to let the magnitude of what she was saying sink it. "Their names are Fatin Ali and Fatima Umar."

The silence was complete. No one moved or even dared rustle her clothing. Ms Hussa motioned the offenders forward. Slowly, Fatin and Fatima walked up to the stage. Every girl in the school stared, wide eyes pointed straight at them.

"They will now come to the front of the stage to repent," Ms Hussa said, gesturing the girls forward.

Fatin and Fatima! Could these hunched figures really be

them? Wadjda was used to their cheeky smiles, the ease of their bodies as they roamed the school, the laughter and secret jokes that seemed to play constantly between them. Now they looked broken, heads hung low, faces blank. Wadjda felt her stomach turn and thought she might throw up then and there.

"To avoid similar situations," Ms Hussa was saying, "you are no longer allowed to bring flowers to your friends at school. You may not give one another letters or autographs. And no one is allowed to hold hands. Do you understand?"

Her voice got louder, resounding through the courtyard. Across the rows of girls, heads bobbed up and down in silent agreement.

"Good. You may go back to your classes now."

The lines of girls broke apart. Masses of students crowded towards the doors, pushing and shoving at one another, trying to get ahead.

Fatin and Fatima turned to leave, too, but Fatin accidentally bumped into a younger girl.

"Don't touch me!" the panicked third-grader screamed. "Don't you dare!"

Wadjda waited for Fatin, always ready with a smart answer, to say something. But she didn't. She just turned, lips pressed into a thin line.

Impulsively, Wadjda started to walk towards her and Fatima. But then she saw Ms Hussa waiting by the stairs. She stopped and glanced at the two girls. They had always been so kind to her. Even when no one else was.

Her eyes went back at Ms Hussa. And, before she could change her mind, Wadjda walked away from Fatin and Fatima, more guilty and uncertain than she could ever remember being in her life.

CHAPTER FORTY-THREE

Blue-painted toenails. Though they looked impossibly cool, a heavy feeling of guilt weighed Wadjda down. She lay sprawled across her mother's bed, staring at her bare feet where they rested against the wall. As Fatin and Fatima's nail polish dried on her toes, memories of the afternoon spectacle at school kept running through her mind, like a movie she couldn't stop.

Her parents' room was decorated sparsely: some flowery curtains, a single, beautiful lamp in the corner. Still, despite its relative emptiness, it was a cosy, inviting room. And even here Wadjda was unable to push away her shame. Over and over, she saw Fatin's and Fatima's faces, emptied of their usual life. How terrible to be humiliated in front of the whole school!

I deserve to die for not standing by them, Wadjda thought fiercely. *For not standing up to Ms Hussa, too, when I might have cleared their names.*

Even thinking about her green bicycle somehow made her sadder.

Her mother was also lost in thought. She sat across the

room, in front of the mirror, straightening her hair. As she worked through her long, thick locks, she sang, her voice pure and strong as ever. Again Wadjda thought that she put to shame any singers on the radio – or anywhere else, for that matter.

"I'll write you a love letter / Tell you how much I miss you," her mother crooned, clamping the flatiron over a lock of hair. As she dragged the iron down the silky length, she leaned in close to the mirror, studying herself in the glass.

"I wish I could cut my hair shorter," she said abruptly, "like Lobna Abdel Aziz."

That would look awesome! Wadjda thought, brightening. Lobna Abdel Aziz was an Egyptian actress who'd made a lot of old black-and-white movies. She was very beautiful, with wide eyes and dark curls in a halo round her face. Sure, her movies were old and boring, but in terms of style –

"Do it," Wadjda said definitively.

Her mother gave her a sidelong smile. In her eyes were unspoken words. Wadjda could read them clearly: *If only it were that simple.*

"Your father loves my long hair," she said, not without a hint of pride, and broke back into song. "I'll write you a love letter / Tell you how much I miss you . . ."

As she sang, she got out a bandanna to wrap up her hair. They both heard the rattle as the drawer opened, the sound of something rolling from the back to the front. Mother blinked, reached in and pulled out a new tube of dark red lipstick.

"What!" Though she turned to Wadjda and raised a sceptical eyebrow, her voice was tender. "Did you buy this for me?"

Wadjda nodded eagerly, proud that something so simple could make her mother happy. Their eyes met in the mirror, and her mother gave her a soft smile. Shyly, Wadjda turned away. But when she looked back at the glass her mother was still gazing at her. It was clear how touched she was. Her eyes shone.

"I'd say thank you," she said, "but I'm afraid to ask where you got the money."

She smiled, pursing her lips as she applied the lipstick. Wadjda smirked and rolled her shoulders against the bed in a sort-of-shrug. *It will remain a mystery*, the gesture said. Her mother shook her head ruefully, returned the lipstick to the drawer and went back to straightening her hair. With her eyes on her reflection, she said, "Your father finishes his shift early tomorrow night. What should we cook? *Margoog*?"

Ew. Margoog again? All those vegetables and meat, mashed together and covered in raw bread dough . . . Wadjda shuddered at the thought.

"I hate *margoog*. And is he going to give me my allowance this month? Or is he going to skip it again?"

Her mother didn't answer. "Your father loves *margoog*," she said simply. "So we'll cook it for him."

Anger jolted through Wadjda's body. Her father got whatever he wanted, and he didn't do anything! He came and went as he pleased. He never talked to her. He just sat around playing video games. And still her mother treated him like a king! It wasn't fair! Without thinking, she lifted her head and snapped, "You should cook me *kapsa*! You know he's paying off his second wife's dowry with my allowance!"

Her mother stopped cold, her whole body stiffening. She'd turned her face away, so Wadjda couldn't see her expression in the mirror. All she could make out were the harsh lines of her mother's body, the way she'd frozen like a statue.

Just like at the assembly, Wadjda felt her ears warming, her face turning red. In that moment, she felt guilty enough to eat a hundred plates of *margoog*.

There was no more conversation, and no more song. Silently, her mother tied the bandanna around her hair, got up and went to the kitchen. Wadjda sat motionless on the bed, staring at the ceiling. For the second time that day, shame crashed over her like a wave.

CHAPTER FORTY-FOUR

The next day, Wadjda moved quietly about the house. She kept her eyes on the ground and made sure her voice was very respectful. At night, she helped prepare dinner and clean the kitchen. She didn't talk back to her mother. She didn't talk much at all. They both knew she was trying to apologize.

When two nights had passed, Wadjda slipped into the living room. Her mother sat on the floor, ironing Wadjda's father's *thobes*. She'd flipped one of the big prayer rugs on to its back, and was using the stiff surface as a board. And – Wadjda's heart lifted – she'd started singing again.

For a moment, she stood in the doorway, listening. Then she padded into the room. Her mother jerked her head up, surprised to see her – and even more surprised to see the Quran in Wadjda's hand.

Tentatively, Wadjda folded her legs and sat, cross-legged, next to her mother. Her mother turned back to her ironing, but continued to sing.

"The handsome man stole my heart with his black eyes / I come closer, he goes away / making me feel hollow / No tears, no words can bring him back. / Oh, my heart!" She drew out the final note, a beautiful low sound, and smiled at Wadjda, who was organizing note cards on the floor in front of her.

Despite the beauty of the melody, Wadjda sighed. There were big circles under her eyes, and the corners of her lips turned down. She looked morose and tired. Concerned, her mother examined her more closely.

"What's wrong?" she said. "You look so –"

"All this work for the competition is killing me!" Wadjda blurted. "Studying, memorizing, reciting – I can't take it any more! And stupid Ms Hussa . . . It's all too much." Her voice broke, and she whispered, "I'm tired."

"What does Ms Hussa have to do with anything? Winning is your business! And you've been working very hard. Don't think I haven't noticed." Her mother smiled encouragingly and added, "Your father's happy that you're doing this. He's so proud of you."

She paused to playfully chuck her daughter under the chin.

"Please, Wadjda. Him being proud . . . That's very important right now."

Was it possible that she'd been forgiven? A glimmer of hope lit Wadjda's eyes. Squaring her shoulders and straightening her spine, she started reciting:

"And of His Signs is that He creates for you mates out of yourselves, so that you may find tranquillity in them; and He has put love and mercy between you. Surely in this there are indeed Signs for a people who reflect."

The words tumbled out of her mouth as fast as she could say them. Phrases blurred together. Though Wadjda got every word right, her pronunciation made it hard to tell. And her mother looked at her lovingly, the way only a mother can look at a daughter in dire need of help.

Turning off the iron, she set it carefully to the side and clasped her hands in front of her.

"Give it a tone like this." In her beautiful voice, she began, giving each phrase a lilting lift, like the verses of a song. "And of His Signs is that He creates for you mates out of yourselves, so that you may find tranquillity in them."

She stopped and nodded to Wadjda. "Go on, try it."

There's no way I can sound like that! Wadjda swallowed hard and took a deep breath. Then she recited again, trying her best to imitate her mother, pacing the words out melodically in rising and falling tones.

"And of His Signs . . ." Wadjda blinked in surprise. She sounded good! "Is that He creates for you mates out of yourselves, so that you may find tranquillity in them."

"Yes, Wadjda, that was wonderful!" Her mother clapped her hands, almost laughing with delight. It was rare that she got to impart wisdom to her daughter. Eagerly, she went on, "Now, do the next lines like this: 'And He has put love and mercy between you. Surely in this there are indeed Signs for a people who reflect.'"

The rich tones of her voice emanated pure reverence. Again, Wadjda straightened her shoulders and followed along. Her voice was stronger now. She let certain words thrum and vibrate, filling the air of the small living room.

"And He has put love and mercy between you. Surely in this there are indeed Signs for a people who reflect." When she finished, Wadjda pressed her palms to the floor to keep from cheering in victory. It was hard to believe that such a perfect recitation had come from her.

"Excellent!" They beamed at each other, a joyful energy passing between them. Then her mother smiled and added, "Your voice is as lovely as your mother's."

Wadjda smiled sheepishly. "I feel shy, though, *Ummi*. I can't recite like this in front of everyone."

"You, shy?" Her mother burst out laughing. "Ha! I only wish that were true!"

Though Wadjda tried to keep a sour expression on her face, she was close to laughing, too.

Suddenly, the window lit up with a huge burst of light. Outside, the long strands of bulbs Abdullah had rigged turned on, one by one. They arched down from the roof towards the empty lot, illuminating the street and sending a magical glow into the dim room. In that surge of radiance, all their past squabbles over the lights were forgotten. Wadjda and her mother looked at each other excitedly, like two schoolgirls sharing a secret.

"You've worked hard," her mother said, rising to her feet and clasping Wadjda's hand. "Come on!"

As one, they raced to the roof to watch the show.

CHAPTER FORTY-FIVE

Side by side, Wadjda and her mother leaned over the barrier wall. Amid the shadows of early evening, the lights made their faces glow, and Wadjda couldn't help thinking how much they looked alike. Dusk softened and rounded her face. It made her eyes look bigger and cast defining shadows under her cheekbones. In this moment, with her arm pressed close to her mother's, no one could doubt that they were related.

Groups of men gathered below, laughing and talking. A light breeze brushed gently through Wadjda's hair, and she shot her mother a look of excitement. The life of their street was in full bloom, and they had front-row seats to the show. In truth, no one really cared who won the election or what the municipal council did. But energy filled the air nonetheless. *Some of it is the novelty of the thing*, Wadjda thought. On their sleepy street, it was nice to see people getting together, to watch the bodies in the crowd mill about and hear the hum of their talk.

Most of all, Wadjda was happy to share this fleeting

moment with her mother. As she watched, Mother brushed a loose strand of hair out of her face and smiled down at the crowded street. They could see Abdullah's bearded uncle, throwing his arms out wide to greet the men as they arrived. Abdullah was there, too, standing at the end of the long reception line, dressed formally in his best *thobe* and *ghutra*. In spite of herself, Wadjda blinked. He looked so handsome! Like a pop star or a football player, but better, because he was Abdullah.

Grinning, Wadjda did another scan of the crowd and spotted her father. He was dressed in his best *thobe*, too, and laughing with another man. Nudging her elbow against her mother's, she pointed eagerly.

"Look!" she whispered. "Father's there. Do you see?"

Her mother's eyes widened, and she searched almost impatiently, squinting into the crowd. "Where? I don't –"

Wadjda pointed again. "Right there!"

"Oh! Yes," Mother's face lit up as brightly as the lights shining over the party. "Look how handsome he is!"

From the corner of her eye, Wadjda watched her mother watch her father. She seemed consumed by the sight of him. Since Wadjda had pointed him out, her mother hadn't looked away, not even for a second. Perhaps it was the power of their secret perch on the roof. Here, hidden from the eyes of the men below, her mother was free to watch her husband's every move.

Wadjda was certainly enjoying herself. Once she'd made sure her mother was distracted, she bent, scooped up a pebble and tossed it towards Abdullah. It bounced dangerously close to his feet. Out of instinct, he flinched away, darting his eyes in every direction to find the culprit.

When he looked up and saw Wadjda, without veil or head covering, her face glowing golden under the lights he'd strung, Abdullah smiled without even thinking about it. As an afterthought, he fixed his *ghutra*, throwing its ends on to his shoulders and spreading out the cloth to show how well dressed and important he was.

Seeing him so proud of his formal clothes made Wadjda giggle. She smiled back teasingly, and then reached up and rubbed at her cheek in an exaggerated motion. The gesture was clear: *You've got something on your face.*

Abdullah paled with embarrassment. His hand shot to his cheek, scrubbing as hard as he could. It was a brilliant trick, but Wadjda couldn't keep a straight face for one second longer. She started to laugh hysterically, waving a mocking finger at Abdullah and mouthing, *Got you!*

A throat cleared to her left. Wadjda looked over to meet her mother's glare. Chastened, she dropped her hand.

And just in time! Down on the ground, the portly bearded man standing next to Abdullah had looked up to see what all the fuss was about. Wadjda and her mother ducked behind the wall, laughing softly, united again by the daring of being out in public unveiled.

When their giggles died away, Wadjda's mother lay back on the roof. Folding her hands on her stomach, she stared up at the stars, twinkling in the clear night sky. Somehow, they outshone all of Riyadh's light pollution.

Again, Wadjda found herself watching her mother. She was still smiling, but now she seemed to be thinking about something far away. Carefully, Wadjda lay down at her side. She could feel her mother's warm arm brush hers. It was peaceful, being here together.

"So, do you love him?"

"Who?" her mother asked shyly. "Your father?"

"No, the neighbour's boy!" Wadjda replied, teasing.

"I don't think *I'm* the one in love with the neighbour's boy," her mother retorted.

Wadjda reddened and tried to laugh the comment off without answering. Her mother laughed, too. To get a better look, Wadjda flipped on to her side, propping herself up on her elbow and resting her head on her palm.

"You didn't answer!" If she was going to get teased, she wasn't letting her mother off the hook, either.

Mother sighed and reached out almost instinctively to run her hands through Wadjda's hair. She smoothed out the knots and tangles with gentle strokes, until each strand slipped freely through her fingers.

"I was in high school when he asked for my hand," she said. "All the girls were so jealous when they saw his picture! He was the first man in my life, and probably the last. And he's a lot of fun, I have to admit."

The words were kind, but there was something bitter in them, too, like an aftertaste of resentment. The look in her eyes, however, left no room for doubt. Wadjda's mother still loved Wadjda's father deeply.

"You're so much prettier than any other women I've ever seen," Wadjda said. "In your red dress, you'll give Father a heart attack."

"No," her mother sighed. She sounded defeated. "He won't see it. He'll be busy in the men's section. But, Wadjda, the man I know . . . He talks big. Of course he does. But he'd never break my heart with another wife. I swear, I don't know who fills his head with this nonsense."

She sat up, eager to change the subject.

"Enough. Let's practise one more time for your competition tomorrow."

Obediently, Wadjda sat and folded her legs beneath her. In that moment, with the soft air brushing her face and the stars bright pinpricks overhead, she was willing to do anything to cheer up her mother.

"Oh, and don't tell anyone about your crazy bicycle scheme," her mother said warningly. "They'll never let you win if they know what you're up to. Now: recite."

Wadjda let her voice flow out of her like a song, felt it carry across the open air of the rooftop and out into the night.

"And of His Signs is that He creates for you mates out of yourselves, so that you may find tranquillity in them; and He has put love and mercy between you."

". . . mercy between you . . ." Her mother rolled the words around on her tongue in a way that made Wadjda think of sipping morning coffee: warm and sweet.

". . . mercy between you," Wadjda imitated.

"Let it come from your heart," her mother said. "Forget everyone around you."

Gently, she clasped Wadjda's hand in hers and placed their joined palms, fingers interlaced, over her own heart. Words spilled from her mouth, full of a sincerity and passion Wadjda had never seen before. A passion her mother had, up until that point, kept locked inside.

Her voice echoed across the empty roof. Above their heads, the election lights swayed gently in the breeze. Beneath her fingers, Wadjda felt her mother's heartbeat.

CHAPTER FORTY-SIX

Wadjda was asleep when her mother came in to say goodbye. She opened her eyes, blinking woozily in the darkness, surprised to see her mother already dressed in her *abayah* and ready to leave for work.

Then she remembered that her mother was going in extra early to open up the school. Wadjda rolled over, frowning and rubbing the sleep from her eyes. They'd have hardly any time to chat – and on such an important day! It wasn't fair.

As if thinking the same thing, her mother sat on the edge of the bed and began to caress Wadjda's hair. Wadjda leaned into her side, pressing her head against her mother's shoulder.

"Now, you've got a big day today," her mother whispered. "So, when you go up on the stage, I want you to say this: God inspire me, make things easier for me, and untie my tongue so I may speak fluently."

Wadjda mouthed the words, struggling to remember them. She was still half asleep, and her voice sounded rough and scratchy. "God inspire me, make things easier for me ..." She paused, forgetting the rest.

"Good," her mother whispered. Shifting away, she began to fix her veil into place. "I'm sorry to leave so early, Wadjda. I wish I weren't the teacher on duty." She shook her head, as if banishing the thought. "But remember now: Untie my tongue . . ."

Wadjda yawned and ran a hand through her messy hair. "Untie my tongue," she mumbled.

". . . so I may speak fluently," her mother prompted.

A car horn honked outside. They both looked instinctively at the door, but Wadjda's mother stayed where she was, smiling down at her daughter. Wadjda brushed her fingertips across the beads on her mother's *abayah*. She wished she could take a fistful of the cloth and hold it in her hands, that she could keep her mother here, by her side.

". . . so I may speak fluently," she finished, voice barely above a whisper.

Her mother bent, kissed her forehead and stood to leave.

"I want so badly to come today," she said again. "But you know the drill: Iqbal, the other ladies, the commute." Sighing, she lifted her *niqab* up over her mouth and nose. Her eyes, still visible, shone with pride.

"I know you'll nail it!" she said fiercely. Then she

slipped out into the hallway, her form a black shadow in the dimness. It seemed to stretch across the wall for a long time before it disappeared.

Wadjda watched her go, then sighed and fell back into bed. As an afterthought, she reached over and touched her father's prayer beads. Her mother had put them on the nightstand last night.

Impulsively, Wadjda gathered them up and held them close, tight in her hands, pretending her parents were there at her side.

On the way to school, she walked as fast as she could, skirting cracks in the concrete, avoiding piles of rubbish, trying all the while not to think about her mother hurtling down the long, dangerous road to work in Iqbal's battered vehicle. This was not the time. Today of all days, she needed to concentrate.

Lifting a note card, Wadjda began to whisper the *tajweed* written there. It was a pronunciation rule that would help her get the Quranic terms exactly right. As much as she'd practised, Wadjda knew in her heart that there was room for improvement.

Remember to sing it, she told herself, and breathed the words out into the air.

"Man yajaala, Mayyjaal, edgham beghunah."

Triumphant, she pitched her father's rock at a bottle, glistening dully on the kerb. *PING!* A perfect shot. The bottle spun like a top and tipped on to the ground. Wadjda smiled, scooped up her rock and continued on to school, lifting another note card from her massive stack.

As she disappeared into the chaotic traffic of the early-morning commute, her lips kept moving, the unvoiced words beating out a silent rhythm in time with her footsteps.

CHAPTER FORTY-SEVEN

So much has changed, Wadjda thought, surveying the room from her perch on the competition stage. *I've changed.*

Her eyes dropped to her sneakers. The black ink was starting to wear off on the toes, showing a flash of the white rubber beneath.

Well, sort of, Wadjda thought, and tried not to smile.

She was standing on the same stage where her class had stood five weeks ago, practising the battle hymn. This time, though, Ms Hussa stood in judgement, arms crossed, sceptically examining the nervous contestant at the lip of the stage.

As Wadjda watched, Ms Hussa raised her eyebrows pointedly. Her patience had run out. She was ready for an answer.

A sign above the stage read QURAN RECITATION COMPETITION, in giant letters. Beneath it sat nine girls, including Wadjda – all that remained of the thirty or so who had originally gathered to compete. It was time for the final questions of the first round. Wadjda's palms were sweating. She kept wiping them against the sides of her uniform skirt, but it didn't really help.

She and the other eight girls sat in chairs along the back of the stage. Three teachers, Ms Jamila, Ms Noof and Ms Hussa, occupied a table to the side, perpendicular to the contestants. Ms Jamila and Ms Noof leaned forward eagerly. Ms Hussa stood in front of the table, holding a portable microphone, acting as MC and head judge.

The entire school had packed into the auditorium for the competition. It was a mandatory event, though. Most of them probably wouldn't have chosen to come. Many girls looked bored, happy to be out of class but disinterested in the events onstage. Girls exchanged whispers whenever a teacher turned her head.

In front of her, Ms Hussa gestured impatiently with the microphone.

"Um, benevolence?" the girl she was questioning offered. From the rising intonation at the end, everyone could tell it was a guess – and not a good one.

"Wrong," Ms Hussa said authoritatively. "Thank you. Please take your seat."

Wadjda would have been devastated by this dismissal, polite as it was, but the girl seemed relieved to be off the stage. She fled down the small set of steps as fast as possible and slumped into a row with her classmates in the audience.

"Next," Ms Hussa called, waving the following contestant to the front. It was Noura, who seemed confident and at ease, even with the eyes of the entire school on her. She straightened her uniform and walked with her head held high, hands clasped demurely behind her back.

Meanwhile, Wadjda was trying to hide what felt like an expression of total panic. Between her fingers was the cool disc of her father's stone. She rubbed it round and round, making circles against her palm. Its firm weight would give her the courage to stay the course, she told herself. It had to.

"What is the meaning of *sadakatouhen*?" Ms Hussa asked, repeating the question that had eliminated the last girl.

"Giving a dowry," Noura said. She sounded fairly confident that she was right.

"Correct." Ms Hussa gestured Noura to the back before she could bask in the glory of the moment. There was no clapping for her correct answer – clapping was considered a pagan habit and strictly forbidden at school events. As a girl, Wadjda had been taught that heathen Arabs used to clap as they went round the Kaaba, the black cube-shaped building in the centre of Al-Masjid al-Haram, the great mosque in Mecca. This, Wadjda learned, dishonoured the most sacred part of Islam's most sacred mosque. Muslims had to do the opposite of the pagans. Hence, no clapping.

Of course, if they saw something they really liked, Muslims could chant "*Allahu Akbar*" instead. But no one in the audience today was anywhere near enthusiastic enough for that. *It'd take more than getting a few questions right*, Wadjda thought, shivering again as she looked out at the great sea of faces.

Ms Hussa had called Salma forward. "What is *Al-Furqan*?" she demanded.

Salma looked less comfortable than Noura, but still Wadjda felt she was the contestant to beat. Noura was all flash and no substance. Salma had a deep well of knowledge. Now she bent over the standing microphone and looked at Ms Hussa, not the crowd. "The Quran?" she said quietly.

"Correct!" Ms Hussa declared. She was clearly rooting for Salma to move on in the competition.

Back in her seat, Wadjda was trying to keep her foot from jittering. It was going up and down like someone working the pedal on a sewing machine. Firmly, she put her hands on her knees, hoping to keep both feet on the floor.

"Next," Ms Hussa called out. "Wadjda."

Her lucky black stone seemed to slip and slide in her hands. Wadjda swallowed hard and stood, readying herself for the long walk to the front. As she neared the microphone, she grew ever more uneasy. The hugeness of what she was trying to do rose up before her. It was like her task was a giant wall, and she was a car, headed for it at top speed, sure to crash. Her heart pounded so hard she could feel it thumping in her throat. Was her forehead glowing from the sweat on her brow?

Then she was at the microphone, and it was time.

"What does *da'ab* mean?" Ms Hussa's voice echoed through the auditorium.

For the space of a breath, Wadjda stood silently. Ms Noof and Ms Jamila exchanged a glance, as if to say that they'd both known this would be the point at which Wadjda would stumble.

"Habit?" Wadjda blurted. Her thumb instinctively sought a button to press, just like when she played her video game.

"Correct," Ms Hussa said, not doing a very good job hiding her shock. "Next contestant."

The next girl approached the front of the stage. Wadjda sat numbly, mind whirling. *I got it right? I got it right!*

The blood rushed out of her face. Air returned to her lungs. *I can do this*, Wadjda thought, *if I stay focused*. For weeks, everything she'd done had been leading up to this competition. If she could keep it together a little longer . . .

"What's the meaning of *zaygh*?" Ms Hussa asked the next girl.

"Weakness?"

"Correct," Ms Hussa said. "Next."

The girl returned to her seat, smiling. Yasmeen walked to the front.

"What is *Hawban Kabiran*?"

Yasmeen took a moment to think. A minute passed. Another. Her eyes swept the crowd desperately, as if the answer might be written on her classmates' faces. At last, she shook her head in resignation and looked up at Ms Hussa. Her eyes told the principal that she didn't know the answer.

"I'm sorry, Yasmeen," Ms Hussa said. "Back to your seat. Next. What is *Hawban Kabiran*?"

A skinny girl Wadjda didn't know shifted uncomfortably before the microphone. It was clear that she, too, had no idea. Grasping at straws, she blurted, "Something . . . big?"

Almost as one, the audience burst into laughter. At the judges' table, even Ms Noof had to suppress a smile. *Wrong, but not a terrible guess*, Wadjda thought. As she'd learned from her game's endless vocab drills, the word *kabiran* meant "great".

"Wrong," Ms Hussa said. "Back to your seat, please."

She surveyed the dwindling number of contestants, clumped in their chairs at the back of the stage. "Next. What is *Hawban Kabiran*?"

With quick footsteps, Noura walked to the front and leaned over the microphone. "Great injustice," she said confidently, and waited, smiling smugly.

"Correct!" Ms Hussa declared.

And then there were six, Wadjda thought, looking at the three empty chairs.

CHAPTER FORTY-EIGHT

Wadjda could hardly believe she was onstage with the finalists. That she *was* a finalist. Yet, somehow, she'd survived the first round – and the second. Only three girls remained, and Wadjda would be the last to read.

Her nerves had given way to a feeling of surreal distance. It was as if she were an impartial observer, watching the action from somewhere far away. At such a long range, what was happening seemed completely inconsequential, a blink of the eye when you considered the grand scheme of things.

The sound of Noura's voice brought Wadjda back to earth.

"We are but peacemakers," she recited, her voice confident but unremarkable. She sounded like one of Wadjda's practice audio recordings. "Now surely they themselves are the mischief makers, but they do not perceive."

Ms Hussa thanked her with a nod and motioned Salma forward. As they passed each other, Noura looked at Salma out of the corner of her eye, smirked and gave her head the most imperceptible of shakes. *Don't even try*, she was saying.

If she'd wanted to shake Salma's confidence, it worked.

Wadjda could see Salma's legs tremble as she stood at the microphone. Behind her, Noura settled into her seat, crossed her ankles primly and looked from Wadjda to Salma like a lion about to feast on two helpless gazelles.

"Please start with *Surat Al-Baqarah*," Ms Hussa said, "from the beginning."

In accordance with recitation protocol, Salma sat and lowered her eyes to the floor. "In the name of Allah, the Beneficent, the Merciful. *Alif Lam Mim*," she said. But her voice shook. She cast a glance towards the back of the stage, her eyes meeting Noura's cold ones. Noura blinked once, twice. *Like a snake*, Wadjda thought.

Salma tried to resume, but she was distracted now and kept stuttering over her words.

"This Book, there is no doubt in it, is a guide to those who guard against evil. Those who believe in the unseen and keep up prayer and spend out of what we have given them." Her eyes darted nervously around. "And who . . . And who . . ."

She stopped. Silence filled the auditorium.

"And who believe . . ." Ms Noof prompted.

Though Salma was shaken, she tried to continue, squeezing her eyes shut and taking two or three deep breaths. When she resumed her recitation, however, her voice was still wavering.

"Who believe in that which has been revealed to you and that which was revealed before you and, uh . . ." she ground to a halt, looking helplessly at her teachers.

Ms Hussa raised a hand. *Stop*.

"That's enough," she said coldly. "Thank you, Salma. Let's continue."

This was it. Wadjda slipped her hand into her pocket, gripping her father's stone. In her head, she recited the words her mother had whispered to her that morning: *God inspire me, make things easier for me, and untie my tongue so I may speak fluently.*

Disgraced, Salma slipped past her and back into her chair at the rear of the stage. Wadjda stayed where she was, silent, awaiting further instruction.

"Wadjda," Ms Hussa said. "Please start with *Surat Al-Baqarah*."

She floated to the front of the stage, feeling oddly weightless, as if her legs had vanished and she was drifting about on a gust of wind. Her brow was creased with uncertainty. When she reached the microphone, she sat, cross-legged, on the floor. The large room dwarfed her, made her feel impossibly small.

Breathe, she told herself. The moment seemed to drag on endlessly: Wadjda, very small on the stage, fighting to make herself steady.

In the crowd, she saw Fatin and Fatima. They were looking right at her. Wadjda wanted to turn away in shame, but something in their sunken eyes and fallen faces gave her the confidence to keep her eyes lifted. She met their stares –

And she let her mouth open. She let the words rise up in her, let them be taken aloft by everything she'd held on to deep inside. From her heart, they poured forth. Words for her bicycle, for her mother and her long commute, for her father and his lonely branch on the family tree. For Abdullah, the way he was always there when she was most in need. For Fatin and Fatima, shrunken and lost. Words for them – and words for her. Words to push back everyone who thought she couldn't do it, to say to all the people waiting for her to falter and fail: *No*.

At first, her voice was soft, but then it lifted, rising and falling in cadence with her words. Her recitation found its rhythm, and the beauty in her tone made the most sceptical girls in the back of the auditorium sit up. Wadjda's voice rang out, soaring above them up to the rafters, growing ever stronger and more intense.

"In the name of Allah, the Beneficent, the Merciful. There is a disease in their hearts," she cried with almost desperate beauty. "So Allah added to their disease, and they shall have a painful chastisement because they lied. And when it is said to them, do not make mischief in the land, they say: we are but peacemakers. Now surely they themselves are the mischief makers, but they do not perceive."

That was the end. Wadjda stopped, blinked. She looked around for some indication as to whether or not she should continue.

The room was completely silent. No girls giggled or whispered. It seemed as if no one even moved. Instead, they stared at Wadjda, a wall of eyes looking up at her in astonishment.

She had done it. There was no doubt left in anyone, not any more.

"Thank you," Ms Hussa said finally. "That was very good."

CHAPTER FORTY-NINE

The call to prayer reverberated from minarets across Riyadh, an echo of overlapping sound as chaotic as it was beautiful. The winner of the Quran Recitation Competition had yet to be announced. Prayer came first. All the chairs in the auditorium had been moved to the front, allowing the girls and teachers to gather at the back.

Most of the students stood about, talking in whispers, retrieving their *abayahs* and wrapping them round their bodies. They had to be entirely covered for prayer. Ms Hussa was in the first row, with the other contestants. A disgruntled Noura stood close by her side, a scowl darkening her pretty face.

Fatin and Fatima had placed themselves away from the group, in the middle of the mosque. They were isolated, a small island in a sea of worshippers. Wadjda spotted them and walked over without hesitation. Fixing her veil properly over her smiling face, she lined up at Fatin's side and unfurled her *abayah*, readying herself for prayer. The cloth rustled in the air as she shook it out. Fatin looked over at her and raised her eyebrows.

"Are you sure you want to stand next to us?" The look she gave Wadjda was full of disgust.

Fatima took Fatin's arm, as if holding her back from a fight, and looked coolly at Wadjda. "Congratulations," she said.

Wadjda blinked, surprised to hear her speak.

"They haven't announced the winner yet," she said.

"You won," Fatin said simply. "And you're their favourite convert, so I'm sure they were all rooting for you anyway."

The girls seemed so defeated. Their eyes were empty. Wadjda stared uncomfortably at the floor, unsure what to do.

When she looked up again, Ms Hussa was searching the rows of girls. Most of them were kneeling now, ready to begin prayer. The principal's eyes landed on Wadjda, and she waved an imperious hand, summoning her.

"Wadjda!" she called. "Come now. We've saved you a spot, up here in the first row with the other contestants."

Wadjda looked back at Fatin and Fatima. This time they looked away, adjusting their *abayahs*. Unsure what else to do, Wadjda dragged her feet up towards the first row of the semicircle.

"Traitor," she heard Fatin mutter under her breath.

Unenthusiastically, Wadjda took her place, kneeling beside Ms Hussa. She felt cramped and uncomfortable, like everyone was staring at her. It was worse than being onstage. The circle of prying eyes trapped her, held her in place.

As if reading her mind, Ms Hussa grabbed the sleeve of Wadjda's *abayah* and pulled her nearer, so that she could whisper in her ear.

"Good Muslims have to line up close to one another so the devil –" she nodded her head towards Fatin and Fatima – "doesn't get in between them."

With that, she placed her right foot atop Wadjda's left, the traditional posture for group prayer. Any open space between worshippers' bodies was forbidden, the imams taught. Those who prayed must form a solid wall, strong and impenetrable. It was unacceptable to let anyone enter into or break the line.

Ms Hussa's stare seemed to beat against the side of her head, but still Wadjda avoided looking at the principal. The call for prayer rang out among them, in concert with the echoes from the minarets outside. It was time to begin.

From the middle of the front row, Ms Hussa acted as *imama* and led the prayer, chanting, "*Allahu Akbar.*" The girls repeated the phrase, speaking in one synchronized voice, their individual tones blending together into one.

CHAPTER FIFTY

And still they didn't know the winner. *This is almost as bad as waiting to buy my bicycle*, Wadjda thought, crossing and uncrossing her ankles impatiently. Though she knew she shouldn't be squirming around, she couldn't seem to stop her body's nervous movements.

Beside her, Noura waited patiently, chin lifted, face seemingly serene. But up close Wadjda could see her fingers fidgeting against her seat. As much as she tried to hide it, she was nervous, too.

At the side of the stage, the judges discussed the results in low whispers. In the audience, the long rows of bored girls shifted and murmured. Despite the wait, there was no apparent hurry to make the announcement.

Finally, Ms Hussa stood and walked to the back of the stage. She reached behind the blackboard for her microphone and clicked it on, sending out a screech of feedback. The principal was the only one in the auditorium who didn't wince. Striding to the front of the stage, she pivoted back and forth, taking her usual dramatic moment to scan the chattering girls below. Annoyed that they hadn't snapped to attention at the mere sight of her, she spoke sharply into the microphone.

"Keep quiet!"

Her voice was like cold steel. Instantly, the girls silenced themselves and sat up properly in their chairs. A smile crossed Ms Hussa's face, and then she began.

"With me onstage are the three finalists in the school-wide Quran Recitation Competition. Two of them will receive award certificates, but only the winner will be awarded the cash prize for first place."

In a last attempt at intimidation, Noura looked over at Wadjda and narrowed her eyes, making her face mean and sly as a viper's. Wadjda kept her gaze steady and straight ahead. Whatever Noura did, it no longer mattered.

"The runner-up in this year's competition is . . . " Ms Hussa stopped, waiting for what felt like half an hour to continue. "Noura Al Markoon."

To her shock, Wadjda felt a rush of heat behind her eyes. As the tears streamed down her cheeks, she realized she was crying. Crying from happiness. She covered her face, swiping at her cheeks, her expression the opposite of Noura's.

Compounding her surprise, Salma rushed over and threw her arms round Wadjda in an ecstatic hug. "You did it!" she whispered.

"Wadjda Al Safan, you are our champion," Ms Hussa said. An uncharacteristic smile spread across her face, too. "Congratulations!"

You did it. Salma's words echoed in Wadjda's mind. Ms Hussa's joined them: *Wadjda, you are our champion!* Was it possible? Yes. She had, and she was.

All those weeks reading and practising, the hours spent listening to Quran radio and playing her game had paid off. The money she'd spent and the work she'd done were worth it.

Exhilarated, Wadjda thought of her green bicycle, gleaming in the sun. After her practices with Abdullah, she could practically feel the pedals spinning beneath her feet.

On unsteady legs, she rose and stumbled up to stand beside the principal. Her face beamed with happiness. Her hands were trembling, just a little.

When she reached Ms Hussa's side, the principal addressed her, but kept her eyes on the crowd. It was like Wadjda was a prop for her big demonstration.

"You are in this spot, Wadjda, because of your devotion and perseverance. I hope all the girls here today learn from your example."

Wadjda nodded a quick "thank you" as Ms Hussa handed her the certificate. She read it over swiftly, eager to get off the stage and out of the school. The praise was nice.

The award looked cool. But neither one was the cash – or her bicycle.

"*Alf Mabruk bint Al Safan,*" Ms Hussa said, using Wadjda's tribal name. She'd called her simply "the daughter of Al Saffon". It was a massive compliment, meant to show that Wadjda had brought pride to her entire family.

I'll take that, Wadjda thought, a grin stealing back across her face.

Standing there, certificate in hand, her name ringing out across the auditorium, she felt strong and big, taller than anyone else in the room. Even taller than Ms Hussa, who towered high above her on her expensive high heels.

"Don't be shy! Tell us what your plans are for the prize money!"

The microphone was thrust into Wadjda's hand. She looked at it nervously, her eyes flicking towards Ms Hussa. The principal nodded, smug and expectant.

Wadjda took a deep breath and scanned the audience. Her gaze slipped past Yasmeen, past the rest of the girls, too. She was searching for –

There. Her eyes settled on Fatin and Fatima. Once again, they were looking up at her. Fatin still had an expression of contempt on her face, but in Fatima's small half smile there was something . . . a glimmer of pride. Maybe she was happy Wadjda had found an escape, had figured out how to work a rigid, unfair system and come out on top. Or maybe she just wanted something to be happy about, some small source of comfort, and Wadjda's victory was that thing.

Their eyes held each other's for only a few seconds. It was long enough.

Ms Hussa nodded impatiently towards the microphone. "Well, Wadjda? What will you do with your prize money?"

Wadjda brought the microphone to her lips, gathered her courage and did what she had to do.

"I'm going to buy a bicycle from the shop down the road!" she announced, smiling mischievously at Ms Hussa.

Giggles and laughter erupted from the audience.

"Wha– what?" Ms Hussa stammered, dumbfounded.

Again, Wadjda looked at Fatin and Fatima. They weren't laughing, like the other girls, but they were smiling bigger smiles than she'd seen since their humiliation at the assembly.

"I'm buying a bicycle," Wadjda repeated, adding matter-of-factly. "One with no training wheels, since I already know how to ride."

Fatin and Fatima *were* laughing now, along with the rest of the crowd. Gales of mirth swept up and down the rows of students, filling the auditorium with sound.

"Now, Wadjda," Ms Hussa said, composing herself

and clearing her throat. "Wouldn't you rather donate the money to our fighting brothers in Palestine?"

Palestine. The word hit Wadjda like a punch in the gut. From birth, she had been taught that this was the one cause you couldn't argue with, the one request you could not refuse. To invoke Palestine was to use a magic word that demanded obedience. All Saudi Muslims knew they had to support this cause without question. Had Ms Hussa said "charity" or "the local mosque", Wadjda might have had a chance.

Palestine? The money was already gone.

Sorrow twisted her heart. The words she wanted to say echoed in her mind: *No! It's my money. I earned it fair and square, by working as hard as I could. And now I'm going to use it to buy my bicycle!*

But, as much as she wanted to shout the words out proudly over the microphone, Wadjda knew she couldn't. The damage was done. By challenging Ms Hussa's authority, she'd broken the biggest rule of all. There was nothing left to do but look steadily back at the principal and wait to see what came next.

Did she regret what she'd said? *No*, Wadjda thought. It *was* her money. And that meant she got to decide what to do with it.

Ms Hussa stared down at her, eyes burning with rage.

Though she was furious, she kept her emotions tightly in check.

"A bicycle is not a toy for girls, Wadjda." Each syllable was clipped and precise. "Especially good Muslim girls, who need to protect their honour."

The words fell hard, tiny lead weights pelting down on Wadjda. The chortling of the crowd stopped abruptly, like someone had put them on pause. Ms Hussa played on that silence, using it to hold Wadjda up onstage and prolong her misery.

"Besides, I'm sure your family won't allow it." She raised her voice. "We will donate the money – in your name – to our brothers and sisters fighting in Palestine."

A cry of outrage rose up in Wadjda's throat, and she silenced it only with great effort. She wanted to scream and shout and demand her money, but –

But she couldn't. There was no way. All she could do was stare at Ms Hussa in disbelief.

The audience was doing the same. As one, they stared back at the principal, shock and anger in their eyes. A silent solidarity had risen up among them, a quiet rebellion that filled their hearts. For just a moment they had come together in their internal rejection of Ms Hussa's absolute power.

"You may step down now," Ms Hussa whispered to

Wadjda through gritted teeth. "And you may all return to your classes," she announced to the crowd.

The microphone turned off with a decisive *click*.

Wadjda stayed rooted, not moving from her spot, unsure what to do. All her energy had been focused on slamming through the school gates, *abayah* flying out behind her, running straight to the toyshop and buying the green bicycle.

None of that would happen now. Her prize money, all those Riyals, was going straight to Palestine. She'd never see it, never feel its weight in her hand, never count the bills into piles on her bed and see her fortune spread out before her.

Distraught, she turned to leave. A hand clamped down on her shoulder.

"I thought you'd changed," Ms Hussa whispered. "But, no, you're still the same conniving little demon you always were. You think you can act however you want and people won't notice? You're wrong. This will haunt you forever."

Infuriated, Wadjda whirled round, shaking off the principal's hand. "You mean like your handsome thief?"

Her voice was ringing and loud – her recitation voice. The crowd of girls close to the stage fell silent, as did a shocked and humiliated Ms Hussa.

Without another word, Wadjda marched down the steps and joined the crowd of girls leaving the hall. Not once did she look back.

CHAPTER FIFTY-ONE

Abdullah peered round the wall of the building just outside the front gate of the girls' school. Where was she? What was taking so long? This was getting risky – he'd been hanging around for almost fifteen minutes. At any second, someone could walk by. The humiliation of loitering so close to the girls' school was immense.

Slipping back round the corner, Abdullah reached up and fixed his *taqia*. No, now it was too far forward. He tugged it back. At his feet sat his backpack, which he'd thrown casually on the ground. Abdullah kicked at the dirt beside it, sending up spurts of dust. They coated his belongings in a fine layer of grit.

His *taqia* slipped back. He adjusted it again.

Finally Wadjda emerged, storming round the corner in a black whirl of fury. She rushed past Abdullah without even looking in his direction. Startled, he grabbed his bag and bike, and ran after her. Her aloofness baffled him. What could she be so angry about? Had she lost?

"What's wrong? Didn't you win?" he asked. "Where's the money?"

"In Palestine!" Wadjda shot back bitterly, never breaking stride.

Abdullah froze in disbelief for a few seconds before he caught himself. Again, he sprinted after her. Despite her rage, he could see that Wadjda was heartbroken. Her eyes were red, like she'd been crying, and her lips turned down at the corners.

Abdullah raced ahead and stopped right in front of her.

"What're you talking about?" he asked confrontationally. Maybe a little grumpiness of his own would snap Wadjda out of her funk. "Don't you have another plan? You always have a plan."

It didn't work. She pushed round him and ran off, leaving him alone in the street, his backpack hanging loosely from his hand, his bicycle propped at his side.

By the time they got to Wadjda's neighbourhood, they were walking together. Wadjda scuffled sadly along, so defeated that she could hardly lift her feet from the ground. The only sound was the rhythmic clicking of the wheels as Abdullah pushed his bicycle along.

"I'll give you my bike," he offered suddenly. It was a big sacrifice. But at this point he was willing to do anything to make Wadjda feel better.

Numbly, Wadjda shook her head. "Then how would we race?"

Her voice broke under the weight of her sorrow, and she pulled away roughly, hurrying ahead of Abdullah and on towards her house. Across the street, a group of workers were collapsing the tent and gathering up the rubbish from the enormous election party. The lights, which had taken Abdullah so long to string, had already been taken down.

Somehow, Abdullah thought, *I have to find a way to make everything OK*. Gathering up all his courage, he put a hand to his mouth and shouted, "Hey, Wadjda!"

She turned to face him, her face droopy and sad.

"You know I'll marry you when we grow up, right?"

Wadjda smiled at him sadly. The expression made her look much older than eleven. Without saying anything, she turned away and pushed open her door, leaving Abdullah alone in the street once again.

CHAPTER FIFTY-TWO

To Wadjda's great surprise, the door to their house was unlocked. Who could be home so early? Was her mother already back from work?

And did it really matter? *No.* She let the heavy door slam shut and dragged herself to the living room, ready to collapse, bury her face in a pillow and cry.

But here she had another shock: her father was there. He sat on the couch, twiddling his thumbs nervously, playing with his blue prayer beads. When he saw her, he startled and ran his hands through his freshly combed hair. It had been trimmed close on the sides and shaped into a cooler, more modern style.

"Hey, finally! You're home." He sounded as if he'd been waiting for her all day. Wadjda gave him a suspicious look. Finding her father at home before nightfall was like discovering a unicorn in one of Riyadh's alleys. It just didn't happen.

"What's up with the new hairstyle?" she asked sarcastically. Her father didn't answer.

"Your mother's been rejecting my calls," he said. Again,

he ran his hands through his hair. "I've been trying her for hours. Where is she?"

It was Wadjda's turn to ignore the question. Without speaking, she pulled the first-place certificate out of her bag, walked over to her father and handed it to him. He looked at her, confused, and started to read. As the words sank in, his face shifted. Confusion gave way to excitement.

"You won?" he exclaimed. "I can't believe it. That's amazing!"

Impulsively, he stood, pulled his daughter close and embraced her proudly. Wadjda rested her head on his shoulder. He felt very strong. A few tears seeped from her eyes, overcoming her best attempts at self-control. Surprised, her father held her out in front of him and frowned, furrowing his brow.

"Hey, why are you crying? You won. You should be happy!"

Wadjda was ready to tell him everything then, about the money and the bicycle, about Fatin and Fatima and Abeer, to let it flow out in a barrage of stories and tears. But, as she opened her mouth, her father's phone rang. Releasing her shoulders, he snatched it up and went to the hallway to talk in private.

The conversation was fast. Through it all, her father kept his body turned away from Wadjda. He didn't look back at her, not once. After a few moments, he whispered something to the person on the other end and hung up. Moving briskly now, he went to the *majlis* and began gathering his things. When he was finished, he knelt in front of Wadjda and put his hand tenderly on her cheek.

"Tell your mother I waited for her." He picked up his *ghutra* and the black cord he used to secure it, the *iqal*. "Tell her I wanted to talk. Tell her . . ."

Wadjda's eyes were fixed on her father's, and she saw the emotion break through his composure. Feeling himself scrutinized, he cleared his throat.

"Tell her I love her."

He forced a smile. For a moment, the boyish light was back in his eyes. He reached down and playfully ruffled Wadjda's hair.

"I'm so proud of you, my little champ," he said.

In the doorway, he turned back once more, the fading sun falling across his face as he flashed Wadjda an apologetic smile.

Once he was gone, the house seemed very quiet. Wadjda collapsed on to the couch. A few more tears rolled down her cheeks, and she angrily wiped them away.

When the phone rang, it took a few seconds to penetrate Wadjda's sorrow. *Brrring-bring, brrring-bring.* By the time she realized what was happening, the call had timed out. A second later, though, it rang again.

Wadjda snuffled, gathering herself. She swiped her hand under her nose and cleared her throat. Then she reached over and picked up the receiver.

"Hello?" Despite her best efforts, her voice was still shaky with tears. "Hi, Aunt Leila. No, I don't know where she is."

Instinctively, she looked around the room, as if her mother might have appeared suddenly while she was distracted. Where could she be?

"Yeah, for sure . . . I'll let her know you called."

Leila hung up, and the dial tone sounded in Wadjda's ear. Sighing, she tossed the receiver to the floor and slumped back on the couch. Her eyes went to the ticking clock on the wall above. She wanted to stay awake and wait for her mother to come home, to pass along her father's strange message. But she was exhausted. The day, with its tremendous highs and lows, had wrung her out like a strong hand squeezing water from a dishcloth.

Slowly, Wadjda's eyes slipped shut. As the clock ticked away above her head, she fell asleep on the couch, still dressed in her uniform.

CHAPTER FIFTY-THREE

When Wadjda opened her eyes, the living room was dark and the clock read nine.

Nine! Starting to her feet, head blurry and confused, Wadjda looked around wildly. *So late!* Why hadn't her mother come to wake her up or take her to bed? She blinked, rubbed her eyes. Had anything been moved? The certificate from the competition still lay on the table in front of her, where her father had set it. Slowly, Wadjda reached down and picked it up.

Somewhere in the neighbourhood, a celebration was going on. *That's funny.* She hadn't known anything was planned. But the sounds were unmistakable, the *crack* of gunshots and *whoosh-bang* of fireworks filtering in through the windows.

No other lights in the house were on, except for a bright line shining out from under her mother's door. Cautiously, Wadjda padded down the dark hallway, poked her head round the jamb – and blinked, caught completely by surprise.

Her mother's *abayah* was thrown carelessly across the

bed. That was normal. But the thing lying next to it was not. A new white lab coat, still covered in a clear plastic wrapper. *Just like* The Matrix, Wadjda thought, lifting up the sleeve and letting it drop. Her mind spun. Where was her mother?

Moving faster now, she checked the bathroom. This room was empty, too. Her reflection in the mirror caught her eye, and she sighed. Her face was red and smudged with dust and tears. Wadjda walked to the sink and leaned in to splash water on her cheeks.

Halfway to the tap, her hand froze. Masses of freshly cut hair lined the inside of the sink. Frowning, Wadjda pinched a silky black clump between her fingers. Before she could examine it more closely, another cacophony of celebratory gunshots and fireworks rattled the house.

No more time to waste. If her mother was home, there was only one place she could be. Wadjda clattered up the stairway to the roof, her heart pounding furiously with every step.

CHAPTER FIFTY-FOUR

The roof was dark, a pool of blackness framed by the lights of the city. Wadjda pushed open the door cautiously. At the far end was her mother, silhouetted against the blackness, smoking a cigarette. Its tip was a tiny blur of red against the gloom.

Wadjda came closer and saw that her mother's hair had been hacked off, a bit unevenly, to shoulder length. The wind sent it twirling and swirling round her neck.

Her mother was staring off into the distance, at what looked like a big party a few blocks away. *That must be where all the noise is coming from*, Wadjda thought. What seemed like a thousand strands of lights illuminated the house, splashing out around it, forming a glowing circle in the otherwise dark streets.

Huge crowds of people were entering the yard. From her perch on the roof, Wadjda could hear their laughter, floating up amid the intermittent *pops* of gunfire. Every few minutes, more fireworks arced up, flecks of sparkling colour cascading down across the silent neighbourhood.

Wadjda walked over and leaned against the wall beside

her mother, keeping her eyes fixed on the party. Her mother glanced over at her, and then discreetly stubbed out her cigarette against the concrete wall.

"I heard the news." She gave Wadjda a sad smile. "Congratulations. I'm so proud of you."

"They didn't give me the money," Wadjda said, her shoulders slumped. The crushing disappointment of that afternoon had given way to a hollow ache in her stomach. She was devastated and tired. The dream of the bicycle was over.

Just like her father had done that afternoon, her mother reached out and tousled her hair, setting the strands askew.

"Forget them." In contrast to the softness of her hands, her voice was sharp. "You don't need their money, anyway."

Wadjda blinked, taken aback. Unsure what to say, she looked out over the edge of the roof, re-examining the scene down the street.

"Isn't that Grandmother's house? But I thought Uncle's wedding wasn't until next month. Right?"

She looked up at her mother, seeking answers.

"It's not your uncle's wedding they're celebrating," her mother said. Her voice was rough, like she was forcing out the words.

Wadjda looked at the party, then at her mother. She thought of the crisp new uniform on the bed. Her mother's choppy hair flowing in the breeze, the cut-off strands filling the sink. The party. She couldn't put it all together, couldn't understand what any of it meant.

And then she did. Her eyes widened in realization, and Wadjda threw her arms round her mother, hugging her with all her might. Panicked anguish jolted through her body as she tried to imagine her mother dancing the desperate dance of the second wives. Her beautiful mother, an object of pity.

Their shared sense of anguish brought them together, and they embraced for a long time. Her mother wrapped her arms round Wadjda's head and shoulders, and Wadjda could feel her body tremble with the pressure of holding back her tears.

Her own hands squeezed tightly, pressing against her mother's back as she tried to pull herself closer – and closer still. It was like being a little girl again. But it was like being a grown-up, too.

Gunshots and excited cries sounded in the distance. Stepping back at last, her mother wiped the tears from Wadjda's eyes with her thumbs and cupped Wadjda's chin between her hands.

"It's all right," she said softly. "He made his decision. It'll be just the two of us now. We'll be fine."

Wadjda looked up at her, more tears welling in her eyes.

"Let's buy the red dress and go over there and get him!" she said, her voice shaky but determined.

"There's no need for the red dress any more," her mother said tenderly. "Besides, I already spent the rest of the money."

On what? Wadjda wanted to ask. But she just watched, a little sceptical, as her mother walked to the other side of the roof and pulled the chain dangling from the bare bulb on the wall. The weak light flickered for a second before illuminating –

The green bicycle!

Impossible! But there it was, parked on the pocked concrete of the roof. It glowed warmly in the small pool of light cast by the bulb.

Wadjda inhaled, but there was no air. It was as if she was seeing the bicycle for the first time. As if the measure of her dreams, of everything she'd worked so hard to do, sat right there in front of her.

It was more than a bicycle now. It was the only risk her mother had ever taken, the only time she'd ever dared to step out of line. Wadjda knew how hard she had worked to fit in, to be like everyone else. All of that was gone now, for both of them.

Time seemed to freeze as she stared at the bicycle. *Nothing will ever be the same*, she realized. Then, catching herself, she sprinted to her mother. Again, she embraced her tenderly. It wasn't desperate and sad, like their last hug. It wasn't a thank-you hug, either. It was a hug that said, *I understand, and I love you.*

"I hope it's the right one," her mother whispered through her tears. "The shopkeeper said he'd been holding it for some spunky little girl for weeks."

Blasts of fireworks lit the sky as they held each other tightly and cried.

CHAPTER FIFTY-FIVE

The next morning, Wadjda swung herself up on to her new green bicycle and set out through the neighbourhood.

Her feet moved her forward. She pedalled at her own speed, on her own terms. For the first time in her life, Wadjda felt the freedom of pure, unchecked movement, and knew the sensation of using her own power to whisk herself through the city. The warm wind slipped under her loose veil and blew her hair back as she swerved down streets and alleys, bumped on and off pavements.

I'll never let go of this feeling, she thought, and pedalled harder.

At her grandmother's house, she braked and slid to a stop at the kerb. The lights still arced over her head, but they were dark now. The street was deserted and quiet. Only a few streamers and stray decorations hinted at the festivities of the previous evening.

Staring at that quiet house, anger welled up inside Wadjda. She wanted to scream at her father, to berate him at the top of her lungs. No, more than that. She wanted to take him by the shoulders and shake him, rattle him around until he turned back into the man he used to be, the man he was before he made this stupid decision. Back when he was just her father, and she loved him more than any other person on earth.

Instead, she stood up on the pedals and pressed down, moving on, away from the scene and everything that went with it. Her mother's words sounded in her ear. *He made his choice.*

I'm making a choice, too, Wadjda thought. It was a choice to be happy, to not let anything stop her. She was making it for her mother, and she was making it for herself.

Pedalling fast, she turned a corner and saw Abdullah playing football with a group of boys. They were behind the abandoned mall, in the same spot where she'd found him smashing windows before their crazy adventure at Iqbal's house. Braking to a stop and hopping off her bike, Wadjda started to approach cautiously. But then, standing up a little taller, she defiantly rolled her bike right past them.

It was impossible to hide her excitement. Wadjda felt like it was visible in her eyes, in the quirk of her smile, the flush of her cheeks. She was glowing with it. After all, she thought, the dream of the bicycle had always been tied up with Abdullah. She could ride next to him now. Together, they could go anywhere their feet could take them.

"Hey!" she called.

Abdullah took his eyes off the ball and looked up, squinting against the sun. Wadjda smiled at him and leaped on to her bicycle. He grinned back, delighted, and waved for the others to go on without him. As Wadjda watched, he sprinted across the dusty car park and dashed to his own bike, waving at her all the while.

He didn't care if the other boys saw him playing with her. Wadjda was his friend, the best friend he would ever have, and he didn't care who knew it.

"Let's go!" he shouted, and jumped on to his bike, pushing hard to catch up with Wadjda as she pedalled away.

His friends watched them go, jaws hanging open in shock. If they had seen an elephant walk on to the field on its hind legs and kick the ball straight into the goal, they couldn't have been more surprised.

But in seconds they were left behind. Wadjda and Abdullah swept through the streets towards the toyshop. As they got closer, they saw the owner sitting in front, sipping tea and chatting with a friend. As the children passed by, he smiled proudly at Wadjda.

Like Abdullah's friends, the other fellow was shocked to see a girl riding a bicycle. He blinked at the owner in confusion.

The old man just smiled and shrugged his shoulders as Wadjda and Abdullah disappeared down the block.

"A new world indeed," he chuckled.

And for the first time in many years he felt more excited for the future than nostalgic for the past.

Round the corner, Wadjda swerved into an alley, sped down it and curved back on to the main street, pedalling as hard as she could. She pushed her bicycle faster and faster, drawing ahead of her friend. Every minute or so, she looked back to see if Abdullah was closing the gap.

"Catch me if you can!" she yelled, and raced past several men on the corner. They turned their heads, looking disapprovingly after her. But Wadjda was already gone.

Putting on another burst of speed, she broke away from Abdullah, who huffed along behind, doing his best to keep up. But Wadjda was already too far ahead. Her feet pushed the pedals furiously. At long last, she was riding her dream, and no one would ever catch her.

There. She'd done it. She'd reached the end of the road, where the highway began. It didn't seem real. Wadjda braked, came to a stop and stood watching the trucks and cars rumble by. A sense of liberty overwhelmed her, a feeling of deep gratitude and happiness.

Nothing comes easy in life, she thought. But whatever price she paid for this moment was worth it.

The cars flashed by. The green bicycle waited, ready to take her wherever she wanted to go. Wadjda looked ahead, fixing her eyes on a point in the distance. She couldn't see it, not clearly, but she knew it was there. That the future was hers.

ACKNOWLEDGMENTS

I would like to express my sincere thanks and appreciation to everyone who helped to make this book a reality, including Rosalie Swedlin, Rena Ronson, Roman Paul, Gerhard Meixner, Namrata Tripathi, Amy Berkower, Craig Emanuel, and with special thanks to Genevieve Gagne-Hawes for her invaluable assistance and support in guiding me through the writing of my first novel.

ABOUT THE AUTHOR

Haifaa Al Mansour is a Saudi Arabian film director and screenwriter, and the winner of an EDA Female Focus Award. Her first feature-length film, *Wadjda*, won the Best International Feature Audience Award at the Los Angeles Film Festival, among other awards, and is the basis of this novel. *The Green Bicycle* is her debut book.